OXBLOOD

OXBLOOD

A VICTORIA ASHER NOVEL

ANNALISA GRANT

OPEN ROAD

INTEGRATED MEDIA

NEW YORK

Cover design by Mauricio Díaz

978-1-5040-1874-6

Published in 2016 by Open Road Integrated Media, Inc.
180 Maiden Lane
New York, NY 10038
www.openroadmedia.com

For Donavan. So much.

OXBLOOD

PROLOGUE

I stumbled, and my knees landed hard in the dirt. I felt a bullet whizz by my face, barely missing my cheek. I scooted back against the large, round bale of hay, hoping to shield myself from the next bullet. Another shot fired. As if I could forget that he was the hunter and I was his prey.

My chest throbbed and my breathing was shallow. Each intake of the manure-soaked air reminded me of where I was: a pasture in the middle of nowhere, with no help for miles. They had taken away everything that proved my identity: driver's license, passport, even the high school ID I still had stuffed in my wallet. I was trapped. All I had left was my fear-soaked adrenaline and the aroma of fresh cow pies. It was too much for my gag reflex. I leaned to the side and heaved twice before I reined it in.

I shook off the nausea and scoped out my options. Going back to the tree line would only put me closer to my attacker. To my left was a long, wooden fence leading to big, empty pastures: perfect target practice for the expert marksman who was stalking me. My only chance of survival was the huge building up ahead. But could I get there without being shot, caught, or both?

I counted four round bales between where I stood and the building. My shoes were slippery and caked with mud. My already questionable athleticism was waning along with my hopes of survival. I could either give up or make a run for it. With how exhausted I felt, giving up was starting to look like a viable option.

He crept closer. He released and then clicked back into place the magazine to his gun several times. I understood. He was the one with all the power. He took his time. He was stronger and faster than I could ever hope to be, and he knew it. This was only a game for him. I felt my strength fading. I had been running from him for hours and I didn't know how much longer I could last.

"Victoria!" he called out, singing my name. It made me cringe, but it was just what I needed. I couldn't give up. I wanted to do more than just survive. I wanted kick this guy's ass.

I shot out like a cannon for the next bale of hay. His gun fired, and I fell to the ground, quickly rolling my body to safety. I heard a *thunk* as the bullet wedged itself into the hay above me. *One bale down, three to go.* Then the final sprint to the building.

I took a few breaths and closed my eyes, but only for a second, and took inventory of my body. My thighs burned from squatting, my calves ached from running, and my arms were riddled with scratches from hay. I couldn't be sure that I wouldn't collapse the next time I tried to move. But, for now, I was still alive.

I made a run for it, the blood pounding in my ears. I expected to hear him fire at me, but he didn't. I reached the bale, then immediately took off for the next, pushing my luck. When he still hadn't fired, I kept running, slipping twice before finally diving behind the last mound of hay. I crouched down to wait.

A small smile of victory crept onto my face, but then faded just as quickly. Why hadn't he shot at me? Why did he let me get this far? I took slow, deliberate breaths as I listened for him. A cow mooed in the distance, then nothing.

It was *too* quiet.

The door to the building was only fifty yards away. I was almost there. I waited for what felt like hours for him to reveal himself. The *squish* of his boot in the mud. The scraping of fabric as he raised his weapon. Nothing. Maybe he was about to round the corner of hay and fire at me—point-blank.

Three, two, one . . . I pushed off the final hay bale and was halfway to the door before I heard the shot ring out. This time, he didn't miss. I fell to the ground, clutching my left arm. I quickly tried to sit up, pulling myself to my knees. My eyes burned, but I refused to let him see me cry.

Within moments, his broad frame shadowed over me. He stared down at me, his gun hovering next to his shoulder, the corners of his lips turned up in a grim smile. I had failed and my fate was more uncertain than ever.

CHAPTER 1

"Hey, Vic! Let me get another cup of coffee before you kick me out," Ray called across the diner. He was a regular, a trucker who stopped in every few days when he got back from his normal route between Miami and the rest of the East Coast. Tall with a balding head and a scruffy beard, he looked every bit the part, too. He was also the kind of guy you knew would be on your side if you ever needed him. That was nice on nights when it was just me, Tiffany, and our boss, Sam, closing up the place.

With bulldog jowls and white hair, Sam was the world's cutest seventy-year-old man. A Vietnam vet, his mind still knew how to defend himself, but his body just wouldn't cooperate anymore.

The Clock had been Sam's dream when he got back from the war. For a while, it was the only twenty-four-hour diner in town—hence "The Clock"—and it was a real hot spot for a couple of decades. But when a chain restaurant with a liquor license opened up a few blocks away, the college professors and entrepreneurs took their business there. After years of only drunks coming in at three in the morning and ordering coffee, money got tight and Sam cut the hours to close at midnight, putting a damper on the catchiness of the name.

It was a classic place. The long counter, lined with padded red-leather stools, faced the semi-open kitchen. Red booths that looked like the backseats of old cars were positioned in front of the windows, and four-top tables were strategically settled in between them and the counter. Sam took pride in the nostalgic feel of The Clock, and it was our adoration for him that made Tiffany and I feel okay about the waitress uniforms he made us wear. Plus, we had to admit that the pencil skirts and button-up shirts with scalloped sleeves were actually kind of cute, in a retro sort of way.

"Anything for you, Ray. And you know I'm not kicking you out anytime soon. You can stay as long as you want," I told him as I finished wiping down a table.

I grabbed the coffeepot and the pie stand and made my way down the counter to his usual spot at the end. "Want a slice to go with your coffee?"

"Sure. Why not?" He smiled.

"Great. I'm having one, too. It's my birthday pie," I told him, and I grabbed the can of whipped cream from the mini-cooler behind the counter.

"Was it your birthday today, Vic?" he asked.

"It's tomorrow, so, technically, I've got another forty

minutes, but I'm starting the celebration early. I'm turning the big two-O," I laughed.

"Twenty. Wow. What are you doing here? You should be out with your friends!" Ray said.

The door to the kitchen swung open and Tiffany appeared. "That's what I told her, but she refused to even let me take her out after work!"

Next to my brother, Gil, Tiffany was my best friend in the whole world. We'd met in high school, and she'd stuck with me through everything that Gil and I had endured. At five foot ten, she was a good five inches taller than me. She was also gorgeous, with long blonde hair and blue eyes and curves in all the right places—nothing like the recent trend of emaciated girls on the catwalk. I kept telling her she should walk around South Beach; some photographer or agent was sure to discover her. But she only shrugged me off, saying she had better things to do.

"A girl's gotta work, Ray. And as for tonight, Tiffany, I'm not a party girl, and you know it," I said.

"Fine. Then let's grab a pie and some ice cream from Sam, and we'll go back to your place and watch movies that make us both *want* and *swear off* relationships." Tiffany gathered the salt- and peppershakers from each table and brought them to the counter where she refilled them.

"Oh! Going back to my place! That'll be new," I laughed. Tiffany practically lived at the apartment I shared with my brother. She narrowed her eyes and shot me a look. "I'm just kidding! It sounds like a perfect plan," I replied. "Sam! Mind if we pilfer a pie and some ice cream for my birthday?" I called to him through the open window to the kitchen.

"You can have anything you want, Vic!" Sam smiled his big, toothy grin and shouted back. "Happy birthday, doll!"

"Thanks, Sam!" I called back to him.

I locked the door to the diner exactly at midnight, and the three of us moseyed out with Ray by our sides twenty minutes later. He pulled a fifty-dollar bill from his wallet and told me to buy myself something special. I tried to refuse, but his insistence was stronger than my resolve.

"You're way too sweet, Ray," I said as I hugged him. Sam and Ray climbed into their trucks, and me and Tiffany in my 1995 Honda Accord. The radio wouldn't turn on, it had crank windows, and the odometer clocked in at 300,000 miles, but the air-conditioning worked, and that was all that mattered in southern Florida. I cranked it on full blast and let the ice-cold air freeze the sweat that had been rolling down my neck.

When Tiff and I pulled up to my building, we did the usual scoping to make sure there weren't any weird guys hanging around. It wasn't the shittiest part of town, but we still had to be careful. Gil and I had lived there long enough to make nice with the neighbors, and besides, we all did our best to keep our noses out of one another's business. Yeah, the crime rate could be better, but it was close enough to campus for Gil and to the diner for me. We'd talked about moving when he finished law school and had started a full-time job. But for the moment, we liked our third-floor walkup in that so-so part of town.

It had been home for the last couple of years—our parents had died in a plane crash five years ago, the crash that changed everything. We had a happy life, but it was ripped away from us without warning. I went into foster care and left every dream I ever had in the last house we shared as a family. It was the hardest thing I'd ever faced, but even harder for Gil, who was a pre-law student living in the college dorms. When he took me in, he couldn't stay there anymore. I offered to quit high school and work, but Gil wouldn't have it. Neither would Sam. It was only after I graduated that Sam gave me more hours.

About a year after the crash, we got a seven-figure settlement from the airline. The paperwork for Gil to take custody of me had just come through, and we moved into our apartment. We agreed to only use the money to pay for Gil's education and to supplement if we were really short. Gil didn't feel as strongly about it as I did, but I had a hard time spending money we had only because our parents died.

In addition to Gil's tuition at law school, we agreed that he could use whatever funds he needed to support himself on his study-abroad program, a six-month research trip to Italy. He was already more than halfway through, so he'd be back to his thrifty spending habits with me in no time.

Gil said Mom and Dad would have wanted me to go to college, too, but I wasn't ready. I wasn't sure if I even wanted to go to college, but I promised Gil when he finished his law degree that we would revisit the subject. If all went as planned for him, it meant I still had a year to

ANNALISA GRANT

figure out what I wanted to do. Thank God Gil was on the four-year plan.

The path up the stairwell to my apartment was always full of smells—the majority of them tantalizing. Mrs. Hobart on the first floor was a baker, so the aroma of cinnamon or chocolate usually seeped through the insufficient weather stripping around her door and windows.

Mrs. Vasquez, directly across the hall from me, was Cuban. The smell of stewing tomatoes and spices wafted from her apartment regardless of the time of day. The fact that it was almost one in the morning didn't matter. Her husband had passed away and her children were grown and living in other states, so I think she liked to wait up for me.

"Hey, Mrs. Vasquez." I smiled as she emerged from her door.

Mrs. Vasquez had been there longer than anyone else. She was a jolly, shapely woman whose apartment had a revolving door; she welcomed anyone who needed a place to stay. She'd already helped three people in our building when they'd gotten evicted. She was kind and probably the only neighbor I could count on to look out for me.

"Hello, *mija*. How was your night?" she asked with a sweet smile and a pat on my arm.

"It was fine, thanks. Tiff and I are just going to spend the night watching sappy movies and eating pie. Want to join us? It's apple!" I said, teetering the box in front of her.

"No, no. I'm watching my girlish figure!" She laughed and shook her generous rump at us. "But I have a little something for you, mija." Mrs. Vasquez walked quickly

12

into her apartment, leaving her door ajar while we waited. When she returned, she was holding a pot of something that smelled heavenly. "I know how much you love it!"

"Oh my God! You made me black beans and rice! I love you!" Tiffany took the pot as I wrapped an arm around Mrs. Vasquez's neck. "You're the best!"

"Now you can eat like a queen for your birthday, *mija.*"

"Thank you so much!" We kissed each other on the cheek and hugged again before she sent us into my apartment to get on with my birthday celebration. It wasn't going to be much of a party, but with pie, ice cream, and black beans and rice, it was certainly going to be better than my original plan: watching the first ten minutes of random shows until the sun came up.

I locked the door behind us, threw my keys and bag on the front-hall thrift-store table, and headed for the kitchen. The only nice thing in our apartment was our living-room furniture. It was a dark blue set with patterned accent pillows, all in a soft chenille fabric. It was heavenly to nap on. Our parents had bought it just a few months before the accident, and Gil and I had been religious about taking care of it.

We had strict rules about no eating on the couch, love seat, or chair; that had always been Mom's rule. Sometimes we would do pizza or popcorn, but we'd always push the coffee table out and put a tablecloth on it.

The rest of the apartment was like the table by the door: pieced together from thrift stores, online ads, and the occasional roadside treasure. Our small, oak kitchen table was a hand-me-down from the woman who used to live in Mr. Hopper's apartment. It was missing a chair and only seated three, but that was fine. There were never more than three people around that table anyway.

Tiffany put the pot of deliciousness on the stove and turned it on low while I put the pie on the counter and the ice cream in the freezer. I scanned Gil's itinerary, which had been magnetized to the fridge since he left. According to the schedule, he had just left Bologna and was on his way to Palermo. I felt a smile turn up the corners of my mouth. I was so proud and happy for my brother, even if I missed him constantly.

"Can I crash here tonight?" Tiffany asked.

"You stay here every night!" I laughed. Tiffany still lived at home with her mom and her mom's flavor of the month. Her mother had always been a magnet for freeloading drug addicts and alcoholics. In a room full of men, the woman had the uncanny ability to find the one guy with a rap sheet as long as your arm. Suffice it to say, Tiffany stayed with me. A lot.

"You're the best, Vic. You know, with Gil gone, maybe I could just move into his room. His bed is so comfy," she said with a dreamy smile.

"How would you know if Gil's bed is comfortable?"

"I've *heard* his bed is comfortable?" she answered sheepishly.

"I don't want to know," I told her. I knew she was joking when she implied that she and Gil had fooled around. The truth was that Gil didn't have time for even a fling. School was his lover and that was okay with him. "It doesn't matter anyway. No one goes into Gil's room without his explicit permission and you know that. The man is obsessed with his privacy."

Gil's room had a tendency to look a bit like a unabomber's lair: piles and piles of research journals organized in a way that made sense only to him. I might have peeked my head in a couple of times after he left to borrow one of his old T-shirts and noticed that he took a dozen blank journals with him. I told him I was sure he could find some there, but he swears by the ones he gets from the student store on campus, claiming they "lay just right" when he writes.

He threw himself into his studies after his girlfriend, Maria, died. We had just lost Mom and Dad two years prior, which made it especially difficult. He became obsessive about school, and I couldn't blame him. We all have our coping mechanisms. Gil is an awesome guy and an amazing brother, but his obsession for the law sometimes trumps his ability to think rationally about things.

"The couch is perfect," Tiffany smiled and changed the subject. "Did you hear from Chad today?"

Chad was my on-again, off-again boyfriend of two years. He was nice enough, but Tiffany didn't like him because he constantly mooched off me. His father was a heart surgeon who'd invented some valve used in valve-replacement surgery. Chad could have had all the money in the world if he'd gone to medical school like his parents wanted him to, but an argument about their unwillingness to replace the most recent car he wrecked, and a rash "I don't need your money anyway" statement later, and Chad was on his own. It took him a year to run out of money, but by then he was too proud to go back and admit he'd been wrong.

We met one night at the diner. He had come in twenty minutes before closing and ordered a cup of coffee. His hair was a mess and there were dark circles around his eyes. He looked like he hadn't slept in days. I asked him if he was okay and I could have sworn he was about to start crying. He said he didn't want to burden me with his problems and called me "ma'am." I refilled his coffee four times, and each time he told me a little more about how he was down on his luck. When the diner closed, he walked me to my car and told me I was the prettiest, sweetest girl he had met in a long time. He was the cutest, most polite guy I'd met in a long time, so it seemed we were made for each other.

Unfortunately, gorgeous brown eyes, sexy abs, and good table manners only go so far. He barely worked and when he did it was only one or two days filling in on a construction gig. After six months of staying at my place and not contributing in any way, I told him he had to man up, grow up, and start helping with the rent and chores. That was when he decided it was better for our relationship if he didn't practically live with me. Eventually, I stopped asking when he'd be back from an out-of-town day job because he usually stayed and mooched off his buddies after the job was done, which meant he wasn't mooching off of me.

The bottom line was if Chad had any idea how much money Gil and I had, he would have tried to put a ring on my finger to get a piece of it. He would be able to maintain his slacker lifestyle and never have to face his parents and admit he was wrong. Life would be a dream for him but a nightmare for me.

Tiffany and Sam were the only ones in my life who knew about the money. Tiffany, because she was there when it all went down; Sam because when things got tough at the diner, Gil and I offered to help bail him out. He wouldn't take the money, but it solidified us as family in Sam's eyes.

"No. He's working a construction job in Fort Lauderdale." I walked to my room, doing my best to disengage Tiffany from further Chad discussion. Lately, most days I could take him or leave him, so whether he called me on my birthday or not didn't really matter. When he did come back, he'd most likely bring me some cheap flowers from the corner store and pour on his charm. I wish I could resist him in those moments, but at the end of the day it's nice to have someone around to cuddle with and buy me flowers. It gets lonely when the only family you have left is in Italy.

"Here, these are yours," I said, returning from my bedroom with a pair of pajamas for Tiffany. "Oh, and I brought you a nail file."

"Um . . . okay. Why did you bring me a nail file?" Tiffany asked.

"You've got a nick in your left thumbnail. You'll want to file it before it tears off," I told her. Tiffany lifted her hand to her face and examined her thumb.

"I don't know how you do that." Tiffany shook her head and got to work.

"Time to get our movie on!" I declared.

I dished out some of Mrs. Vasquez's black beans and rice into two bowls and grabbed two cans of generic soda from the fridge while Tiffany pushed the coffee table out and threw a tablecloth over it. We sat on the floor, leaned our backs against the couch, turned Netflix on, and searched for sappy movies that carried no hope of ever becoming reality for either one of us.

By four in the morning, we had eaten the whole apple pie and half the carton of ice cream, watched a Rachel McAdams and an Audrey Hepburn movie, and spent the night sufficiently laughing and crying. Tiffany cozied herself up on the couch with a pillow and her favorite of my blankets, and I tucked myself into my queen-size bed.

When Gil left for Italy, I moved my picture of him from my tall, five-drawer dresser and put it next to the one of Mom and Dad on the night table. I looked at both photos, feeling desperate because I missed everyone in them. I said good night to the silver-framed photo of my parents, as I had every night since they died, and then looked at the calendar that hung above the small wooden desk I'd had since middle school. It was officially Sunday, which meant I was due to get an email from Gil that night.

Over the months he's been gone, I've lived for that Sunday email. Gil told me about seeing the Colosseum and Trevi Fountain, and how the research was hard but he knew it was going to pay off in the end. It was exciting and I was so happy for him.

I woke to the delicious smell of coffee and bacon. It was a rarity that someone else was cooking for me. I lay there in bed relishing in the luxury of it. After a few moments, I stretched and twisted my body then dragged myself to the kitchen.

"What is all this?" I asked. The pale yellow kitchen walls felt neon to my morning eyes. The sun streamed through the window.

"This is your birthday breakfast," Tiffany answered, handing me a cup of coffee. Still in her pajamas, her hair was in a messy bun on top of her head. "Cream and three Splendas, right?"

"You know me so well." I yawned and nodded sleepily as I took the first sip. "Mmmm, this is good. Thank you, Tiff. This is so sweet of you. What time is it?"

"It's a little after two," she answered. "I figured if we served breakfast all day at The Clock, then we could have breakfast at two in the afternoon if we wanted."

"Good point. And when is breakfast ever a bad idea?" I chuckled. "I don't remember, are you working tomorrow? Somehow I got today and tomorrow off."

"Yeah, I'm on for the closing shift tomorrow, but I'm all yours today, baby," Tiffany kissed the top of my head and returned to egg-scrambling duty.

They smelled heavenly, the cheese melting on top like

molten lava, and I couldn't wait to dive in. Gil used to make breakfast for me every Sunday morning our first year here. He would read the paper, and I would read novels I'd check out of the library. I used to think those were activities we did because we enjoyed them. After a while, I realized that we both read because we didn't know what to say to each other—terrified we'd mention Mom or Dad and one of us would fall apart. Sometimes talking seemed like a dangerous venture. But each day became a little easier, and one day Gil said he read something Dad would have found funny and neither of us cried.

"Do you want to go window-shopping at Aventura today?" Tiffany asked. Window-shopping was mostly all we did at the mall, although Tiffany tried to convince me on several occasions that the sales were of apocalyptic proportions and important enough to break out the debit card to the settlement money. If I wouldn't use the money for a car that was younger than me, I certainly wasn't going to use it for a great price on a pair of Prada shoes neither of us had an excuse to wear—even if they were totally badass grommet, suede, peep-toe booties.

"Sure. And maybe we can have dinner at The Cheesecake Factory," I suggested. "Gil usually takes me there for my birthday. Just because he isn't here doesn't mean I can't still go."

"We're going to have a perfect day!" Tiffany squealed.

After enjoying my birthday breakfast, I checked my email to see if Gil had written yet. It was usually in my inbox around noon—but I had no new messages. Maybe he was waiting until tonight to send it at the exact time I was born. Last year, he held out and didn't say anything about my birthday until exactly nine forty-two at night.

I tied my hair on top of my head and took a quick shower. It wasn't much, but the slate blue paint on the walls, the scented candle, the knock-off version of the expensive shampoo and shower gel, and the rain shower-head Gil gave me for Christmas last year made my bath-room feel like a spa.

Tiffany pulled an outfit from the extra clothes she kept in my closet, and we got ourselves as swanky as we could get for the upscale mall. Dressed in the designer jeans from the consignment store and some trendy costume jewelry I found at Versona, we transferred our things from our junkie purses to the knock-offs we bought at the flea mar-ket last summer and drove to Aventura.

We tried on clothes and acted aloof with the store clerks. I used to feel badly, but they seriously treated you like you were Julia Roberts in *Pretty Woman* if you didn't. Well, I suppose *all* the stores weren't like that. We hit Hot Topic, where Tiffany bought an ironic boy band shirt.

When we walked through the makeup and fragrance section at one of the high-end stores, Tiffany, of course, told one sales clerk that it was my birthday.

"We normally only do partial makeup to feature products from our line, but you have to let me do everything!" The girl, not much older than me, clapped her hands together in excitement while I rolled my eyes. Tiffany gave me a shove and told me to sit down and enjoy being taken care of.

"Fine, but I better not look like one of those Real Housewives when you're done," I said with a laugh. I never dressed up or went anyplace nice, so I rarely wore makeup. Sometimes Chad and I went to a movie, but I usually cooked dinner for us at my place. I may have rolled my eyes as the makeup girl started, but it actually felt pretty good to relax and let her wave her magic brushes over me.

When my face had been thoroughly blended with foundation, my cheeks made rosy pink with blush, and my eyes detailed with shadow, eyeliner, and mascara, she turned me around to face the big mirror.

"Oh my God, Vic! You look phenomenal!" Tiffany said with wide eyes.

I did. My naturally tan skin glowed under a light powder of blush. And my brown eyes, which I always thought were just plain brown, popped with the eyeliner she used. To round out the picture, my long brown hair fell over my shoulders and framed my features in a way I had never seen before.

"It's a shame I can't afford to buy all of this," I whispered. "Thank you. It was definitely a treat." An inner voice that sounded an awful lot like Tiffany's spoke up. *You can afford it, Vic. You just choose not to.* I just couldn't use the settlement money to buy something as frivolous as makeup. In fact, I couldn't imagine using the money for anything.

"We're having our free-gift-with-purchase promotion right now. Maybe you can get just one or two things and then you'll get a whole loot of goodies! I would suggest getting the foundation powder and the eyeliner. This one just really made your eyes pop." The sales clerk held up the two items in my color palette with a huge grin on her face. "The free gift is eye shadow, lip color, our famous moisturizer, and a cosmetic bag. What do you think?"

I did the math in my head and realized the bill would come to fifty dollars. I hadn't spent that amount on makeup in all the years of my life combined.

"C'mon, Vic. It's your birthday," Tiffany encouraged. "Ray gave you fifty bucks last night. You should use it! *And* you'll get all the other stuff for free." She smiled at me warmly and I knew that this wasn't about *stuff*. It was about Tiffany wanting me to do something nice for myself because I never did.

I twisted my mouth and looked down at my fidgeting fingers for a moment before glancing at myself in the mirror again. "Okay, I guess . . . I mean . . . it *is* my birthday, and Ray told me to buy something nice for myself."

Tiffany threw her arms around my shoulders from the side and pressed our ears together, forcing us to look at our reflection. "You look unbelievable!"

"Whatever," I said. I leaned my head in toward her and closed my eyes. I treasured Tiffany. She was like family, and if anything ever happened to her or Gil, I didn't know what I'd do.

We had just left the store when I noticed two guys following us. With broad shoulders and thick, wavy hair, they could have been attractive had they lost the gold chains and creepy thin mustaches, or whatever the fuzz on top of their lips qualified as, but they both looked like total jerks. And having already seen one of them fold a twenty-dollar bill over a stack of ones told me that no makeover was going to change their scamming ways.

"Hello, ladies," the short one said. "How are you today?" His slight Cuban accent revealed itself with the way he rolled his *R*'s and the way he lingered at the end of the word *today*. "We were wondering if you were already under representation with a modeling agency. We're with a premiere modeling agency from New York and we're here scouting out beautiful women like yourselves."

Oh, please. I looked at Tiffany, and we both rolled our eyes.

I gave them the once-over. "You're modeling agents?" I asked. The taller one cocked his eyebrow and nodded while the short, creepy one gave a resounding "*Mmm-hmmm.*"

"Really? Who have you worked with?" I asked with a smile as I played along.

"Let's just say that we've worked with one of the most famous Victoria's Secret models out there," the tall one said.

"Wow. That's impressive. Which one?" I challenged.

"We're not at liberty to share client information," the short one said.

"Oh sure. I totally get it. So you've got, like, a card you can give us?"

They patted the sides of their linen pants before reaching into their matching jackets, pretending to look for something that all four of us knew wasn't there.

"We seem to be all out. But if you give us your numbers, we'll be happy to call you from our office and set up a meeting." The shorter of the two raised his brows at me expectantly.

"Go away. Neither of you is even carrying a wallet. I watched you fold a stack of ones under a twenty and shove it into the inside pocket of your jacket," I said to Señor Creepy. "Not to mention, both of you are wearing gold chains—and I use the word *gold* loosely—that are literally turning your necks green. And don't get me started on the Bruno Magli loafers you're wearing from three seasons ago."

I grabbed Tiffany and left the Mario Brothers standing in the middle of the mall, completely befuddled by my response. Mission accomplished.

"How do you do that?" Tiffany asked. "I mean, how did you know that about the wallet and the money? Hell, I didn't even see those guys before they approached us!"

"I'm just observant. They were standing in that small hallway where the restrooms are outside the store," I told her. "I saw one of them fold the money and put it in his coat pocket. I could see the outline of the money, too."

"And the shoes!"

"You can take credit for that. Having a shoe whore for a best friend has finally paid off."

"I can't help it. An evil fairy cursed me with expensive taste and no money."

25

We walked and laughed and window-shopped all the way to the restaurant. I knew it was dumb, but it felt kind of nice having a bag in my hand as I walked through the mall. Not that I never shopped. I just usually found my necessities at Target. But this was a bag filled with things that I didn't really need, and it felt pretty good. It even made me think that maybe enough time had passed and Gil and I could start using the money for things other than his tuition. Getting out of our apartment would be the first thing we would do, that's for sure. But I quickly lost my resolve, and my mind went back to the place it always did when I thought about the money: profiting from my parents' death was not only disrespectful, but gross.

The Cheesecake Factory with Tiffany was really great. Half the fun was flipping through their twenty-five–page menu and figuring out what we were going to gorge ourselves on before we dug into two huge pieces of cheesecake. I hadn't done a birthday dinner with her since before my parents died. I had kept it just Gil and me because it seemed so strange not to have Mom and Dad there. This time, though, I felt like I had taken a baby step into a place where special days didn't feel so empty without them.

"Oh, *mija!*" Mrs. Vasquez swung her apartment door open just as we reached the top of the steps upon returning home. "I forgot to give you something!" She reached inside her apartment and pulled a box through the dingy doorway. As she handed it to me, I noticed a small red line on her wrist. A burn, the third one this week. "This was delivered for you yesterday. I knew your brother wouldn't forget your birthday."

I turned the box around and examined the package. It was wrapped in brown paper, my name and address written in Gil's chicken-scratch handwriting. And there were red and blue stamps with Italian words. The corners of the paper were rough and frayed from its journey.

"I told him not to get me anything. He doesn't listen," I said, laughing as I tucked the shallow box under my arm. "Thank you for rescuing the gift. I don't know what's in it, but I'm very thankful you kept it safe."

Tiff and I entered my apartment, and I dropped my bag on the table by the door before we flung ourselves onto the couch, both stuffed beyond reason. It was getting late and I could see myself surrendering to a food coma any second. But opening Gil's gift trumped everything else.

"What is it?" Tiffany asked eagerly.

"He said he would send me something from Italy since he wouldn't be here for my birthday, but I told him not to worry about it." I rolled my eyes as I tore the paper wrapped around the shallow box. "I have no idea what it could be."

"Well it sure ain't a pair of Prada shoes straight from Milan," Tiffany laughed.

I let the paper fall to the floor as I removed a small gift box. I shimmied open the lid and found one of Gil's leather-bound research journals.

"Oh, that's sweet. He sent you a diary," Tiffany said in a sappy tone.

I felt my eyebrows scrunch together. Gil knew I wasn't into journaling. I picked up the book and felt the smooth faux leather in my hands and let my fingers trace the embossed design. I opened the cover to see if Gil had written a note—but what I found made my blood run cold.

"Oxblood," I whispered, reading the single word written in bold letters across the otherwise empty cover page.

I examined the emblem on the cover again and walked into Gil's room.

Screw his rules, I thought and picked up one of the journals off his desk. The designs were exactly the same. *Why had he sent me one of his journals?*

I flipped through the pages of my gift and searched for an explanation. They were filled with his handwriting, but none of the few sentences I skimmed made sense. My heart was pounding inside my chest as I lifted the front and back covers up like a bird, shaking the book with hope that some kind of note would fall out telling me why Gil had sent me something he explicitly told me never to touch. But nothing fell from the pages.

"Something terrible has happened," I whispered. "Gil is in trouble."

CHAPTER 2

Tiffany wrapped her arm around my shoulders, trying to calm my nerves. She understood how big a deal it was that Gil would send me something so personal, but only I understood the gravity of our family's code word for "the shit has hit the fan." I flipped through the book again looking for clues. The pages were filled with oddly drawn trees with bare branches.

"What are those drawings?" Tiffany asked.

I traced my finger along the lines of the crudely drawn pictures. "They look like trees. But I don't understand why he would send me a journal filled with leafless trees."

"Who's Noah Brown?" she asked, pointing to a name written on one of the branches.

"He's a cousin of ours. Lives in New York," I told her. I stared at the picture and willed my brain to comprehend what I was looking at. Each branch had a name written on it, and as the pages progressed, more branches appeared with new names on them. I recognized the names, but their connection to one another on the trees made no sense.

They were family trees.

"Maybe it got lost and someone found it and returned it," Tiffany suggested.

I examined the first and last pages in hopes that she was right and that I had just missed an obvious clue.

"His name isn't in it and there's no address, Tiff," I countered.

"So . . . what's 'oxblood'?"

"It's a color. A shade of dark red. It was our mother's favorite. She used colors to describe feelings: chartreuse for happiness, ebony for sadness. Mom always said oxblood was actually a muddled-up conglomerate of other colors. That's what she said about problems, too. So, *oxblood* always meant something was very wrong," I explained.

Worry filled every inch of my heart and I knew I had to do something. What was Gil up to? How had a simple research trip turned "oxblood" dangerous?

I grabbed Gil's itinerary from the fridge and darted into my room for my laptop. The thirty seconds it took the screen to flicker on seemed like an eternity. I went straight for my inbox.

Still no email from Gil.

I'd heard from him last Sunday, but his email was shorter than usual. Still, everything seemed fine. He told me about the progress he was making on his immigration law research and how working on a culturally diverse team could be challenging, but it wasn't anything he couldn't handle. He even shared a funny story about mixing up the Italian words for *door* and *port*—*la porta* and *il porto*—when giving another student directions. There was nothing to indicate there was any problem, except now it was almost ten o'clock and I still had no email from my brother.

"He's supposed to be in Palermo right now, but the postmark is from Bologna." I quickly googled a map of Italy and found that these two cities were nowhere near each other.

"That doesn't mean anything. It can take weeks for a package to come from overseas. And, look, he was in Bologna right before Palermo," Tiffany pointed out on the itinerary. "I'm sure everything is fine. You'll get an email from him any day now when he finds out the university in Bologna sent the journal to his home address. And he'll explain that he wrote the . . . what is it . . . the '*oxblood*' code for some random reason."

"If they were sending it to him here, why was it addressed to *me*? And Gil would never use the word *oxblood* randomly. Seriously, Tiff. We hated when our mom made us use her color chart to describe our feelings. He's not going to start using it again on a whim." Out of reasonable answers, Tiffany looked at me and shrugged and squeezed my shoulder.

I found the last email Gil sent and replied to it again. First, I yelled at him in bold, capital letters to emphasize how freaked out I was. Then I told him to contact me right away to tell me what was going on. He knew what sending me a journal would mean, let alone using that word.

I went back to Gil's itinerary and began emailing the law school department chairs at the universities directly. Gil didn't leave phone numbers because he said it was silly to waste an international call.

I pretty much cut-and-pasted the same message to the seven email addresses he left me. I told them who I was, that there was a family emergency, and that I needed to speak with Gil as soon as possible. I didn't want to sound like a crazy person just in case Tiffany was right and there was nothing to worry about, but I definitely wanted them to have a sense of urgency.

"You're going to feel really silly when Gil replies and gives you a completely reasonable explanation for this," Tiffany warned. "Why don't you try to get some sleep? I'm sure you will have heard from one of the universities or Gil by morning."

"I can't sleep, Tiff," I protested.

"You can't just sit here and stare at your inbox all night. There's nothing you can do about anything, if there is even anything to have something done about. . . . You know what I mean." Tiffany knelt down next to me by the desk and covered my hands with hers. "I know you're afraid of losing him. You're not going to lose him, Vic."

Fear was rushing through me, the same fear from the day Gil said he was going to Italy for his exchange program. After losing Mom and Dad, I couldn't handle the thought of losing Gil, too. But he went back and forth a couple of times for interviews before he actually began his six-month project, and I slowly acclimated to the idea. To think that he got all the way to Italy only to have something horrible happen to him filled me with dread.

I stared at the screen for thirty minutes, repeatedly refreshing my inbox, before I conceded to Tiffany's insistence that I sleep. I shut down the computer, changed into my pajamas, and crawled into bed.

It took longer than usual to fall asleep because my mind was imagining terrible things. I understood Gil's desire to go to Italy to study. We had talked about wanting a better life. We knew it was what Mom and Dad would have wanted for us. Gil was going on this trip to make him a better lawyer. I may have even been a bit jealous—he was in one of the most beautiful countries in the world, and I was waiting tables at a diner in one of the worst parts of Miami—but I was happy for him.

Not going to college was my choice so it wasn't like I could complain. I knew college wasn't for me. Maybe my feelings would change once Gil was done with law school. Perhaps I'd find something I could be passionate about the way Gil was about the law. Until then, I felt fine about getting by on my street smarts.

But I missed him. All the time. What was Italy *really* like? Who was he meeting? What exciting things was he experiencing? Was he touring the Colosseum and tossing coins into Trevi Fountain? I wanted so desperately to hear the *ping* on my phone telling me I had an email. One from Gil, apologizing for making me worried, for forgetting to write.

That email never came.

What did come were seven emails from seven universities in Italy that had never heard of Gil Asher. They were all very sorry for the confusion and offered to contact me if they heard anything from him.

"Can't you just call his cell?" Tiffany suggested as she handed me a cup of coffee. She offered to make me some breakfast, too, but I had absolutely no appetite. It was barely after eight in the morning and too early to eat anyway.

"His phone doesn't work internationally. I wouldn't let him spend the extra money to have temporary service abroad," I told her. "I don't understand what's going on."

"Why don't you contact his professors here? If he's on this exchange program, surely they'll have some information. Maybe all those professors have teaching assistants who answer their emails, and they just didn't know who he was?"

"*No one* has heard of him? That's crazy, Tiff. You're right, though. I should just call and talk to his professors here. I've never met any of them, but he talks about his favorite one, Professor Engskow, a lot. If I can't get in touch with him, I can at least call the school and talk to someone in that department."

I spent the next thirty minutes on hold listening to the University of Miami's prerecorded commercials for everything from their biology degrees to their prestigious law degrees. Twice a woman picked up and asked if I wanted to leave a message or speak with someone else, but I refused to become a lost piece of paper on someone's desk or get the runaround from a random teaching assistant. I was determined to speak directly to Professor Engskow as soon as was humanly possible.

"Miss Asher?" the voice on the line said through the speaker on my cell phone. "I'm Jim Engskow. How may I help you?"

"Yes, Professor Engskow, I need to speak to you about my brother, Gil," I told him.

"Oh yes! How is Gil?"

"Well, I don't know. See, I'm having trouble contacting him in Italy and I wondered if maybe you or someone in your department could help me reach him at the university in Palermo where I think he's supposed to be right now." I tried not to let it, but desperation filled my voice, making me talk too fast.

"Oh, I'm sorry you're having trouble connecting with him, but he didn't leave any contact information with us. Well, at least not with me. But I'd be happy to ask around the department. I didn't realize he was going to be in Italy! When he said he was taking the semester off to dive deeper into his thesis paper, I just assumed he would be burying himself in books and interviews locally."

"Wait. What? He's on an exchange program with the universities in Italy." I hoped to jog Professor Engskow's memory.

"The law department at the University of Miami doesn't have an exchange agreement with any university in Italy, Miss Asher."

"But . . . he went to Italy to interview for the program.

He said the university told him it was required for such a competitive internship," I explained.

What the hell was going on? Nothing was making sense. Before the six-month visit, Gil had taken three trips to Italy for what he told me were interviews and meetings to finalize the exchange program. What had he really been doing? More importantly, why would he have lied to me?

"I wish I could be of more help," Professor Engskow said. He sounded concerned.

"Well . . . um . . . thank you for your time, Professor Engskow. Sorry to have bothered you," I said with a shaky voice.

"It's no problem at all. I'll ask around. If I hear anything, I'll be sure to contact you."

"Thank you."

"Okay. We can worry now," Tiffany whispered.

I put the phone down and tried to think, but I was completely out of ideas. Did Italy do APBs? Would they even care enough to do one for an American citizen?

That's it! "Gil is an American citizen missing in a foreign country. The FBI or the US Embassy or somebody has to do something, right?"

"Oh my God! Yes! They have to!" Tiffany sat down in front of my laptop and began googling the number for the FBI. "Holy crap! There's a field office here in Miami. We should totally go down there. If you're there, if they see you, Vic, they'll have to help!"

"Okay. First, let me find a recent picture of Gil so they have something." I grabbed the laptop from Tiffany and began searching my Facebook pictures for a good one of Gil. I only had to scroll down a few times before I landed on one of Gil from his birthday last February. I got dressed while it printed.

Tiffany and I were out the door and following the Hugh Jackman–sounding voice on her phone's GPS in no time. In forty minutes, we were parking outside the FBI's Miami field office. It was a square white concrete building, and I assumed they were going for discreet when they designed it. The only thing it had going for it was the line of palm trees in front, standing like lazy soldiers.

It felt surreal walking up to the front desk to tell the receptionist that I needed to report my brother missing in Italy. Like I was watching someone else live an alternate version of my life. Finally, the last piece of my old existence was getting ripped from my hands.

Apparently, my idea of emergency and the FBI's were two different things. Tiffany and I waited thirty minutes in the stark white waiting room before an agent graced us with his presence.

"Miss Asher? I'm Agent Stokes. Please follow me." Agent Stokes was a tall, older gentleman who looked to be about fifty. His eyes were dark and his aging face was mapped with lines—proof, I guess, of the stress of being an FBI agent. As he approached, I could see his left arm was stiffer than his right; it didn't swing with the same ease when he walked. There was a faint scar next to his left eye, too, and I wondered if that side of his body had been injured on an assignment.

We walked down a long, industrial-looking hall and stepped into a waiting elevator. Agent Stokes pushed the number two, and we quickly traveled up. Tiffany and I followed him out of the elevator and down the hall to a conference room.

In the center of the room, there was a large, dark wooden table with twelve chairs tucked neatly under. A huge modern art canvas adorned one end of the long room, while a television hung opposite it. The inside wall was made of glass. The windows overlooked the parking lot, and I could see cars zooming along I-95 and the Ronald Regan Turnpike. When I turned around, Agent Stokes was closing the door behind Tiffany.

"Would you like to have a seat, Miss Asher?" he offered. I sat down and my shorts slid up my thigh. *Why didn't I think about wearing something more professional,* I chided myself. Then I instantly took it back. I was here to find my brother, not interview for a job. "How can the FBI be of assistance to you?"

"Well," I began. My voice seemed small. Tiffany put her hand on my arm and gave me a nod of support. "My brother is missing in Italy."

"I'm so sorry to hear that. How long has he been gone?" the agent asked. He flipped open his legal pad to an empty page and my hope that he was going to take the case rose.

"He left three months ago for what he told me was an exchange program between the University of Miami and several universities in Italy. He's a law student with a focus on immigration law and was there for research. I lost contact with him, and now I can't find him."

"Did you try contacting the universities in Italy, or his professors here?" he asked as he scribbled something on his notepad.

"I did," I said hesitantly. I didn't want to admit it, but evidence was mounting that Gil dropped off the map of his own volition. Evidence to anyone who didn't know him, that was. "That's what was so strange. I emailed the universities in Italy where Gil said he'd be, and none of them had heard of him. And when I called the university, the professor I spoke to there said that they didn't have an exchange agreement with any Italian universities and that he had no idea Gil was in Italy."

"I see," Agent Stokes said. He dropped his pen and my heart went with it.

"But there's also this." I pulled the journal from my bag and laid it on the table. "He's incredibly protective of his research and has always forbidden me from even breathing near it. But then he sent me this. It's one of his research journals. For him to have packaged it up and sent it to me from Italy . . . well, I can't begin to explain how out of character that is for Gil. And there's more." I opened the front cover. "He used a code word from when we were kids. We *only* used it when something was terribly wrong."

Agent Stokes took the journal and flipped through it, showing no emotion at all as he read a few pages.

"Have you read this?" Agent Stokes said.

"Not completely," I answered. "Well, I looked to see if there was anything that jumped out at me like a note as to why he would send it to me, but I didn't find anything."

Agent Stokes nodded. "Well, it doesn't appear that there's anything illegal in here, so that should put you at ease. Honestly, it looks to me like a regular journal. Maybe even a memoir of sorts. Here's something about a summer vacation up to the Tampa Bay area."

"What?" He passed me the journal. The page opposite was another one of his crazy family trees. I recognized a few of the names, but closer examination of it revealed that the tree was filled in with people we knew but were certainly not related to, unlike the tree I had examined at the apartment that was filled with family members.

"I don't know what's going on with the journal. But you have to understand that none of this makes sense . . . really. It is completely out of character for Gil. It's some kind of sign." Tiffany tried to reiterate the magnitude of this act, but it was clear Agent Stokes was not getting it.

"I can see that you're genuinely concerned about your brother. But sometimes people choose to disappear on purpose. He gave you false information about why he was going to Italy and now he's fallen off the grid. There's no evidence of foul play or that anything illegal has happened. I know this isn't what you want to hear, but in my professional opinion, it looks like he *wanted* to disappear."

My face became hot as I listened to Agent Stokes shoot down my hopes at finding Gil. I didn't know if I wanted to scream or cry. Seeing I was visibly shaken, he said, "But if you have a recent picture of him, I'll send it over to our attaché office in the US Embassy in Rome and ask them to keep an eye out."

"But they won't do anything?" Tiffany asked for me.

"I don't have any evidence to indicate that he's disappeared under suspicious circumstances. I'm sorry."

"I understand." I took the picture of Gil I printed out and handed it to the agent. "I appreciate you being willing to do this much."

"I wish I could do more. This is my direct line here." Agent Stokes pulled out his business card and handed it to me as Tiffany and I stood up. "If anything else comes up, please don't hesitate to contact me."

I took a deep breath and extended my hand to shake his. "Thank you for your time."

He escorted us back to the lobby, we thanked him again, then walked back out into the Florida sunshine. I immediately crumpled up his card and threw it in the trash.

I didn't say anything as Tiffany drove us back to my apartment. My mind was too busy working out my only option. By the time we walked through the door, I had made my decision. It would be the stupidest, or the bravest, thing I'd ever done, but I didn't have a choice.

I sat down at my kitchen table while Tiffany poured lemon-lime soda into two glasses filled with ice.

"Well?" She sat down and pushed a drink in front of me.

I knew what I had to do. "I'm going to Italy to find my brother."

CHAPTER 3

I began tossing clothes into a small suitcase at random. I went for versatile jeans and T-shirts, and even my one fancy black dress—when I found Gil, I was going to make him take me to a really expensive restaurant to apologize for making me travel halfway around the world. I tossed in the strappy pair of heels I'd worn with it to graduation two years ago, too.

"You cannot go to Italy, Vic!" Tiffany said sternly from the bedroom doorway.

"Why not?" I challenged, still throwing clothes from my dresser into my suitcase.

"You know you're going to have to get on a plane, right?"

"I know that, Tiff."

"And you know you're going to have to break into the cash that was only for emergencies, right?"

"This *is* an emergency."

"And you know you have no idea where he is or even where to start, right?"

"Are you going to continue stating the obvious or are you going to be a supportive friend?" I darted from the closet to the bathroom to the suitcase on my bed.

"I am being a supportive friend. Vic, listen." Tiffany took me by the arm and stopped my feverish movement. "What about asking Agent Stokes if he can give you a contact in Italy who will help you?"

"Agent Stokes already said there was nothing he could do. If the shoe were on the other foot, Gil would drop everything to come find me. He already proved that when he rearranged his whole life so I didn't have to keep living in foster care. I have to do the same for him." Tiffany conceded and let go of my arm.

I walked back into the closet and pulled down the small, fireproof safe Gil and I kept all of our important documents in. I pushed aside our birth certificates and our parents' death certificates and reached for my passport. Three months before it expired. Thank God for the family cruise to the Bahamas a month before the crash; otherwise I'd have to sneak into Italy.

"Are you just going to show up at the airport and hope to find a flight?" Tiffany's voice was trembling.

"There's a flight to Rome at two fifty-five. It's eleven now. If we leave in the next twenty minutes, I'll be there in plenty of time. If I can't get on that flight, then I'll get on the next one or with another airline. I have to do this, Tiff."

She sighed. "Well, I guess it's good that you never

touched any of that money because this is going to be one hell of an expensive search party."

I threw my arms around her neck and hugged her fiercely. "Will you please discreetly explain the situation to Sam?" I said. "And you can stay here while I'm gone and use my car. Okay?" I said hopefully.

"Of course." She smiled back.

There was a knock at the door.

"That's probably Mrs. Vasquez. Do you mind getting it while I finish packing?"

I walked into my bathroom and opened the small cosmetic bag that had come with my gift-with-purchase yesterday at the mall. I gave a little chuckle at the timing of actually having a *travel* makeup bag.

When I got back into the bedroom, Tiffany was there and with a look of annoyance on her face.

"What's wrong?" I asked.

"You are not going to believe who decided to show up," she said with an eye roll.

"Hey, babe! You got anything to eat?" Chad's voice bellowed through the apartment, startling me. Of all the days for him to show up!

"What are you going to tell him?" Tiffany questioned with raised eyebrows.

"I don't know. Maybe I can just get him to leave." I'd spent the last two years pretending I had barely a dime to my name. How on earth would I explain going to Italy?

I steeled myself and walked into the kitchen. I found him bent over with his head in the refrigerator looking for food I didn't have. With Gil gone, I'd been working more hours and eating at the diner. He stood up, and I was taken aback for a moment. He had gotten a haircut. Without the shaggy brown hair covering his face, I could see his blue eyes and his striking jawline. I smiled just a little at the sight of him.

"'Sup," he said when he saw me.

I shook my head and brought myself back to the moment. "Hi. There are granola bars in the cabinet. You can take the box with you on your way out," I said with as sweet a voice as I could muster.

"On my way out? I just got here, babe! Aren't you happy to see me?" Chad put his arm around my waist, pulled me to him, and kissed me hard on the mouth, distracting me from my mission.

"Oh yeah. I'm super-happy to see you. It's just that Tiffany and I were on our way out."

"Where're you going? Can't it wait?" He cocked his eyebrow.

"We are . . . house-sitting for a woman in Davie and we have to meet her at her place before she leaves," I told him.

"For who? How 'bout I come with you and check the place out?" he said a little too excitedly.

"She's a customer from the diner," I answered quickly. "So you have to go because I have to finish packing and we have to be there in less than an hour." I pushed Chad out of the kitchen, grabbing the box of granola bars from the cabinet along the way.

"Seriously?"

"Seriously." I kissed him quickly, shoved the granola bars into his hand, and shut the door behind him.

I turned to Tiffany. "Go watch out the window to make sure he leaves."

Tiffany scurried to the window while I finished packing. I printed another copy of Gil's contact information so I could leave a copy for Tiff and stuck it in my purse. Since his connection with the universities turned out to be a lie, all I had to go on was the list of hotels.

"He's gone. Damn! His car is an even bigger piece of shit than yours!" Tiffany laughed as she entered my bedroom.

"Thank you. Okay. I think I have everything. Oh my God! I can't believe I almost forgot the two most important things!" Back in the closet, I pulled the safe down again and retrieved the debit card attached to the airline settlement money. Then I grabbed the journal and shoved it in my purse on top of my tablet. "I'm going to need these."

There was no time to deal with my cell phone company and get international service, so Tiffany would have to rely on email. Plus, I left her the hotel address and phone number in Bologna on the fridge if she needed to reach me. I'd email her again when I moved on to the next hotel. Tiffany's lead foot got us to the airport in record time. She wanted to come in with me to make sure I got on the flight I wanted, but I made her go.

"How are you going to get from Rome to Bologna? Are they even close to each other?" Tiffany asked as we pulled my suitcase from the trunk. Bus fumes made my eyes water, and the loud roar of their engines made it difficult for us to hear each other.

"I have no idea, but I'm sure I'll figure it out when I get there," I shouted.

"Be safe," she said with her eyes locked on mine. "And don't forget your self-defense moves, okay?"

We'd spent hours watching YouTube self-defense videos and practicing the poses—the hope being that we'd never actually have to use them. "I'm going to be fine!" We hugged at the curb, and I rolled my suitcase into the airport. It was surprisingly empty, so I weaved my way through the tape like a lonely rat in a maze and approached the counter.

"I need a ticket to Rome, please," I said, not believing those were actual words leaving my mouth. "I think there's one that leaves at two fifty-five?"

"One moment. Let me see what I have available." She typed away on her keyboard, looking for a seat while I crossed my fingers and toes. "I'm afraid the only seat I have is in first class. Would you like that?"

Holy hell. First class? I knew I was going to be spending a lot of money on this, but I hadn't planned on being a Rockefeller. "How much is that ticket?" I cringed.

"I'm afraid a same-day ticket for this flight in first class is ten thousand, two hundred and fifty one dollars," she answered politely.

My heart may have stopped for just a moment before I answered "What? There wouldn't happen to be another flight out at the same time with a different airline that wasn't quite so much, would there?"

"You're welcome to check with the other airlines, but I'm afraid unless we're rescheduling a passenger who already has a ticket, I don't have access to that information." She smiled sweetly.

I didn't have time to walk the ticket counters and compare prices. I would have to take the flight she offered. I shook my head at the ridiculousness of my being disappointed that I was flying first class to Italy. Anyone else would be thrilled.

"I'll take the ticket." I handed her my passport. Before I knew it, she was christening my debit card with an ungodly amount of money. This trip was already killing me, and I hadn't even left Florida yet.

"Do you have a return date?"

"Um, can the ticket be open ended?" I asked. I hadn't thought about how long I was willing to traipse all over Italy in search of my possibly missing brother.

"I'm sorry, I can't do an open-ended international ticket. But you can change the date of your return if you need to. There's a two-hundred-dollar fee, but it would give you some more flexibility," she suggested.

"All right then, how about two weeks from today? I can extend it if I need to anytime?"

"Yes, ma'am," the agent said kindly.

Ten minutes later, the agent was saying something about a first-class lounge while handing me my ticket. I passed through security without a hitch, found my gate, and collapsed into a seat. It was at that moment that reality hit.

What am I doing?

Was I really about to get on a plane to Italy? With my elbows on my knees, I buried my face in my hands. Where should I even start looking for Gil? Was I expecting him to be waiting for me at the hotel in Bologna? Or maybe he'd be at the corner café drinking an espresso and eating a pastry? Tiff was right; this was crazy. I didn't speak any Italian and, so far, everything Gil had told me was a lie. I was embarking on what was already feeling like a wild-goose chase.

I took a deep breath and tried to calm myself. I was here now. Wild-goose chase or not, I couldn't turn back. If I had to chart a course with the geese in Italy, so be it. My best option seemed to be the bank account. I could look up where and when he made withdrawals and trace his steps that way. I didn't want to pull that up in the airport terminal so I decided the privacy of my hotel room in Bologna would be best.

I pulled out my phone and found that I could take a train from Rome to Bologna, about two hours away. I didn't know where the train terminal was from the airport, but it couldn't be far. The distance from the station to the hotel in Bologna was another question, but I was sure I'd be able to hail a taxi.

I looked at my ticket and read the words *First Class* on it again. As if the whole experience wasn't surreal enough. I, who had sworn off flying forever, was not only flying, but flying *first class*. I felt guilty, but Gil and I had agreed that we would use the settlement money for things that were incredibly important, and I couldn't think of anything more important than finding him.

Gate D30 had only a few people milling around, but the terminal was bustling with travelers. Down the hallway, I spotted people going in and out of what looked like a secret club. It was a large, heavy-looking wooden door. Suddenly, I remembered the ticket agent telling me I had plenty of time to relax in the lounge. I felt awkward, but my curiosity got the best of me so I got up and made my way to the American Airlines Business/First Class Lounge. I walked straight in like I knew what I was doing.

The attendant checked my ticket and told me to enjoy the complimentary food and beverages. There was even a bar with a bartender. I filled a plate with some mini–hot dogs, cheese, crackers, and baby carrots. I got a can of Coke from the bartender and chose a plush leather chair in the far corner of the room where I could watch people come and go and eat my snacks in peace.

A few men came in and made a beeline for the bar. They all ordered bourbon and loosened their ties as they sat down. I couldn't tell if they were together or not, but they seemed friendly with one another from the handshaking and smiles that were going around. I watched them for a few minutes before focusing on the bartender.

He was a good-looking guy, probably in his late twenties, early thirties, cordial and friendly with everyone he spoke to, including me. His personality put me at ease. Something about him made me feel like I wasn't the only one in the room who ate off-brand mac and cheese and PB&Js for dinner more than once a week. He caught me looking at him and smiled. I smiled back. Nothing flirtatious, but it did make me think of Chad. I quickly dismissed that thought and focused on food and people-watching.

One of the men pulled out a deck of cards and invited the others to play blackjack. He then proceeded to cheat his ass off. He won all but three of the twelve rounds, and only because he gifted the wins to the three other guys. By the time they were done, Five Card Stud had more drinks coming to him than he deserved.

I was enjoying the snacks and the quiet, mentally preparing myself to get on a plane, when one of the card players came over and sat in the leather chair next to me. He was average height with brown hair, and he was wearing a gray suit. He wasn't a particularly good card player. He folded almost immediately if he had terrible cards, but rubbed the back of his neck when he was dealt a great hand. I could tell by the condition of his suit that he was a family man— there was a tiny patch of glitter and green finger paint on the left cuff. And there was a small indent on his left ring finger where his wedding band should have been.

"Hello," he said.

"Hello," I said out of sheer politeness.

"I'm Stefan."

Really? That was the fake name he was going with? I contemplated telling him my name was Regina Phalange but decided against it in case he was on my flight.

"Vic."

"I'm assuming that's short for Victoria?"

I nodded and went back to my crackers.

"Where are you traveling to today, Vic?" he asked.

This guy really was dense. Getting me to talk to him was like pulling teeth, but he was oblivious.

"I'm going to Italy to see my brother," I told him.

"Surely, a beautiful girl like you isn't traveling alone." He cocked his head to one side and leaned his elbow on the arm of the chair toward me.

I put my plate of food on the coffee table in front of us, crossed my legs, and faced him.

"Look. You seem like . . . well, you seem like a nice guy. And even though you're a married man hitting on me here in the lounge at the ever-so-romantic Miami airport, I'm going to help you out. Your buddy dealing the cards is cheating," I told him. "The win you had was a gift."

"What? I'm not—" Stefan stumbled.

"You have kids, too, don't you?"

He nodded slowly, embarrassed.

"How do you know he's cheating?" he whispered, obviously avoiding being called out about his personal life.

"He's cold-stacking the cards. Did you see how many times he shuffled the cards in that fancy way? Not like you or I would shuffle them. He's watching for high cards and keeping track so he gets them," I explained.

"Yeah, but *how* did you know he was doing that?"

"My dad used to play cards with his buddies every week-end at our house. He taught me how to watch for things, what to look for."

"That son of a bitch! I play cards in here with him twice a month, and he wins every damn time. Do you have any idea how many free cocktails that man has consumed? Too many!" He laughed. "You've got a real talent there, Vic. You could work for the Nevada Gaming Commission."

"I don't think so," I chuckled. I picked up my plate of food and ate a piece of cheese.

"Um, about the other thing—"

"I'm sure you travel a lot and get lonely. Just don't forget that she's probably lonely, too."

With a tight-lipped smile and a nod, Stefan left me to rejoin his friends. He suggested another game and offered to deal, but Cool Hand Luke wasn't interested in a game he couldn't control, so he left the lounge.

When it was time for my flight to board, I clutched my purse and headed for the gate. The man scanned my boarding pass and told me to enjoy my flight. *Right.* I took baby steps to delay my progress but all too soon I crossed the threshold into the hall that would lead to my nemesis.

The closer I got to the plane, the narrower the tunnel seemed. The walls were suffocatingly close, the ceiling claustrophobically low. The air felt like it was getting thinner. I stopped and leaned my head against the wall, closing my eyes and trying to breathe deeply. Maybe a flight attendant would have to sedate me and drag me to my seat. I focused on putting one foot in front of the other, then on my anger at Gil. He knew how much I hated to fly. How dare he make me do it?

With small steps, I finally made it to the open hatch door. The overly pleasant flight crew welcoming me onboard was reminiscent of an old *Saturday Night Live* sketch. But seeing how nervous I was, a flight attendant led me to my seat and helped me get comfortable. I was happy to see it was a single seat by the window. No neighbor meant I could freak out in relative privacy. She showed me the food and drink options, and I wondered if there was a legal drinking age in the air. A first-class flight to Italy seemed as good a time as any to get drunk for the first time.

It felt like only seconds later we were taxiing from the terminal to the runway. My hands were sweating, my heart was racing, and I was beginning to feel dizzy. I must have looked pretty bad because the same flight attendant who seated me came to check on me.

"Miss? Are you okay?"

"I'm not a fan of flying," I told her.

"Is it the takeoff or the landing that gets you?"

"It's the being in a hollow metal tube thirty-five thousand feet in the air and crashing in a fiery blaze that gets me." I considered telling her about my parents' death but thought it better not to bring it up. My sarcasm would have to do for the time being.

"I see," she said slowly. Surely, it was not the first time she had heard the fears of a passenger. "You know, when I was a little girl, my mom used to do this thing with me whenever I was scared. It could have been when we were flying somewhere, or if I was getting a shot at the doctor's office. I would close my eyes, she would grab my hand, and we would name all the Disney princesses together until the scary thing was over.

"I still do it. I hate takeoff. So, when I'm sitting there, waiting for it to be over, I shut my eyes really tight and whisper their names. Sometimes I have to say them more than once." She raised her eyebrows and gave me a sweet smile. "My name is Janine. Don't hesitate to let me know if you need anything at all."

"Flight attendants. Prepare for takeoff," the captain said over the intercom.

"That's my cue," she said, and walked up the aisle, gripping her hands into fists.

I'd been so preoccupied about finding Gil in Italy that I hadn't put a lot of thought into the logistics of getting there. I took a few deep breaths to calm my nerves so the air marshal wouldn't have to restrain me. Although, maybe he had something that would knock me out for the duration of the flight?

The engines roared in preparation for takeoff. The way I was knotting and gripping my hands together made me sure I would land in Rome with several broken fingers.

Gil. Gil. Gil. Gil, I chanted to myself. I had to stay focused on why I was doing this. *Gil. Gil. Gil.*

The plane picked up speed on the runway and so did my heart. Outside my window, the tarmac was racing by. I thought, *Maybe this won't be so bad.* But then some flaps adjusted on the wings, making a whining sound, and I knew I *wasn't* going to be okay. My breathing became shallow, and I was overcome with the need to get off the plane. Now. I peeled my eyes away from the dizzying landscape outside my tiny, fragile-looking window, and toward the kind flight attendant, Janine. Her eyes closed up tight, and her lips were moving silently.

There was no turning back. I had to find Gil.

With that, I shut my eyes and began to whisper, "Cinderella, Snow White, Aurora, Ariel . . ."

CHAPTER 4

Dinner was served almost immediately after takeoff. This first-class thing was no joke. I had never been treated so well by anyone without having to put on a show. Up there, it didn't matter that I was wearing jeans, a T-shirt, and a hoodie. The fact that I had been able to afford a ticket was good enough for them.

I ate well: filet mignon with some kind of wine sauce, green beans, and roasted potatoes. Who knew airplane food could be so good? For a second, a jolt of excitement passed through me. Here I was, flying first class, on my way to Italy! But the feeling left just as quickly. I wasn't about to embark on a posh European vacation. I had to find Gil and bring him home.

I knew I should try and get some sleep to prepare for what was ahead, but I was restless. Despite my nerves, I managed to doze off for a few minutes a couple times, but I eventually gave up trying. I pulled my bag from the floor and onto my lap, and took out Gil's journal. I had to read it. Gil sent it to me for a reason, and if I was going to find him, I had to know exactly what that reason was.

I decided to start at the beginning. The word *oxblood* glared at me from the front cover. What was Gil telling me? And if he was in such grave danger, why wouldn't he involve the local police?

I found the first oddly drawn family tree. There were names on branches, three on each side. At the top was a block with a big question mark in it. I recognized the uncles and aunts, a few distant cousins, and even some family friends, but they didn't connect the way Gil had laid them out.

I shook my head in confusion. It wasn't dated, so I didn't know if this was a journal he started back home or since he had arrived in Italy. When I began to read, I became even more confused. The first pages described our great-uncle Ricky on our father's side hosting a dinner party. He lamented having ordered a specific cut of meat from the butcher, but the butcher couldn't get it to him in time. Two pages later, they were attending the butcher's funeral.

I flipped several pages ahead and found more fake memories of a life Gil and I never lived. There was the vacation in Tampa, where he wrote about spending the Fourth of July on Pass-A-Grill Beach, until storms forced everyone under the picnic shelters across the street. But another family who was already there said there wasn't enough room under the shelter for everyone, and the men in both families basically duked it out until Uncle Ricky and cousin Mikey declared our family the winners.

It wasn't that we never took vacations. But they weren't *these* vacations. In the journal, people who were our parents' friends were referred to as aunts and uncles, and friends Gil and I had growing up were brothers and sisters. He drove a car we never owned and studied foreign languages I'd never even heard spoken in my life.

Husbands presented wives with jewelry at every family gathering and went hunting for weird animals with guns that sounded more like weapons of mass destruction than anything. "Aunts" and "uncles" were dying and leaving their family businesses to their children. They had unexplained accidents, and one even disappeared without a trace. Some of the uncles and cousins became ruthless businessmen and started companies of their own, firing employees left and right for divulging trade secrets. And while Gil was writing as if he had observed all the events, I had yet to be mentioned anywhere.

My eyes hurt after poring over most of the journal. It was so confusing I gave up three quarters of the way through. What was he trying to tell me? Was this how he did his research? In bizarre fictional stories? I wondered if the stress of losing Mom and Dad and then Maria finally broken him.

I snapped the journal shut, my thoughts confused and my hopes dashed. The sun was setting outside my window, illuminating the sky with a red-and-orange glow. Dark clouds just below us made the scene more wicked than magical.

I closed my eyes and tried to focus on my plan of

attack. I would start at the hotel in Bologna where, supposedly, Gil had last been. At least I knew the journal had been mailed from there. At the hotel, I would review our bank account. And it wouldn't hurt to ask the front desk clerks if they remembered Gil, either.

I didn't even know how much time had passed since Tiffany and I left my apartment and headed for the airport. Now, I was getting out of a taxi in front of the Marriott in Bologna. It was a plain gray building with a beautiful glass-door entry. The lobby was sleek and simple, with an odd square bench centered on a rug, surrounded by pillows. I wandered through the lobby and into the lounge, pulling my suitcase behind me. It was late in the afternoon, and there were only a few people: a young couple holding hands and kissing in between sips of wine, an old woman with a billowy scarf on her head sitting in the corner knitting, and a super-hot blond guy playing feverishly on his iPad.

There must have been some part of me that hoped Gil would be there, casually writing in one of his journals. We could laugh and call this whole silly trip off, and he would take me to his favorite café and explain everything over cappuccino. But Gil wasn't there, and suddenly I felt exhausted by the weight of my impossible task. Did I really think it would be as easy as hopping on a plane and walking into a hotel lobby? My heart sank even further.

As I approached the reception desk, I remembered another major problem: My entire Italian vocabulary consisted of high-end fashion brands and drink sizes available at Starbucks. Stating my desired destination was all I had to do at the train station in Rome and with the taxi driving here in Bologna, but I had a sinking feeling that saying "Prada" and "*venti*" to the receptionist wasn't going to help me find my brother—or get a room.

"Hello," I said tentatively. "I was wondering if you had a room available."

"*Buon giorno!* Welcome to the AC Hotel. I would be happy to assist you today," the girl behind the counter said as she smiled brightly. She had dark hair and fair skin, and her young features made me wonder if she was even old enough to have a job.

"Thank you so much." I sighed with relief.

"Of course, miss. So you do not have a reservation?"

"Um . . . no, so I'm really hoping you have a room available for the next few days." I used as desperate a tone as I could, hoping to magically make an available room pop up on her screen.

She typed away, searching for a room with not much of an expression on her face until she spoke again. "Yes. I see that we have a few rooms available, but they are all junior suites. Would you like to reserve one?"

A junior suite? First I'm flying first class, now I'm booking a junior suite? *Just go with it, Vic. Next you'll be having a limo drive you around Italy!*

"Yes, I'll take the suite," I told her without even asking how much it was. I handed her my passport and debit card. I looked around the lobby aimlessly while I waited and took note of where the restaurant was so I could get something to eat later. The woman who was knitting in the lounge had relocated to the lobby, and the hot blond guy got in line behind me.

He smiled politely at me, and I returned a small, tight-lipped smile back at him. I laughed to myself thinking about what Tiffany would have done if she were here. He was definitely right up her alley. His dress pants fit him perfectly, and the sleeves of his white button-up shirt were rolled up past his elbows. The top buttons were undone, revealing his sharp collarbones and a slice of smooth chest. His hair was a stylish mess on top, and he had the most striking blue eyes.

"Here are your room number and card key along with the instructions for accessing the Wi-Fi. Is there anything else I can help you with, miss?"

"Actually, there is. My brother stayed here a few weeks ago. He's six feet tall, dark hair, brown eyes, mid-twenties, kind of looks like me. I wanted to surprise him. I wondered if you ever spoke to him, or maybe knew where he went when he left here?"

"You don't know where your brother is?" the girl asked curiously.

"He's on a little self-discovery journey. You know, backpacking around the Mediterranean." She nodded and smiled. "His name is Gil Asher," I added.

"Let me see," she answered, clacking away at the computer again. "I see here that Mr. Asher checked out two weeks ago. I remember him. He was very nice—and handsome. Hard to forget," she said like it was a secret. "He seemed fine when he checked out, but he was quite insistent that I mail a package to America for him right away."

"*You* mailed the package?"

"*Sí.*" She smiled.

"Did he say anything else?"

"No. Just that it was extremely important that the package go out immediately."

"Well, thank you. I appreciate your help." I couldn't think of anything else to ask, but maybe if I rested for a bit and let the jet lag run its course, I would come up with something.

I followed her directions to the elevator and made my way to the fourth floor. I found my room at the end of the hall and entered, letting the door close by itself behind me as I took in the room.

"It's sad when a hotel room is nicer than your own apartment," I mused aloud.

The room had wood flooring and furniture in gray hues. It was sleek and modern, just like the lobby. Gray tile covered the walls of the bathroom, where I noticed a shower curtain was conspicuously missing. *Well, showering is going to be an adventure*, I thought.

I rolled my suitcase into the separate bedroom and tossed it on the bed before I plopped myself down next to it. I had no idea what time my body thought it was. All I knew was I was weary from traveling and worrying. I heaved myself up and pulled my laptop from my bag. I followed the instructions and was on the hotel's Wi-Fi within minutes. A quick Google search later and I learned that

Italy was six hours ahead of the eastern seaboard. That meant that my body thought it was mid-morning. I would be okay for a little while, but if I didn't rest, I wouldn't be able to keep my eyes open come dinnertime.

Before my eyelids betrayed me, I pulled up the bank account and saw that Gil had paid for his hotel rooms at each of his stops over the last three months. Genoa, Rome, Palermo, Venice, and Bologna. There had been a few cash withdrawals as well. Only a few hundred dollars here and there. The last transaction was at this hotel—two weeks ago.

I checked my email but didn't find anything new from Gil, the universities, or Tiffany. I sent her a quick email to let her know that I had arrived safely and gave her my room number in case of an emergency. I signed off with a string of *X*'s and *O*'s and shut both the laptop and my eyes, surrendering to whatever tomorrow would bring.

I dreamed I found Gil shopping in Milan with a woman he met and married on the fly. He told me he wanted to start a new life in Italy. When I asked him about the journal he sent, he said it was his way of saying good-bye to me forever, that giving me a piece of his imagination was the best thing he could think to leave me with. When I asked about the woman he married, he told me it was none of my business and that I needed to go home to Miami, go to college, and start a new life, too.

I cried and begged him to come home with me. I told him how alone I would be without him because he was my only family, but he just took me by the shoulders and told me it was my turn to live the better life we had always talked about. He said I had to stop being so afraid and be the badass girl he always knew I was.

He kissed me on the forehead, turned, and walked away with his beautiful Italian wife on his arm. The crowd thickened and, before I knew it, he was gone.

A loud knock on the door to my suite woke me from that terrible dream. I must have cried in my sleep, too, because my eyes and pillow were both wet. The numbers on the clock next to the bed told me that it was seven-thirty. I hoped that my short nap would be enough to begin getting me adjusted to the local time.

I opened the door and found the hot blond guy I had exchanged smiles with in the lobby staring at me.

"Hi," he said with a cute smirk.

"Hi. Can I—" Before I could finish, he was pushing me back through door and into my room, something hard pressing against my belly.

I took a deep breath to scream.

"Don't," he hissed. "Look down."

I glanced down. Pressing into my stomach was the muzzle of a pistol.

"If you scream, I shoot," he said, his English accent recognizable now. "You answer my questions honestly and you get to live. Nod if you understand."

I didn't know if I should nod or not because I *didn't* understand what he was doing there.

He stepped back but kept his gun pointed at me. "Who are you? Why are you looking for Gil Asher?" he asked.

"My name is Vic and Gil is my brother," I said. "Do you—do you know him?" I was so terrified I could hardly think, but even so, the fact that this guy with a gun, who'd just barged into my room and assaulted me, was asking about my brother didn't elude me. What would Gil have to do with someone like this? I was scared as hell, but I couldn't believe I would find my first link to Gil so quickly.

"Did you miss the part when I instructed you to answer my questions?"

"Yeah, well, I have a few of my own," I challenged with misplaced bravery. My heart was still racing as his piercing eyes bore into me.

He cocked his head, surprised by my defiance, and stared at me for a moment.

"Prove he's your brother," he demanded after a moment's thought.

"Um, my cell phone has some pictures of us on it. It's in there on the table." I pointed to the bedroom.

He stepped to the side and waved his gun toward the bedroom. "Go get it."

When I came back with the phone, I already had one of Gil and me at his going-away party pulled up. My captor took the phone from me and swiped through the photos, which included a mix of me with Tiffany and a couple of Chad.

He shook his head as he closed his eyes. He finally lowered his gun and shoved it into the back of his pants and leaned against the wall. I felt my body relax and let out the tension-filled breath I had been holding.

"What are you doing here?" he asked.

"I'm looking for him. He's disappeared. I tried to reach him at the universities where he said he'd be, but no one has heard of him," I explained. I didn't tell him about Gil's weird journal because I didn't know who this guy was or if I could trust him. I didn't know if he was looking for Gil to harm him, or if he was looking *out* for Gil. "Your turn. How do you know my brother?"

"Gil was . . . *working* for me, for lack of a better term," he answered.

"Doing what?"

"I'm not at liberty to say. But I can tell you that I'm looking for him and will send his ass home as soon as I find him." He pushed off the wall and pulled out his cell phone. "Stay the night. Enjoy the food here—it's pretty good—and I'll get you on the first flight out tomorrow."

"Wait a minute," I said, my head spinning. "Who are you? What's happened to my brother?" I steeled myself. "I'm not going anywhere until I understand what's going on!"

"You remember that gun I had earlier, right?" he said in his snarky British accent.

"Look, if you need to shoot me, then do it, because if I don't find Gil my life is over anyway. He's the only family I have left." I choked back the lump in my throat that was forming because my body wanted to cry. I had gotten this far. I couldn't start falling apart now.

He shoved his hands into his pockets as he took me in and sighed resolutely.

"Well . . . why don't we start over?" He held out his hand to greet me officially. "My name is Ian Hale. And I'm a friend."

CHAPTER 5

I shook Ian's hand hesitantly, and we stood there for a moment evaluating each other. Now that we had been formally introduced, and Ian's gun was tucked away, I wanted to believe that he was an ally of Gil's. I had started this venture flying solo, with almost no leads. I certainly wouldn't say I trusted this Ian Hale, but I couldn't deny that discovering him might make finding Gil much easier.

"You've had a long trip and you're probably getting hungry. Why don't you let me buy you dinner?" he offered with a crooked smile. "There's a place not far from here."

"That's very nice of you, but unnecessary." It's true, I was starving, but I wasn't about to go anywhere with this guy quite yet.

"We can walk there," he said.

"Um, okay then." Walking was good. I had a better chance of escape on foot if Ian decided to wield his gun again. But mostly, I had a ton of questions, and a public place felt like a better location to get them answered.

I grabbed my bag, Gil's journal tucked safely inside. Ian held the door for me as we walked out of the building. It was a nice evening. Clear skies and a cool breeze. The streetlights were on the opposite side of the street, making our walk a bit too shadowy for my taste. We walked a block in silence before Ian spoke.

"Why did you come all the way to Italy just because you couldn't reach Gil? That seems pretty extreme."

"How was Gil working for you?" I replied.

"Do you answer every question with a question?" He smirked with a cocked eyebrow.

I gave a nervous laugh. "Only when I've traveled thousands of miles to find my missing brother."

"What makes you think he's missing?"

"Because I know Gil. He . . . did something very out of character. Something that I interpreted as a call for help. When I tried to find him, I discovered that he hadn't been entirely honest with me. I have no idea where he is and I'm pretty sure he's in some sort of trouble. I knew I had to do something; I'm not a sit-around-and-wait kind of girl."

"I can see that. What did he do?" Ian asked.

I didn't answer, but instead looked at Ian over my nose as if to say, *You think I'm really going to spill everything?*

"You're smart not to trust me. Not because you can't, because you certainly can, but it will serve you well to not trust people you've just met."

The hostess began to seat us near the center of the

small, crowded restaurant, but I requested, with some awkward pointing and head nodding, the back corner table instead. Once we were settled, our waitress came by and took our drink orders.

"*Vino rosso, per piacere*," Ian said in perfect Italian.

"Proper English and Italian? Impressive," I teased.

"If I wanted to impress you, I'd make sure you knew I also spoke Russian, German, and French." He flashed another crooked smile.

I didn't want to be so disarmed by Ian's charisma, but his piercing blue eyes gazing into mine was making it difficult—and his strong jaw and day-old beard weren't helping. His thick, messy hair told me he couldn't be any more than twenty-six, if that. I knew he was dangerous, but he was hot, distractingly so. Less than an hour ago, he'd held a gun to my stomach and now he was buying me dinner—and flirting.

"Mission accomplished," I said softly as I looked over the menu.

Although there was a hotel down the street, the restaurant clearly did not cater to tourists. Every word on the menu was in Italian, and I couldn't read a stitch of it.

"I think you're going to have to do some translating here," I said sheepishly.

"Are you a picky eater?" he asked, not looking up from his menu.

"Not really. I'm not a fan of weird things, but I'm pretty open to almost anything." French food had some adventurous dishes like escargot and foie gras, and most Scottish dishes were based on a dare. Italian food, though, seemed safe.

"Good. I'll just order for you," he said. I nodded in agreement.

When the waitress came back, she had a bottle of red wine and two glasses. She set the glasses down, poured each of us a glass, and left the bottle on the table. After a quick conversation with Ian, she walked back to the kitchen.

"Okay," I muttered.

"So," Ian said before he took a sip of his wine.

"So?" I countered.

"The wine is good. You should have some," he told me.

"I'm not old enough," I told him. Not that Tiffany and I hadn't enjoyed a drink or two, or more, in my apartment. It's just that I had never dared to drink out in the open.

"You don't look under eighteen," he said, taking another sip.

"I'm twenty."

"Then have a sip, Victoria."

"It's Vic," I corrected.

Ian twisted his mouth as he considered my name. "I like Victoria better."

No one had called me Victoria since I was twelve years old. When I turned thirteen, I told my mother that Victoria was too proper, and Tori was too preppy, and from that point on, I wanted to be called Vic. To me it was a stronger, more commanding name.

"Who *are* you?" I said as I took a sip of wine. It was

better than any wine that Tiffany and I had ever had, which wasn't saying much since the wine came in a box.

Ian crossed his legs and sat sideways in his chair like an old movie star. He leaned on the table with his elbow and looked at me intently. I wanted to believe Ian was a good guy. Gil wouldn't have worked with him if he didn't trust him. If everything Ian had said was true, then he was my only hope of finding my brother.

"What would you like to know, Victoria?" he asked slyly.

"Really? You're going to answer any question I ask? And answer it honestly?"

"I didn't say that. I asked you what you wanted to know. But if you're really Gil's sister, and you're anything like him, I'm fairly sure I can trust you with the truth."

"That's not very guarded of you, Ian," I said. He raised his eyebrows and wineglass to me before taking another sip.

"My job is to read people. I have to know within a matter of seconds whether I can trust them or not," he explained.

"So at what point in time were you *fairly sure* you could trust me? Was it before or after you had a gun to my chest?"

"It was in the hotel room, when my gun didn't stop you from asking questions, and every moment since then."

The waiter brought our food, giving me the perfect excuse to unlock our gaze and regain my composure. I had a sneaking suspicion that his endgame was to seduce me into jumping onto the first flight back to Miami. But if he thought that a cute accent and a gorgeous face was enough to make me leave the country without my brother, then it was time to look for another job, because he was reading me all wrong.

But that could wait. On the table in front of me was possibly the most incredible-looking bowl of pasta ever made. Just the aroma wafting from the dish made my stomach growl with anticipation. A rich, meaty sauce on a bed of ribbons of pasta. It looked delicious, and I wanted to eat it more than I'd ever wanted to eat anything. I gaped in a carb-induced frenzy.

"It's traditional Bolognese. *Buon appetito.*"

"Thank you," I smiled softly. I pierced the pasta with my fork and blew on it for a moment before I put it in my mouth. I began to compare it to Sam's spaghetti sauce—the recipe I swore no one could ever hold a candle to—and immediately felt bad because it wasn't even a contest. The flavors exploded in my mouth, and I involuntarily let out a little moan.

"Well!" Ian responded with a sexy smile. "That's definitely a good sound."

I blushed, embarrassed. "Yeah, it's really good. I can't afford to eat like this at home," I admitted.

"Yet you can afford to fly to Italy," Ian challenged me. I put my fork down and took another sip of wine, which made the food taste even better. I didn't know if I should tell Ian about the airline settlement, but then decided that he probably wouldn't care. Ian didn't come across like the type who was out for the money; I got the feeling that his MO entailed something much larger. And perhaps telling him would assure him of my ability to finance my own journey to find Gil?

"Well, I choose not to eat like this at home." I paused, carefully choosing my words. "Do you remember the crash of Northwest flight eight-fifteen?"

"Was that the flight that crashed on the runway six years ago?" he asked, a worried look crossing his face.

"Five. My parents were on that flight." Throughout the years, the responses after hearing that my parents had died in a horrific plane crash varied from apathy to tears. I was curious what his would be.

"I'm really sorry, Victoria. I know that must have been very difficult for you," he said. His face was soft and compassionate, but not condescending. His eyes connected with mine, and I knew the next thing out of his mouth wasn't going to be another suggestion of how going gluten-free or doing tai chi in the park would change my perspective on life.

I nodded. It always seemed strange to say thank you. "The crash was a pilot error. Turns out the airline let him work too many shifts in a row. So, along with the other one hundred and seventy-four families, we received a settlement from the airline that was more money than anyone really needs."

"And so it's been just you and Gil then. No wonder you're here." Ian leaned forward. "That's . . . That's really something." He looked like he wanted to say something else, but then he shook his head slightly and picked up his fork.

"I wasn't asking for your sympathy. I just wanted you to know that if me sticking around is a matter of money, I can carry my own weight," I told him resolutely.

"Money is not an issue, Victoria," he replied without looking at me.

There was an awkward silence, so I turned back to my food as well. In between bites, I took in the restaurant, admiring the simple decor. There were paintings hanging on the taupe walls and two marble statues of women draped in robes flanking the entrance to the kitchen. There were also decorative maps of Italy featuring different regions along the wall behind Ian. Families told loud, animated stories, emptying bottle after bottle of wine as they laughed. Couples sat close, kissing and holding each other while deep in deep conversation. Public affection like that would get lots of stares back home, but here, no one but me gave them a second look. Dining out in Europe did not appear to be a quick experience. Sam would kill me if I let a table sit as long as these servers did.

"So, what did Gil do that was so out of character?" Ian asked as the waitress cleared our plates.

I made a hard line with my lips, still feeling the need to keep the existence of the journal under lock and key.

"Don't worry. I'm not going to ask for details, Victoria. It doesn't really matter. You'll be gone tomorrow, and as soon as I find Gil, I'll be sending him home, too," Ian said matter-of-factly.

"I already told you that I'm not leaving without him," I replied defiantly.

"And I already told you that you're not staying."

"What was Gil doing for you that you granted him permission to stay?" I countered.

"Trust me, I would have sent him home in a flash had he been honest about having a family." Ian's voice turned hard and almost angry.

"What are you talking about?" I asked, confused.

"In my line of work, there can be no family or friends to whom you matter, because your death can't matter." Seeing the pained look on my face, Ian leaned back in his chair and calmed his tone. "I'm sorry. That was . . . That was brash."

Ian continued with a softer approach. "When I asked Gil if he had anyone to go home to, he said no."

Gil was passionate beyond reason about law. He would go days without sleep during a research streak. He once dug through 130 years' worth of archives to find a precedent that would convict a defendant—for a *case study*. It didn't shock me that he denied my existence. Gil could be so single-minded and goal-oriented that the rest of the world disappeared. And based on what Ian said, it was clear that Gil had gotten himself into something pretty deep.

"It doesn't matter," I began.

"It does matter! Do you know how many people would love to have someone to go home to?" Ian's reply was passionate.

"Then help me. Help me find him and bring him home," I pleaded. "What was Gil doing that could get him killed? And what is it that you *do*? Please, Ian. It's your turn to explain. I need answers."

Ian watched me for a moment, considering his options. I stared back at him, willing him to make up his mind and let me help find Gil. He bit his lip and ran his fingers through his hair.

"I don't know if you can handle this, Victoria. I wasn't sure Gil could, either, but he was already in deep and there was nothing I could do." He sighed. "I want to help you. I just don't know if—"

"Shut up," I snapped. Ian creased his brow in surprise and confusion at my cutting him off. I rested my cheek in my hand and pulled my hair down from the ponytail it had been in, letting my long hair fall to shield me from the rest of the restaurant. "The guy at my nine o'clock has been at my twelve and one since we got here. He keeps moving closer and hasn't had a bite to eat," I whispered.

Ian's eyes got bright and a surprised expression came over him. He probably thought I was overreacting and nervous, finding everyone suspicious. But then the faintest smile appeared on his face.

"I take back what I just said." The smile on his face widened, confusing me.

"I don't understand," I replied.

Ian turned toward the guy and motioned for him to come. He nodded and pulled up a chair at the end of our table. "Victoria, this is Damon Pazzia. Damon, this is Gil's sister, Victoria."

"*Piacere di conoscerti,*" Damon said as he took my hand

and kissed it. If there was a poster boy for the classic Italian male, it was Damon. He had dark hair and eyes and rich olive skin. He was just like Rudolf Valentino in all those old movies my mom used to watch.

"He's very pleased to meet you," Ian laughed.

"I can see that. Does he speak English?" I asked.

"He does. He likes to lead with the Italian, though, don't you, Damon?"

"The ladies, they like the Italian," he answered with a smoldering look. "Wait. She is Gil's sister? Gil has a sister?"

"Yes," Ian answered.

"That is not good," Damon said in his Italian accent, his eyes turning dark.

"No. Why don't you go back and see if we've got anything new? I've got to figure out what I'm going to do with Victoria," Ian instructed him.

"I know what I'd like to do with Victoria," Damon said in a sultry voice that made me blush.

"Go!" Ian demanded. Damon kissed my hand again and exited the restaurant.

"You have to figure out what you're going to do with me?" I questioned him, annoyed by the implication that I was something to be done with.

"You surprised me. Damon is a chameleon, a shadow. He's followed the pope into the Vatican and gone unnoticed." Ian looked around the restaurant and then back at me. "They were going to seat us in the middle of the room. But you preferred the corner. You like the vantage point it gives."

"Yeah," I said in a short breath.

"What else have you noticed?" he asked curiously.

I paused. "The couple to your back right is having relationship problems. Every time she gets up to use the restroom, he checks his phone."

"That's not unusual. Maybe he's looking for the latest football score," Ian proposed.

"Does the latest football score cause a bead of sweat to form on your upper lip, or cause you to adjust yourself?" I said confidently.

"Go on." He smiled.

I leaned back in my seat and narrowed my eyes.

"The slight limp tells me our waitress is nursing a blister on her right foot. The man eating alone at your nine o'clock lost his wife not too long ago. He keeps spinning his wedding ring and rubbing it like a genie's lamp in hopes of bringing her back. You shoved the capers in your dish to the side, which tells me you like the flavor they add, but not the taste of them directly, otherwise you would have requested they make the dish without them." I smirked at him triumphantly.

"Is that it?" he challenged.

"No. You suck at Candy Crush."

"What? No I don't! I mean . . . How did you . . ."

"Were you, or were you not, playing Candy Crush on your iPad when I saw you in the lounge at the hotel?" I leaned forward and rested my forearms on the table.

Ian huffed a smile and licked his lips as he looked away

from me for a moment. "Well, Victoria Asher. You may not be headed back to America as quickly as I thought."

"I'm pretty sure that's what I've been telling you," I countered.

Ian asked for the check and paid for our dinner. I knew it hadn't been a date, but it was nice to be on the receiving end for a change.

The night air had turned chillier by the time we began our walk back to the hotel. It was only a few blocks away, but I was kicking myself for leaving my hoodie in my room.

"I'd offer you my jacket if I had it with me," Ian said apologetically.

"Really? Guys still do that?" I asked disbelievingly. Chad was certainly not the chivalrous type. The last time we went to the movies, I had to buy the tickets *and* the popcorn, and then I proceeded to freeze to death in the theater. After spending half the movie viciously rubbing my arms and sending him death glares, I finally asked for his jacket, but he just shrugged and told me that I should bring one next time. I used to see Dad do sweet things for Mom, and Gil hadn't dated anyone since Maria died and he became obsessed with school—or whatever it is he's obsessed with.

"Where I come from, they do. My mum taught me to believe that women deserved to be treated like princesses and queens," he said with straight conviction.

"Well, you do come from a place where they have *actual* princesses and queens."

"It's more than that." Ian looked at me softly, and there was something in his eyes that melted me. Pain. A lost love, perhaps. I held his eyes for another moment. Suddenly, something clicked and I was sucked into the whirlwind of Ian Hale. Who was he? Where did he come from? And what did "more than that" mean?

Ian walked me back to the hotel, and we rode the elevator up in silence. When we reached my room, I slid the card key into the slot and opened the door when the light turned green. Before I could say thank you and good night, Ian stepped past me and into my hotel room, making himself comfortable on the couch. Resting his ankle on his knee, he looked at me with anticipation. When I didn't respond, he got playfully irritated.

"Really? You're not going to say anything? That's disappointing," he chuckled.

"You're kidding, right? What am I supposed to say? You are officially the King of Mixed Messages. One minute, you're saying you can't tell me anything. The next minute, you're saying that anyone who joins your club has to be alone in the world just in case they get killed. Then you're telling the Italian Don Juan that you have to decide what you're going to do with me. If you could choose which side of the street you're driving on, then I could hitch a ride. Until then, I'm sorry if I'm a little skittish about asking the wrong questions from the man who held a gun to my chest within the first sixty seconds of meeting me!" I crossed my arms and waited for his response.

"Okay, first of all, it's not a club." He stood and planted himself two feet in front of me.

"Seriously, Ian! Look, if I were honest, you were really nice tonight, you know, after you put your gun away. Being out with you actually put me at ease in the midst of all this craziness. But I have to get back to why I'm here, and I'm still really hoping that you're going to help me."

"Hey, hey, hey." Ian closed the gap between us and rubbed my arms to soothe me. "I'm sorry. If *I'm* honest, I had a lovely time tonight, too. There are parts of me that I don't get to access very often, at all really, and it was nice to feel like I was just a bloke out with a pretty girl." I blushed at his compliment and looked down for a moment to compose myself. "I can assure you that finding Gil is our focus."

"Thank you." Gratitude welled up in me, and I found myself up on my toes and wrapping my arms around Ian's neck. I felt the strength of his body against mine and Ian instinctively put an arm around my waist. The scruff of his five o'clock shadow brushed my temple, causing me to tilt my head and bury my face in the crook of his neck. He smelled like mahogany and lavender. It was intoxicating.

I landed back on my heels and caught a look of sweet surprise on Ian's face. I was pretty sure there was a hint of pink on his cheeks. "I'm sorry. You Brits aren't very big on the affection thing, are you?" The words stumbled out of my mouth, revealing my embarrassment.

"My grandmother wasn't very big on the '*affection thing.*'

I happen to enjoy it very much," Ian said with a smile, and this time we both blushed.

"So, now what?" I asked, regrouping.

"Well, if you're going to stay—it's obvious I'm not going to be able to put you on the first plane home—there are a few things you should know. Like what, exactly, it is that I do."

CHAPTER 6

I sat in the oversize chair with my back to the window and faced the entry to the suite. Ian sat catty-corner to me on the couch. He rubbed his hands together like he was going to start a fire. Worry painted his face as he started and stopped speaking more than once.

"Get to it, Ian," I said impatiently. "I'm sure you've had to explain before."

"It's difficult because you're different," he answered without hesitation.

"How am I any different?"

"First of all, I don't find myself needing to explain my job to anyone very often. Secondly, you're different because you didn't seek this out. You didn't come to me wanting to sign on to what I'm about to tell you."

"But my brother did?"

"Yes and no." Ian let out a heavy sigh. "It's not easy to understand, Victoria, and it will sound very farfetched. I can assure you, though, that everything I'm going to tell you is true. I know you want to stay to find Gil, but if after you've heard what I have to say, you may change your mind. If so, I'll get you on a private plane back to Miami and I will personally make sure Gil isn't far behind." Ian leaned his elbows on his knees and rested his head in his hands. He stared at me while I processed what he just said.

What if I really couldn't handle what he was going to say? What would I do? I knew that I wouldn't leave Italy without finding Gil, but what if Gil didn't want to come home? What if tracking down Ian and disappearing was part of his plan, just like Agent Stokes said? That would mean Gil had abandoned me on purpose. That thought scared me more than anything else.

"Thank you, Ian, for considering my feelings. But as I've repeatedly said, I'm not going anywhere without Gil. I came here to find him, and that's what I'm going to do." I pressed my lips together, to keep from crying, or smiling, or both.

"You're sure about this?" he asked, reconfirming.

"Get on with it already!"

He nodded to himself a few times and then locked his eyes on me.

"My team and I work for INTERPOL," he began.

"That's it? Your big I-don't-know-if-you-can-handle-this secret is that you work for INTERPOL?" I didn't hide the look of disappointment and then confusion at Ian's secrecy from my face.

Ian shot me a look. "To be specific, we work for a secret

division within INTERPOL. We do what the other agencies don't want to do, or can't do. Usually because, in order to accomplish what needs to be done, some very serious laws have to be broken. Don't get me wrong. INTERPOL is not above breaking a few laws. But when it goes beyond what they can do without their hands becoming *visibly* dirty, they call on me and my team to get the job done."

"What do you mean '*visibly* dirty'?" I asked. Instead of replying, Ian looked past me and out the window. "If you're not going to be straight with me, then I guess I'll have to find him on my own."

I started to stand when Ian stopped me. He looked at me with surprise. Did he really think his broad explanation was going to be good enough?

"We do a lot of things. Protection. Surveillance. We make sure secrets stay secret. And, well, sometimes it's necessary to become embedded in an organization in order to take it down from the inside out. Implode it, so to speak."

"Don't law enforcement agents do that all the time?"

"Yes, but these aren't your inner-city street gangs where you send an agent into their hideout with an unmarked laundry van parked a block away listening in. These are international drug and gun dealers, kidnappers for hire, human-trafficking rings. Really bad people doing really bad things. Things . . . happen, Victoria."

"People die," I said, connecting the dots.

"Yes." Ian leaned back on the couch and unbuttoned the second button on his dress shirt, seemingly satisfied that I was beginning to understand the depths of his job.

"Have *you* killed people?" I asked. If this was Ian's line of work and Gil had been working with him, what the hell was my brother doing?

"Yes. But they were all bad," he answered with just a hint of a smile.

I stood up and paced the room a few times. I chewed and swallowed the information and considered where Gil fit in. Had Ian trained Gil to be some kind of killer for hire? Why on earth would Gil become a professional hit man? Could I stand behind a team that killed people?

I shook my head. At the moment, I didn't have the luxury of questioning Ian's morals, or even my own. What mattered now was getting Gil back. And Ian seemed like the best way in.

"Okay," I said. I turned to face him, trying hard to put on a brave face.

"Okay what?" Ian sat up and cocked his head at me.

"Okay, I'm in."

"You're *in* what?"

"I'm in whatever your international fight club is so that I can find out what my brother is doing and bring him home."

"This isn't something you get to decide if you're in," Ian argued.

"Gil did. You said he was already in too deep and you didn't have a choice but to let him stay on and do whatever it is he's doing. Consider me in too deep, because I'm not leaving."

Ian stood up and took command of the space between

us. He was so close that I could feel his breath on my face. I looked up at him boldly. His nostrils flared and his chest heaved with frustration. After a few tense seconds, he shook his head. "You are exasperating, you know that?"

"It's part of my charm," I said with a sugary smile. "Now, please tell me how Gil fits into all of this, and then how I'll be helping." I waited for Ian's response, but he maintained his silence. "Why did my brother come to you?"

Ian paced the room, wrestling with how to give me the details of my brother's secret life. He took a deep breath before answering.

"Gil didn't come to me, it's more that we stumbled upon each other. My team was given an assignment two months ago. We were to embed ourselves in the Cappola crime family to figure out what they were illegally importing and exporting. I had been trying to get close to Antony Cappola so I could bend his ear on some interesting loopholes, only to find out Gil had beat me to it. When Antony said he had solid information from another source, I knew it had to be Gil. We had every piece of intel on the Cappolas, and there was nothing in there about your brother.

"It took me a couple of weeks, but I got close enough to Gil to know he wasn't one of them. He was working his own angle. So I cornered him and we had a little conversation. He told me that he was an American law student doing his thesis on immigration law. He knew the system was corrupt, but his objective was to find the legal loopholes that were making it easier for countries to export illegal products into the States. I told him that was the stupidest thing I had ever heard, but knowing what he knows about the law put him in a position to help the Cappolas. As much as I hated it, he was already in the mix. There was no way I could kick him out and then come in and gather the same information he already had without looking suspicious."

"So you asked him to work for you?"

"For the record, I didn't exactly have to twist his arm. He was quite insistent on finishing what he started. And you have no idea, as a outsider, what it takes to gain the trust of a mob family. The fact that Gil was able to do that in such a short amount of time was genius. For me to come in and do what Gil had already done would have been far too suspicious and would have blown our whole operation. We agreed that he could stay as long as he provided me with the information he was gathering—and that he had no family to go home to." With that, Ian gave me a sharp glance.

"And how, exactly, is my brother supposed to defend himself if he gets found out?" I asked, ignoring Ian's jab.

"He said he had some gun training before he came to Italy."

"I'd say that's not true, but it's obvious I have no clue what my brother has been up to."

"My team also gave him some training. Not enough, but at least enough to give him a chance," Ian said. "He was supposed to meet me at this hotel two weeks ago. He didn't show, and I found out he'd checked out three days earlier. We've been watching the Cappolas, but they've practically been hermits. With the exception of the help, no one has come or gone from their estate since. Damon is working on getting some eyes inside, but at this point, we don't even know if Gil is still with them. I've been sitting on the hotel hoping he would come back or that someone would come looking for him. I didn't expect that person to be you."

"Is this Cappola family especially violent? Could they have found out he was working with you and killed him?" The words left my mouth like a nightmare. I never imagined having a conversation about the possibility of my brother being murdered.

"No more than any other crime family. They're known for your standard money laundering and extortion, and a little import-export business. But things in the last several months have begun to escalate, and we're seeing connections between the Cappolas and another family known for having their hands in more dangerous activities."

"Where does Gil come in?" My breathing was getting shallow as I realized Gil was in deeper than I could comprehend.

"Gil said the Cappolas mentioned a man I know only as Paolo. Gil didn't catch all of their conversation, but heard them say Paolo was looking for something of value. I've been watching him for almost a year, and Gil's information was the first lead I'd had on him in three months. So I sent Gil back in to find out what he could about his connection to the Cappolas. Based on how out in the open he is, I don't think Paolo is in charge of the operation. I want

Paolo's boss, and he's good at hiding." Ian looked disappointed.

"What is Paolo looking for? Why do you have your eye on him?" I asked.

"He's been linked to drug and arms trafficking—so it could be that he's on the hunt for new products—but he was also photographed coming out of an all-girls boarding school in London two days before three students went missing."

"You think he had something to do with their disappearance?" Ian nodded. The vein in his neck was pulsating, and his jaw was set. It sounded like he thought this Paolo guy didn't agree with his belief that women should be treated well. "But what else did Gil find out about him?" I asked.

"Only that Paolo was planning on meeting with the Cappolas in Bologna. Gil disappeared before he could tell me when. So, as of now, Paolo could be anywhere."

Ian took my hand and led me to the couch. We angled ourselves toward each other, our knees touching. "Once I told Gil who Paolo was, he made it his personal objective to get the proof we needed to bring him down. He thought that if he could become of service to the organization as a whole, then he would rise in the ranks. He'd already found favor with the Cappolas. If he's not still with them . . ." Ian hung his head and a bolt of fear ran through me.

"Just say it."

He looked into my eyes. "I can't tell you that Gil isn't dead."

I couldn't think that way. I'd come too far and I had

OXBLOOD

too much to lose. "You can't tell me he isn't alive, either,"
I countered.

"Hope is a dangerous thing, Victoria."

"No. Hope is a glorious thing. Hope is what put me on
a plane I swore I'd never get on. Hope is what keeps me
talking to you instead of running to the US Embassy or
back to the airport. Because, right now, you are my only
hope of finding my brother."

Ian looked at me like he had never heard such opti-
mism. Maybe he hadn't, or maybe it had been too long
since he had. Until I knew for a fact that Gil was no longer
breathing, I wouldn't give up. I *couldn't* give up.

"My home is with Gil, and until I find him, I have
nowhere else to go." I put my hand on top of Ian's resting
on his lap.

"I don't know, Victoria," he said quietly.

"I'm not a fragile little doll, Ian. I can handle myself."

"Yeah, I could tell that when I was able to back you into
your hotel with a gun shoved in your gut," he replied. His
tone changed quickly from soft to defensive.

"Because I should have known that a gun-wielding
Englishman was going to come knocking on my door?
Why are you being so difficult?" I stood up with a fury. He
quickly stood, too, towering over me, a look of frustration
plastered on his face.

"Because if we find Gil, I don't want to be the one to
tell him that I got his sister killed! You have a life! You have
people back home who care about you! This is a lonely and
dangerous job, Victoria. I wouldn't wish it on anyone."

93

"I'm not asking for this to be my life, Ian! All I want is your help in getting my brother back. If that means I have to become a part of whatever it is you do, I'll do that for as long as I have to. I know I sound like a broken record, but I'm not going home. All that's there is my shitty apartment, my less-than-mediocre job at a diner, my *one* friend, and my freeloading boyfriend. I will miss Tiffany, but I would rather be here where I feel like I'm accomplishing something than merely existing day to day and wondering if I'll ever see my brother again.

"Train me. Put me to the test. If I fail miserably, you can send me home. But don't sentence me to a life of worry without at least giving me a chance. I know I can do this." I took an infinitesimal step toward Ian, closing the gap between us, and lowered my voice. "You said there were agents who would give anything to have someone to go home to. Why do I have a feeling you were talking about yourself?"

Ian turned his head away and looked down. My hand cupped the side of his face, pulling it toward me. For a minute, we were inches apart, his frustration melting at my touch. His expression was soft, the dim light pooling in his eyes. We stood there for a moment, our breathing barely audible above the faint sounds of the traffic outside.

"Help me find my someone."

Ian backed up and leaned against the wall, putting himself a good four feet away from me and my emotions. He studied me with contemplative eyes, then pulled out his phone and began typing and swiping away. Two minutes later, he shoved his phone back into his pocket.

"Let's go."

"Where are we going?" I asked, confused at his sudden change of heart. I thought for sure I was in for some more arguing; I even began formulating my next rebuttal.

"You're going to meet the team," he said.

The Ian who had connected with me on a personal level, the one who took me out to dinner and asked me if I was cold, was gone. In his place was the other Ian, the gun-wielding Englishman who killed bad guys and infiltrated Italian Mafia families. The transformation happened so quickly that my heart got whiplash. I quickly pushed those feelings down. I needed Ian the professional. I needed his training and his expertise. Now was not the time to linger over how handsome, charming, or even funny he was. *Vic, get it together.*

Determined, I grabbed my bag and said, "Great. Let's go then."

I followed Ian around the corner of the building to a sporty, black unmarked car. I stood there for a moment at the back of the car, not sure which side I should be walking toward: left or right? I had been too tired when I plopped myself into the cab from the train station to the hotel to notice where the driver was.

"Get in. Italy drives on the right side of the street. Most of the world does, actually," Ian said as he opened my car door and I stepped inside. He went to his side, jumped in, and drove quickly through the back lot and onto the street.

"I knew that. I just forgot for a second," I declared in an embarrassed excuse. We drove for a few minutes before

I spoke again. "If I ask you something, will you answer me honestly?" I said softly.

"It depends on what it is." Ian didn't move his eyes from the road.

"Why was Damon at the restaurant tonight?"

"I've met many beautiful women who have played the innocent and then didn't hesitate to use me as a human shield," he answered. "I had to be sure you weren't there to kill me.

"If I ask *you* a question, will you answer it honestly?"

"I have no reason not to answer you honestly," I said.

"If he's a freeloader, why is he still your boyfriend?"

"What?"

"Inside the hotel, you said that you had your best friend and your freeloading boyfriend to go home to. If he's a freeloader, why is he still your boyfriend?" His tone was softer again.

"I don't know," was all I could muster. I asked myself the same question all the time. Chad was not someone I'd ever imagined myself with, and certainly not someone my parents would have chosen. He was entitled and lazy and thoughtless. He left his family over a silly dispute about money, and I would give every cent for one more day with mine. "Why?"

"I told you. I have a thing about women being treated respectfully. Freeloading boyfriends do not treat women as they should." He gripped the steering wheel, his knuckles turning white.

"Well, I guess, sometimes a freeloading boyfriend is better than . . . I don't know what it's better than."

We spent the next thirty minutes in silence. We had left the bright city streets of Bologna behind and now only small, dark buildings dotted the side of the road. Eventually, we stopped at what looked like an abandoned factory. It reminded me of the buildings near the diner, and I couldn't help but wonder how many people lost their jobs when this place shut down.

Ian pulled out his phone and got busy typing. I watched him, waiting to see if the softer Ian was going to show up again, the Ian that charmed me over bowls of pasta.

We sat in silence. A car passed by behind us, its headlights shining on Ian's face long enough to reveal a scowl that had replaced his crooked smile.

His phone beeped. He read it and nodded. "It's time to meet the team."

CHAPTER 7

I followed Ian to the side of the building, where we entered through a rusted-out metal door that looked like tetanus waiting to happen. He pulled the door open, his biceps stretching the fabric of his shirt. He took the two flights of stairs two steps at a time, me scurrying after him. I did my best to keep up, but my breathing was labored and my chest was beginning to burn. Ian didn't wait; I guess the testing had begun.

We walked down a dark hallway and into an office area. It was empty, the only light coming from a single bulb dangling from the ceiling. The desk in the corner was coated in what looked like thirty years' worth of dust. And there were cobwebs. Lots and lots of cobwebs. It looked more like a good place to hide a dead body than the secret hideout for an INTERPOL team.

Good, Vic. Because impetuously getting on a plane and flying to Italy wasn't enough, finding yourself in what could be a serial killer's lair is what is really going to make this trip memorable.

We arrived at another door, this one simple wood, and finally, Ian turned around to face me.

"Do I even need to ask if you've changed your mind?" he said with a hint of disappointment.

"Nope." I answered him assuredly. From here on out, there was no way in hell I was going to show Ian I was anything but strong and confident.

He nodded with a straight face and opened the door. It was like Dorothy walking into Oz. The entry room had been one big dustbowl, but this room was clean. Really, really, clean. The air smelled different, too, like it was purified, and the temperature was perfect.

One wall was filled with six flat-screen televisions tuned into different news stations from around the world. A large table held several state-of-the-art computers and big, glowing monitors. On an opposite wall was a giant map covered in little red pins. I couldn't help but wonder what the pins represented: Dead agents or living targets?

The far end of the room looked shrunken. The wall was shorter than it should have been, and there was a misplaced seam on the ceiling. They were clearly hiding something behind a faux wall, and I made a mental note to find out what. You could still tell that the building used to be a factory, despite the high-tech retro fittings.

When I finally broke my gaze and turned to face the room again, I was greeted by two new faces, along with Damon, who seemed to have melted out of the corners of the room.

"What are you? Ninjas?" I said sarcastically.

"I like this one," the guy who wasn't Damon said. He was a little taller than me. At first glance, one may have thought he was just stocky, but I could see he was deceptively strong. There was something about the way he carried himself: back straight and shoulders squared. "Adam McKenzie," he said as he extended his hand.

"Vic," I replied.

"Everyone, this is *Victoria*," Ian told them. "She's going to begin training with us tonight for her *brief* stay. She is also Gil's sister." Bug eyes and shocked expressions came from everyone.

"Whaaaat?" the girl standing between Damon and Adam said. She looked at me for a minute with a cocked head and then shook my hand. "Oh yeah. I can see that."

"Those darn genetics." I laughed nervously.

"I'm Claudia Kho and I cannot tell you how great it is to have another pair of boobs around here!" She laughed, flipping her long black ponytail. Her big brown eyes seemed to glow when she smiled.

"Way to keep it classy, Claudia," Ian said as he walked to the other side of the room. "If you can keep your crassness to a limit, please get Victoria started on Phase One."

"You got it, boss," she called across the room to him.

"Wait, Ian!" I called as I followed him across the room. "What is Phase One? I thought—"

"You thought what, Victoria?" Ian asked. He stopped in his tracks and turned to me. He looked at me with a hard face, and I could tell that it would be a long time before I saw the smiling, joking Ian I had been with earlier.

I swallowed hard, caught by Ian's challenging gaze. "I just thought I would be more of an extra pair of eyes. Phase One sounds like you're initiating training."

"I am. And as long as you are here, you will follow my directives. If you don't like that, you are more than welcome to leave."

If Ian was going to play tough, I would too. I lifted my chin, turned on my heels, and beelined over to Claudia. She was seated in front of a computer, her eyes glued to a slew of code. She typed something in then spun around to face me. I looked at her and then at Adam and Damon. Not a single one of them could have been more than twenty-five.

"You're all so . . . young," I commented with astonishment.

"Yeah. We're like the *Jump Street* division of international secret organizations," Claudia quipped. She reminded me of Tiffany and I could see us becoming friends, if we were allowed. "That would sound cooler *IF WE HAD A NAME!*" she yelled in Ian's direction.

"We are not an after-school club, Claudia," Ian called back. Claudia and I raised our eyebrows and laughed. "And we have a name."

"R-14 is not a real name!" she replied.

"Phase One, please."

"So what's Phase One?" I asked curiously.

She held out her hand, palm side up. "I'm going to need all of your identification. Passport, driver's license, credit cards. Anything on you that would identify you or connect you to the outside world."

"But how will I pay for anything? I mean, I haven't checked out of the hotel, and I still need to eat." This was all moving a little fast. One day I was working at the diner, and the next I was in a top-secret clubhouse being asked to hand over everything that proved I was me.

"As long as you pass through training, you won't need any of those things while you're with us." Claudia's delivery was straight and sure.

Training, I thought to myself. All I wanted was to find my brother. How did I end up in the middle of Command Central for a secret division of *Jump Street: INTERPOL Division*?

"So," Claudia continued. She pulled something up on her computer as she spoke. "How'd you come to find yourself in the company of Mr. Congeniality over there?" She nodded toward Ian and smirked.

"Ian knocked on my hotel door and held a gun to my stomach," I told her.

"Always the charmer," she said flatly.

"He made up for it with dinner, though."

"You went to dinner with Ian?" She raised her eyebrows like it was the craziest thing she had ever heard. I nodded in reply. "Well, this is going to be interesting," she smirked.

"Interesting? Why is this going to be interesting?"

"Gather round, everyone," Ian called to the group before I could get an answer from Claudia. "Victoria, have you given Claudia your identification?"

"Oh, um . . . no. But I'm a little concerned about—"

Ian cut me off. "What did I just say about my directives? Team, what happens if my directives aren't followed?"

Claudia, Damon, and Adam answered in unison. "You die."

"Do you have any questions about that?"

"No. I've got it." I pulled my wallet and my passport from my purse and handed them to Claudia. I told Ian I could do this, and by God, I was going to do it.

I kept Gil's journal hidden. That was one card I wasn't quite ready to put on the table.

"All right then. Damon is going to work with you on honing your observation skills and your intuition. You did well at the restaurant tonight but could have done better," Ian said.

"You seemed pretty impressed," I retorted.

"Maybe. But you have to be better." He paused like he wanted to say something else, but then changed his mind. "Claudia will give you the rundown on some of our tech: Who we monitor. How we monitor. And what we do with what we find. And Adam will work with you on weapons training."

"Whoa. *Weapons* training? Is that entirely necessary?" I asked nervously. "I've already got some pretty solid self-defense moves." I wasn't there to be a soldier or a spy. I just wanted to get my brother back.

"We all have our specialties. But we all also have to be trained to defend ourselves and one another. And you're going to need a hell of a lot more than self-defense moves to do that."

Ian's eyes locked on mine. He was challenging me to back down. His tone was strong and commanding, but his eyes told me so much more. They pierced through mine, screaming to let him take me out of this place. I would sooner die than back down and give up.

"Got it."

"Good. Then let's get started," he said.

"Wait. What exactly is *your* expertise, Ian Hale?" I asked, loud enough for all to hear. Claudia looked away embarrassed, like I had just called the teacher out for getting a question wrong.

Ian closed the distance between us so tightly that I could smell the faint scent of his cologne again. "My *expertise* is keeping this team alive. Is that okay with you, Miss Asher?"

My brazenness left me quickly and all I could do was nod. I closed my eyes as he walked away and chastised myself. *Get your head in the game, Vic. If you want to find Gil, you're going to need Ian's help. Stop being a smart-ass and start playing nice.*

"C'mon. You look like you could let off some steam." Adam tugged at my elbow and brought me to his side of the room. "Welcome to my sanctuary." He smiled wide and sat on the corner of his desk, gripping the edge with his hands. "Hit me, baby, one more time," he called. Before I could ask what Britney Spears had to do with weapons training, the faux wall I noticed earlier moved to the side, like a sophisticated sliding glass door. Soon, the wall was completely gone, revealing dozens of guns and knives of all shapes and sizes.

"Wow."

"Impressive, right?" he said with glee.

"It's something," I said.

"Don't stroke his ego!" Claudia called from behind her computer.

"What? No secret button under your desk?"

"That's so cliché," he smirked.

"And Britney?"

"Who doesn't love Britney?"

I took in the wall of weapons, attempted to still my increasing heartbeat, and tried to mentally prepare myself for what I was about to do. After Ian's explanation of what his team did, I understood that the instruments before me would be the difference between keeping myself alive and Ian finding me in a pool of blood.

"How much experience do you have with guns?" he asked.

"Does hearing nightly gunfire on my street count as experience?"

Adam chuckled and shook his head. "Well then, pick one out and we'll go from there." Adam opened his arm toward the wall of weapons in a showman's gesture of invitation.

"Shouldn't I start off training with something a little less intense?" I asked nervously.

"This is as low key as weapons training gets," Adam said plainly.

"Then, in that case, I would feel much better if you applied your vast knowledge of guns and picked one out for me."

"Okay. I'll select a few and we can see what feels right." He picked several and laid them on the table in front of me, pointing to each one. "For you, because we're looking at defense, not marksmanship, any of these will be good."

I looked at the guns lined up before me on the broad table. Adam could probably rattle off the differences between all of them the way I could with burgers and pie at Sam's. I wondered if I'd even be able to grasp them properly but then realized that that wouldn't be the issue—pulling the trigger would be. I was sure Ian wasn't planning on using me in tactical operations, but clearly I wouldn't be immune to having to make a fatal decision—especially if Gil was in the kind of danger we thought.

I watched Adam ready each gun, and was paralyzed by fear.

"Hey," he said, laying a gun down and putting a hand on my shoulder. "It's going to be fine. You're not even going to touch one of my babies until we've sufficiently covered gun safety. It'll be so ingrained in you that Yosemite Sam will make you cringe."

"Okay then. Where do we start?"

"We'll start with the basics. What is the first rule of gun safety?"

"Don't talk about gun safety?" I joked. Adam snickered and then raised his eyebrows, prompting me to take the question more seriously. "Try not to kill anyone?"

Adam didn't look amused. "The first rule of gun safety is that the gun is always loaded. Even if it isn't, it is. The second rule of gun safety is that you keep your finger out of the trigger guard until you're ready to shoot. Also, always keep the gun pointed down until you're ready to shoot. It's much better to be shot in the foot than the leg or crotch. Especially the crotch.

"Finally, the most difficult rule is that when you point your gun at something, be prepared for that thing to die. Whether it's the particleboard you're going to obliterate in training or a human being, when you pull that trigger, you will *end* whatever it is you're pointing at. Got it?"

"Sure."

"There is no 'sure.' Do you understand?"

"Yes. I understand," I replied with as much courage as I could muster.

Adam nodded and then proceeded to go over everything from the difference between guns with a hammer and a striker to the proper tactical stance for shooting. Before I knew it, an hour had passed and I still hadn't fired a shot.

When he deemed me ready, Adam took me into the basement of the building, where a shooting range had been set up. Paper targets had been affixed to particleboard posts. Adam picked up the nine-millimeter Glock and showed me all its parts again. The barrel. The handle. Where the magazine clicked into place inside the handle. He showed me again how to properly wrap my fingers around the handle, but my palms were sweating and I was terrified that it would slip out of my grasp and explode on the floor.

"So . . . where are you from, Adam?" I asked.

"Well, that was random," he said. "You wouldn't be stalling, would you?"

I rolled my eyes. "No," I lied. "I was just curious as to where you were from. I mean, Ian's British and Damon is from around here, I'm guessing. What about you?"

He waited a moment before he answered. "Canada."

"Oh, cool."

We stared at each other for a moment with tight-lipped smiles. I was hoping Adam would elaborate, but it was obvious he was just waiting for me to quit stalling.

Finally, Adam took my hand and put the gun in my palm. Then he molded my fingers around the handle. We went over the load-and-make-ready movements, then he handed me a pair of bulky headphones and told me to put them on.

"These are tactical headphones," he said. I could hear him clearly. "They muffle the sound of gunfire but allow you to hear your surroundings. Can you hear me okay?"

"Yes," I said a little too loudly. Adam laughed.

"You ready?" he asked.

"No, but I'm doing it anyway," I told him. At that moment, Ian appeared through the doorway. A current of nervousness shot through me so intensely that my teeth hurt.

"How is she doing?" he asked, barely acknowledging me.

"She was just about to have a go at it," Adam answered.

"Great. Let's see it then." Ian folded his arms in front of his chest and waited.

OXBLOOD

I pushed down every ounce of fear I had and replaced it with every scrap of courage I could muster. I didn't have to get it right. I just had to look like I had the nerve to keep going. I raised and aimed my weapon.

"Is the shooter ready?"

I took a few deep breaths like Adam taught me.

"Yes."

"Fire when ready."

CHAPTER 8

I spent two days in that building and on the surrounding property in intense training.

Ian and Adam worked me like a dog, making me shoot targets in the basement over and over again. For Ian, nothing I did was good enough. Even when I hit a bull's-eye on my first shot, he was quick to dismiss it as beginner's luck. "Things won't be this easy in the real world," he added condescendingly. "The targets are moving and you won't have the time to prepare—or Adam to walk you through each step." All I could do was grit my teeth and put my headphones back on. At least those were proving to be useful at drowning out the gunfire *and* Ian's disappointment.

"Again," Adam would say after I emptied each magazine.

During the day, Adam took me outside for tactical training. The old factory building was situated on a large pasture. I couldn't see them, but the sound of cows mooing in the distance broke the silence as we walked to the end of the meadow and into the woods. Along the way, we passed several mounds of hay. A long fence of wooden posts connected with chicken wire enclosed the area directly behind the building.

"You have to be aware of your surroundings while staying hidden," Adam said. "This is your next lesson." He held out his arm as if to welcome me to the forest. We were a good twenty-five yards inside the woods. I could barely make out the pasture through the trees.

"How is the forest my next lesson?" I asked.

"Close your eyes and count to twenty," he said. I shot him a look, but the expression he retaliated with trumped mine so I did as instructed. When I opened my eyes, Adam was nowhere to be seen. I turned around, twigs and leaves crunching beneath my feet. I looked everywhere, even up in the trees. I don't know how he did it, but he had disappeared without making a sound.

"Ha-ha, Adam," I said. "You can come out now. I get it. You're the master of hide-and-go-seek!"

I waited for him to appear and elaborate on the lesson, but a full minute went by and he still hadn't appeared. It was dead silent, and I was starting to get creeped out. I swallowed hard and wondered, yet again, what I had gotten myself into.

I took a step toward the tree line and heard a gun go off, and then a bullet whizzed past me. I spun around looking for its origination but only saw trees.

"They're rubber bullets, but they still hurt like a bitch," Adam called from his hiding place.

"What the hell, Adam!" I called out to him.

"I'd run if I were you."

I mistakenly went deeper into the woods thinking I could hide, but Adam's aim was excellent and a forest full of trees wasn't going to be enough to protect me. I had to make it back to the building. At the tree line, I decided my best plan was to run from one bale of hay to the next, then dash into the old factory for safety—all without getting caught or captured.

As I made a run for my first hiding spot, I felt the swish of air as another bullet missed me—undoubtedly, on purpose.

"I swear to God, Gil. When we make it out of this, I'm going to kick your ass." With one more look behind me, I made a run for it.

When we walked back into headquarters, I was nursing a welt on my arm the size of a golf ball. I had been moments away from reaching safety when Adam reminded me just how inexperienced I was by hitting me intentionally. Though Ian had instructed him to give me the fast-track training, I felt like I had come a long way, so it was discouraging to be caught at the last minute.

"Don't sweat it, Vic," Adam said. "For someone who's never had any kind of training, you're doing remarkably well."

I winced going down the stairs to the basement. "Yeah, well, I'm determined. I have to find Gil. There are no other options." Adam nodded. "And I don't have *zero* training. I'll have you know, I'm at the top of my class at the Asher Home School of Self-Defense."

"I'm sure! Which is why we're headed to the mats."

Unlike Ian, Adam valued my DIY self-defense skills and helped me hone a few moves, like using your assailant's charging force to flip them to the ground and head-butting your attacker from behind hard enough to do some damage. He tried to teach me how to throw a punch, too, but I couldn't muster enough force to make it useful.

The whole experience was very *Die Hard.* I was tired and dirty and I smelled awful—and, surprisingly, I loved every second of it. Something inside me lit up when I was training with Adam. I felt like I belonged there.

When it was time for Damon to work with me, I had to force my eyes to stay open and my chin from drooping to the desk.

"Your observation skills must be as keen when you are tired as they are when you are rested," he said as he stood next to me. We were in another room in the basement. I sat at a table while Damon's tall, dark, and handsome stature shadowed over me.

He pulled out images that reminded me of those Hidden Pictures pages in *Highlights* magazine from when I was a kid. All the cards were big, like the size of a regular piece of paper, and the images varied from advertisements to actual photos. At first, they were easy. I had to find what was off about a picture. They became harder as we went along; missing objects got smaller and scenes became more chaotic.

Next came the pictures with scenarios.

"This woman is asking you for directions to the nearest bathroom so she can change her *bambino*'s diaper. Do you believe her or not?" Damon said, his Italian accent ringing in my ears.

In the photo, a woman was standing next to a large fountain. There were a few people scattered around her, sitting on the fountain's ledge or walking across the square. It looked like it had been taken somewhere in Italy based on the architecture. She was wearing a simple black T-shirt, jeans, and flats. Her auburn hair was long and brushed behind her shoulders. The photo appeared to have been taken from a distance.

"Well, based solely on this image, since there's no baby anywhere in sight, I'm going to say no," I replied.

"Good," Damon said. "This woman proceeded to take a hostage and then demanded the release of her boyfriend who had recently been arrested for an attempted terrorist attack."

Damon moved on to more challenging scenarios. One after another, he put photos in front of me and asked detailed questions about each scene.

I knew we were winding down when he put an image of a cream-colored strapless gown with a slit up the length of the leg and asked, "Where will you hide your gun in this dress?"

"That has nothing to do with being observant, Damon," I quipped.

"Maybe not, but I'm very curious." He raised his eyebrows and then winked at me. Strangely enough, it relieved some of the stress that had been building up.

We took a short break to eat *caprese* sandwiches that

Claudia made in a kitchen I had yet to see. There was no small talk. No talk at all. We ate in silence. Well, everyone else ate. I inhaled my food like I hadn't eaten in weeks.

After lunch, I continued training with Damon. Another hour or so later, I thought I was going to lose it. Anger was burning inside of me. I was angry with Adam for shooting me when I was so close to victory. Angry at Ian for making me go through his spy training. But most of all, I was angry with Gil for leaving me. My mother would have used the word *coal* to describe this feeling. "Coal is dark and dirty, but inside of it there is something beautiful that can only come from the trial it faces," she would say. If she were here now, I would call it bullshit. This anger sucked, and I was having a difficult time seeing the something beautiful. It was finding Gil, of course, but I had a feeling our relationship would never be the same.

"Which one is our guy?" Damon asked as he slapped down a picture of a group of people. It looked like a run-of-the-mill Italian family portrait. Father, mother, children.

"They're all just standing there in a posed shot. How am I supposed to figure that out?"

"You have to know who the imposter is. We take months, sometimes years, and embed ourselves into the enemy's family. We become so much a part of who they are that they don't pay attention to the tiny details. *You* have to pay attention to the details, Victoria." Damon's eyes bore into me as he spoke.

It was an impossible task, but I picked up the eight-by-ten photo to examine it more closely.

"Put it down. You don't always get a better angle. Use the one you've got. What do you see?" Damon said.

I took a breath, sat up straight in my chair, and looked again.

"There are four men, one of them is much older and is most likely the father of the group. The other three seem to descend in age so I'd say they're his sons," I said as I began by stating the obvious. "There are five women. One is clearly the older man's wife. Two of the other women are wives of the other men, and the other two women are daughters."

I studied each person in the photo again and pointed to one of the men in the middle after a moment. "This guy. He's not one of the sons so he must be one of us."

"Why?" Ian said from behind me. I was surprised to hear his voice, as I hadn't seen him since he stopped torturing me during my gun training with Adam.

"The father and his two sons have rounder shoulders, little paunch bellies, and hairy chests. By the way, that gaping-shirt look is not attractive. This guy has broad shoulders. He's fit and trim, and his chest is as bare as a *Men's Health* model," I answered.

"You could say some brothers don't match up exactly to their family," Ian challenged.

"But could you also say that they color their hair? His roots are starting to grow in. He has hazel eyes while everyone else has brown." I yawned involuntarily, making my eyes water. I rubbed them and said, "Next."

"We're done for now," Ian said. "Good job, everyone.

Get some rest, and I'll have an update for you soon. Claudia, can you initiate Phase Two with Victoria, please?"

Ian walked away, and I got up to meet Claudia at her station. "What, exactly, is Phase Two? Because I thought I just spent the last two and a half days going through phases two through twenty." Hours ago, I would have fist-bumped this win with Adam, but my arms were too sore to even consider it.

"Well, Phase Two is a good sign if what you want is to be part of this team." Claudia said, chuckling as she tucked her thick black hair behind her ears. "Phase Two means I temporarily wipe you off the face of the earth."

"What?" Her statement hit me like a cold shower, momentarily perking up my exhausted body. "How on earth do you *temporarily* wipe someone off the face of the earth?"

"I don't really wipe you out. I just make you invisible. It's like an electronic cloaking device. If someone tried to look you up, it would be like you didn't exist."

"Um, he said to *initiate* Phase Two. Is it a process or is it immediate? I mean, I feel like I should email my friend back home to let her know I'm okay." My heart welled up at the thought of dropping off the planet and Tiffany not knowing I was okay. I knew that pain well. That pain had brought me to Italy. "And what about the hotel?"

"I've already changed the name and payment on the reservation to one of Ian's aliases. I don't know how long you'll stay there, but as far as the hotel is concerned, Victoria Asher was never a guest."

Claudia looked at me sympathetically. I wondered if she remembered the day she disappeared and if it was painful for her. "And once I make you invisible, you won't have an email address."

"Oh. Yeah, I guess that wouldn't be good," I whispered.

"Tell you what. If you want to send your friend a final email, I can set up a dummy account. Your name can't be in any part of the email address. You'll need to think of something so she'll know it's you. And you'll need to dictate the email to me so Ian doesn't catch us," Claudia added in a hushed tone.

"That would be great, Claudia. Thank you." I gave her a tired smile as I recited Tiffany's email address, and she set up the dummy account. "Send it from . . . Prada." Claudia gave a little chuckle and began to take my dictation. "Dear Tiff, first off, I'm great. I'm going to be out of pocket for a bit, but please don't worry. I have to shut my email down, but everything is fine. Once I find Gil, I'll explain everything to you. Thanks for taking care of my place. I'm wiring money to Sam. Please ask him to pay my rent and whatever else he needs with it. I love you and I'll see you soon. Hugs . . . Vic. P.S. Don't go into Gil's room."

I looked at Claudia as she hit send. "Thank you. I also need you to wire money from my account to my boss." She nodded and I gave her some of Sam's information.

"It's done," she said.

"Wow. You've got the world at your fingertips." Claudia's workstation had several monitors and black boxes with wires and cables connecting everything together. The screens glowed and the ports on the boxes blinked with green lights. I considered myself relatively computer savvy, but all this was beyond me.

I sat in the chair next to her desk and started to lay my head down on top of my arms like a bored elementary-school kid, but stopped myself. I couldn't look too defeated or Ian would surely use it as an excuse to make me repeat Phase One.

"I wouldn't have it any other way," Claudia said. "I've had a computer attached to my fingers for a long time. It got me into some pretty hot water, which is when Ian found me. He's a good man to know, Vic. He'll be hard on you, and it will seem unfair and unreasonable, but it'll keep you alive. And it will hopefully lead you to Gil." She put her hand over mine.

"If he'd quit being so difficult, I think I'd have an easier time. He's been hot and cold since the moment I met him. One minute, he acts like he wants to be my friend. The next, it's like he's doing everything in his power to break me."

"I'm not sure Ian knows how to be anyone's friend," Claudia replied.

Claudia's statement made me sad. How tragic to do what Ian did and not have anyone to decompress with. I'd be lost without Tiffany to bitch to about my day—and I was just waiting tables.

"Ian is hardcore when it comes to having no family connections in this line of work," she told me. "Gil was already embedded in the Cappola family when Ian found him. He was in deep, so Ian didn't have me run the standard background check because it wouldn't have mattered. And to find out that Gil lied about you? Well, that's got Ian fuming."

"Is that why he's being so rude to me?"

"He likes you and he doesn't know how to deal with that."

"He's not acting like it." I rolled my eyes.

"All I know is that when Damon came back from the restaurant, he said he saw Ian smile. *Really* smile. We need those moments, Vic, but we don't get them. It's probably better that we don't. It's going to hurt when you leave."

"I guess that makes sense. All of this . . . it's insane. I just spent the last two and a half days learning how to shoot a gun and play the mastermind version of I spy." I pulled my hair down and ran my fingers across my scalp. My entire body ached, and I was on the verge of tears. So what if I could shoot a paper target from the safety of the shooting range? Or notice if a cup was upside down in a picture? What if, out there in the real world, where it really mattered, I wouldn't be able to defend myself or the team? The reality of the huge risk I was to the team hit me hard. But even more terrifying was the thought of Ian cutting me loose. I imagined being drugged and thrown in a plane and waking up in my apartment in Miami thousands of miles from Gil without any hope of ever seeing him again.

I looked around for Ian, hoping he might be ready to take me back to the hotel. I wanted a hot shower and a warm bed. I had no idea what time it was, but I planned on sleeping for as long as possible. He and Damon were huddled over a table, their eyes on a laptop, so I walked over to the maps hanging on the wall.

There were maps of Russia, the United States, France, Germany, and, of course, Italy. I stopped in front of the US map and stared at Florida, running my finger along the tiny spot where Miami would be. I hoped Tiffany was safe and that Mrs. Vasquez was keeping her well fed with black beans and rice. I said a little prayer that she would understand my email and not totally freak out.

I looked at the map of Italy. *Huh. It really is shaped like a boot*, I thought as I found all the major cities: Rome, Milan, Venice . . . It was funny to think that while others were looking at the map of Italy and romanticizing, I had been here rolling around in the dirt, shooting guns, and determining the best hiding places for weapons.

"Are you ready?" Ian said sharply, surprising me from behind.

"Yeah," I replied as I looped my bag over my shoulder. I reached in to make sure Gil's journal was still there, wondering if Ian had felt the need to snoop while I had been training.

"Think maybe you can give me an idea about what our next move is in our Gil search?" I asked innocently.

"We're not *searching* for Gil," he said as he began to walk away from me. I darted around to get in front of him.

"What do you mean we're not searching for Gil? That's the whole point of this!"

"No! That is *not* the whole point of *this*." He raised

his arms out to the side, indicating to the team and the resources at their disposal. "The *point* of this is to provide safety and security to the world! The *point* is to do things in the shadows that the rest of the world thinks only happen in James Bond movies. We have things to accomplish here. Things that we can't just abandon because your brother has gone AWOL!"

"I came here to look for my brother," I told him through gritted teeth.

"Well, good luck putting up posters like he's a lost puppy. Don't come crying to me when you've blown his cover and you find out the mob tied cinder blocks to his ankles and dropped him in the ocean."

"I asked you to help me find my brother. The next thing I know, you're bringing me here and training me like a dog. You let me believe we were going to go out there and find him!"

"Gil could literally be anywhere in the country, if he's even still *in* Italy. At this point in time, it looks like he did what he set out to do. He's not with the Cappola family anymore. They probably already moved him up the ranks with another crime family. He could have spent the last two weeks traipsing all over Italy with any number of people. We don't *go and find* Gil because we have no idea where he is. We do our job and hope to God we'll cross paths with him."

I rubbed my eyes, too tired and angry to argue. I was about to tell Ian to take me back to the hotel when my eyes caught the map of Italy. I stared at it for a moment feeling something churning inside me. I stepped to the side and cocked my head to the left and that's when it clicked.

He could have spent the last two weeks traipsing all over Italy.

"Oh my God. That's it!" I said softly.

"What are you talking about?" Ian turned around and followed my eyes to the map of Italy. "What are you looking at?"

"Gil hasn't spent the last two weeks traipsing all over Italy. That's what he's been doing since he got here." I pulled Gil's journal from my bag but didn't open it right away. "Claudia, can you pull up a map of Italy and a map of Florida?"

"Sure. Any kind in particular?" she asked as she began the task.

"Just make sure they both have all the cities on them," I instructed.

"Are you going to tell me what you have in mind?" Ian asked.

"Just hold on," I scolded. "I'm assuming you can do something cool like lay the map of Florida over the one of Italy," I said to Claudia.

"Please. Your average sixth grader can do that," she scoffed. Claudia did as I requested and Florida was a little smudge over Italy.

"Make Florida bigger." She enlarged the map little by little until it almost perfectly lined up with Italy. "Okay. Stop there." I examined the aligned maps more closely. "I know where Gil has been, and maybe even where he is now."

"Explain," Ian demanded.

Hesitantly, I held out the journal. "This is the out-of-character thing he did. It might not mean anything to you, but for him to let me look at his research, let alone send it to me . . . it's monumental."

"So what's in it?" Ian stepped forward.

"It's a bizarre story filled with weird family trees and tales of trips we never took as kids. It didn't make any sense to me until now. I think he was trying to connect the dots covertly. See," I said as I flipped a third of the way into the book, "here he talks about a trip to Tampa that we never took. But you can see that Tampa is Rome on the map."

Ian stepped closer to the map to see what I was seeing. "Give me another location."

I flipped through the journal again. "He talks about an uncle who lives in Tallahassee."

"That's Genoa. Another."

"The Keys."

"Sicily."

"That's just the beginning. He talks about people in our lives who are not actually relatives as uncles, aunts, and cousins," I told Ian.

He turned around and had one arm crossed over his chest. He twisted his lip with his other hand before holding it out for the journal.

"May I see it?" Ian asked.

I set the journal carefully into his waiting palm.

He read a few pages and examined the family trees that had more people added to them as the journal went on.

"He's a genius." Ian lifted his eyes from the journal and locked them on me.

"How is he a genius? This seems like he went to an awful lot of trouble," I lamented.

"Because he knows you. For whatever reason, he couldn't get the information he's hidden in here directly to me. He sent it to you knowing you'd never sit still. He knew you'd come after him, and that I would find you. He also knew I would send you home, but clearly he underestimated you. It may seem convoluted, but it was the safest way to get whatever is in this journal to me."

I smirked at Ian's comment and then half-smiled at the immense trust Gil had in me. I was happy that I hadn't let him down. I also had to admit that it felt pretty damn good unlocking a piece of the puzzle for Ian.

"What do you need us to do?" Damon asked.

"Gather everything we have on the families known for illegal import and export first," he said matter-of-factly. "Adam, get my bag from the office," he continued.

"And me?" I asked.

"I'm taking you back to the hotel, and we're going to tear this journal to shreds. Between the two of us, we're going to figure out what information Gil was collecting," Ian said to me. He shoved his laptop into his backpack. "Ready?"

I felt like I had crossed over the threshold from trainee

to official member of this team. This was it, the break I had been hoping for. My questions were about to be answered. As soon as we decoded the journal, we'd find Gil and our lives would get back to normal. But was normal what I wanted? And why did the thought of leaving Ian and his team make me sad?

CHAPTER 9

Ian closed the car door for me and I immediately leaned back on my headrest. I was just going to close my eyes for a minute. Before I knew it, the car door was opening again and Ian was reaching in to lift me up.

"I'm awake," I yawned, as Ian's arms slipped under my knees.

"Oh . . . Right. Good," he stammered, moving back. He held out his hand and helped me from the car. We walked in silence to the side entrance and directly to the elevators.

"What time is it? Or, maybe I should ask what day is it?" The elevator doors closed in front of us. I leaned against the back of the elevator and started to close my eyes again. Sleep was begging me to embrace it, and I began to teeter.

"Whoa there!" Ian chuckled as he caught me. "It's five o'clock on Friday afternoon. I'd ask if you're hungry, but it's clear that what you need is sleep."

"I am hungry, but I need a shower, too."

I could barely hold myself up, so Ian put his arm around my waist and all but carried me to my room. He felt just as strong as I remembered from our impromptu hug. I liked having him close. The way he took command of dangerous situations made me feel safe, and I couldn't deny it was pretty sexy, too.

"I'd be grateful if you *would* shower." A hint of a smile flashed from the corner of his mouth. "And I could stand to close my eyes for a bit myself."

Ian locked the door behind us and untucked his dress shirt.

"I'm sorry I was so hard on you." He shoved his hands in his pockets. "You did really well, Victoria. You should be proud of yourself."

"Can I ask you a question?"

He nodded slowly.

"Claudia said you had her run a thorough background check on everyone on your team. Have you run one on me?"

"Yes."

"What did you find out?"

"Things you already told me. Things you didn't."

"Such as?"

Ian looked past me to the window and then back at me. "Such as . . . Gil isn't the only family you have left."

That's what I had been waiting for. "So?"

"So I hoped you would tell me on your own."

I sighed. "My mom's family is in New York. My parents

were flying there for my grandmother's birthday—her seventieth—when the accident happened. My grandparents ran a restaurant that my great-grandfather started back in the early forties. My mom's brothers ran the kitchen, and her sisters did everything else. That was their life, and they expected it to be Mom's life, too. But a month after they got married, Dad got a promotion that moved them to Miami. They blamed Dad for separating them and were angry with Mom for choosing him over them. No one in the family had ever moved away from the Bronx. When I was a kid, we would go up occasionally to visit them, but they treated us differently. They didn't even play the doting grandparents card to try and sucker my parents into moving back or visiting more often. Our cousins got game systems, and we got holiday sweaters. Ugly ones. They were never really interested in us, so I wasn't surprised when they wouldn't take me in after Dad and Mom died. I spent a year in foster care until Gil could work out how he could take care of me himself."

I untied my shoes and slipped them off. "Anyway, a few years later, my grandmother died and Gil and I went up to New York for the funeral. Gil said it was our duty since Mom couldn't be there. It took us two and a half days to drive because I refused to fly. When we arrived, they treated us like royalty. It was disgustingly fake. We knew they had heard on the news how the surviving family members had received settlements from the airline in excess of 'seven figures.' I told Gil I never wanted to go back there again.

He promised we wouldn't. It took a two-sentence conversation for us to decide that from then on it would be just me and him."

I finally sat down on the couch, my whole body melting into the cushions. Ian sat next to me. His eyes were soft. These weren't the eyes of the sergeant who made me do the same drills over and over again. This was a man who had a story, perhaps one as devastating as mine.

"I'm sorry that you and Gil had to make that decision. Family should be there for one another, not treat one another like property." Ian took my hand in his, and I knew I had to say what had been on my mind.

"We can be friends, Ian. We can do the whole badass spy thing *and* be friends."

"I wish that were true, Victoria. But you can't have friends in this line of work." Ian stood and propped himself against the wall.

"Why not? How can you put yourself in potentially fatal situations and not trust and protect one another?" I stood up, too, and immediately regretted it. My thighs were still burning from the combat stance Adam and Ian had made me repeat ten thousand times.

"We're colleagues, not friends. People stay by their friends' sides when they're dying. We can't do that. If anyone is too hurt to move, we have to leave him behind until we can go back safely. Sometimes, that's days later. You hope that the person has been able to find a way to survive in the meantime, but that's not always the case," he explained. "Friendship is a luxury."

"But eventually you go back. Even if it's just for the body."

He nodded.

"Call it what you want, but that's friendship."

Ian swallowed hard and looked away. "I'm going to call down for something to eat. Is there anything you're in the mood for?"

Claudia was right. It was clear that Ian struggled with the concept of friendship. When was the last time Ian had had a friend? Not a teammate or ally, but a true friend?

"I'd be super grateful for a burger—and a piece of cheesecake if they have it." I bit my lip, only slightly embarrassed at how quickly I ordered the two things a girl is never supposed to order. But after what I had just endured, there was no way in hell I was ordering a salad and a glass of water.

"I'll see what I can do," Ian smiled as he looked around the room.

"The menu is on the nightstand next to the phone in the bedroom," I told him.

Ian took a step toward the bedroom and stopped. "May I?"

"Um . . . Yeah. Of course," I replied. *Did he just ask permission to go into the bedroom?*

Ian slipped into the bedroom, and I watched as he sat down on the side of the bed near the phone and looked over the menu. I left him there and walked into the extra bathroom.

I decided to take a shower after we ate in case room

service was super fast. I had no plans of rushing through a wonderfully hot shower, not even for a burger and cheesecake. In the meantime, I had to wash my hands and my face. I felt so incredibly grubby. I took my shirt off so I could wash my neck, too. I knew it was impossible, but as I looked at myself in the mirror, I could have sworn the muscles in my arms were more defined. It was a strange sensation to feel as weak and fatigued as I did, and to feel strong, too. I liked it.

I shut the lid of the toilet and sat down, feeling a burning relief when I closed my eyes. Suddenly, there was a knock at the door and I jerked awake. Was the food already here? Had I actually fallen asleep sitting on the toilet?

"I've got it," I called to Ian, throwing my shirt back on and heading out to the door. I turned the handle in anticipation of dinner, but was greeted by the last person I thought I'd see. "Oh my God. Chad?"

"Hey, baby!" Chad stood there with his arms open wide and a smile that could light up the room. I don't think I had ever seen him that happy.

"What . . . what are you doing here?" I was stunned.

"I came to see you!" Chad pushed his way past me and sauntered into the living room.

"How did you know where I was? Where to find me?"

"You said you weren't going to be at your place for a few days so I thought I'd do you a solid and clear your fridge of anything that might go bad. Mrs. Vasquez let me in. That's when I saw the contact info on the refrigerator door. When I asked her, Tiffany said you were meeting up with Gil. I found it odd that the college would pay for you to come out here. It only took a few more questions for Tiffany to spill the beans. You've been holding out on me, baby!"

Chad sat down on the couch and rested his ankle on his knee and spread his arms across the back of the couch.

"Okay. So you know how *I* got here. How did *you* get here?" I questioned as I crossed my arms.

A little of Chad's smugness dropped from his face. "I borrowed the money from Sam."

"You did WHAT? How could you do that? Sam doesn't have that kind of money!" I shouted.

"But you do. I told him you'd pay him back," he said as if it were obvious.

That was the last straw. It was one thing to take advantage of me but something entirely different when it came to Sam.

"Of course I'm going to pay him back, but—" I began.

"Darling? Is everything all right out there?"

I turned to see Ian emerge from the bedroom, his shirt undone. He stepped to my side and put his arm around my waist.

"Who the hell is this?" Chad demanded as he stood.

"I'm Ian," he said, extending his hand. "I'm Victoria's, well, we haven't really defined that yet, have we, darling?" He looked at me with soft and loving eyes.

Chad's nostrils flared. "Who is this guy, Vic?"

"Ian is a friend of Gil's," I said, thinking quickly. "We started emailing a while back and hit it off."

"You've been cheating on me with some British dude you met online?"

"I wouldn't call it cheating. I mean, you're hardly ever around, and when you do show up, it's only because you want something. Did you even remember that my birthday was on Sunday?"

"I was . . . I was busy. I'd been working. I'm sorry I forgot. Happy birthday," he said insincerely. "But that doesn't mean you should go hooking up with some guy you met online like a slut!"

Before I could respond, Ian had Chad's face pressed against the wall and his arm crooked and twisted behind his back.

"I'm going to give you one chance to apologize to Victoria. She is a beautiful and bright woman with more courage and strength than anyone I've ever known. If you were too foolish to recognize that when you had her, that's your loss."

"I'm sorry! I'm sorry!" Chad winced, and Ian let him go.

I slid up to Ian and took his hand. I held it tightly and Ian squeezed it back, letting me know he was right here with me.

"So that's it? You're ditching two years with me for this guy you just met?" Chad challenged.

"Go home, Chad. And I mean, go *home*. Go back to your parents, and let them send you to med school. Become a doctor. Find a girl whose birthday you won't forget."

Chad thought for a moment before he spoke. "I flew all the way here for this?"

"I didn't ask you to come here—and plus, we both know the real reason you're here."

Ian cleared his throat and broke the silence. "I think you need to leave."

"Don't you think that's up to Vic?" Chad narrowed his eyes at Ian. I stiffened my arm and held my grip on Ian's hand to keep him from charging forward.

"I think that Victoria has made it quite clear that she doesn't want you here."

"Oh really?" Chad challenged. Ian started to say something, but I cut him off before he and Chad got any deeper into their pissing match.

"Would you like us to have someone take you back to the airport?" I asked bluntly.

Chad darted his gaze from Ian to me. His eyes widened, and I wondered how he could possibly be surprised at how this had all played out.

"No," he said after a beat. "I got it." Chad shook his head at me and then turned quickly. "Good-bye, *Victoria.*" I swallowed hard as I watched the door close behind him. I heard it click, then turned the top lock and bolted the door. I turned back to Ian, who was buttoning his shirt.

Ian sat next to me on the couch as we both stared at the opposite wall and considered what had just happened. I thought about what a grand gesture flying to Italy to see me would have been had my relationship with Chad been different. His bravado when Ian entered the room with his shirt undone might have carried weight if he'd ever been bothered by guys hitting on me in the past. I thought about how he called me a slut, something I'd never heard him say before. But then I thought about the lovely things Ian said about me. I knew it was just for show, but it felt good to hear them.

"Are you all right?" Ian asked.

"Yes."

"Are you sure?" Ian turned his body to face mine, and our eyes met. He looked concerned, worried about me.

Feeling the way I did around Ian was starting to bother me. I was there to find Gil, not a new crush. But the way Ian gave me his full attention when we were together made me realize I could say or do anything and it would be okay. When he came from the bedroom and slid his arm around my waist, his hand ever so subtly gripping my hip, my heart had begun to race and heat rose inside me. In my two years with Chad, I had never felt that way.

I nodded. "I will be. He just surprised me, is all. Thank you for all of that. I don't know that you needed to slam him against the wall, but thanks just the same."

"He deserved to have more than his face smashed into the wall for what he called you."

After Ian's apology for not having a coat to give me the night we met, his insistence in the car that women be treated well, and his response to Chad's derogatory comment, I couldn't hold my curiosity back any longer.

"What's the story, Ian? I know plenty of guys who treat women well, but you . . .you're passionate about it."

"Why does there have to be a story? Why can't I just be

a guy who firmly believes that every woman deserves to be treated well?"

"Because no guy really believes that," I said plainly. *Except my dad*, I thought to myself. But I'd come to understand that the way my dad treated my mom was an anomaly. I'd never seen another man treat a woman that way.

"I'm sorry to hear you say that. Perhaps I'll be able to change your mind." Ian rested his arm along the back of the couch and took a lock of my hair between his fingers. His eyes darted between mine as if he were searching for something, and he wet his lips.

I was certain he could hear my heart beating like a drum inside my chest. Just as Ian rested his other hand on my leg just above my knee, there was a knock at the door.

Ian stood abruptly. "That must be the food."

I leaned back and took a few deep breaths while he answered the door. Thank God for room service. No matter how badly I'd wanted to kiss Ian, I couldn't lose focus on finding Gil. Besides, as soon as we found him, I'd be returning to Miami.

I pushed the coffee table forward and sat on the floor.

"What are you doing?" Ian asked as he pushed a cart into the room.

At first, I didn't know what he was talking about, but then I remembered that not everyone sat on the floor to eat. "Oh, just habit. My mom had this rule about not eating on the couch. The only way we were allowed to eat in the living room is if we sat on the floor. Gil and I still do it at home."

"The floor it is, then." Ian smiled.

I looked at the plate Ian set in front of me. Before I could ask, he answered my puzzled expression.

"They had fries, but the closest thing I could get to a burger was Millefoglie di angus. It's beef in a puff pastry," he explained.

"At this point, food is food."

We ate in silence until there wasn't a morsel of food left on either of our plates.

"You should get some sleep," Ian finally said. "I'm going to need you alert when we go through the journal."

"Yeah, I'm pretty tired. Actually, *tired* doesn't even begin to describe it." I stood up and my whole body screamed at me. "Owww!"

"Are you all right?" he said, jumping to his feet.

I rubbed my neck in a vain effort to bring some relief. "I'll be fine. Nothing a hot shower and a cozy bed won't fix."

Ian moved my hand and replaced it with his, massaging my neck and shoulders. I closed my eyes and let him work out the knots.

"You know," I said, not opening my eyes, not quite trusting myself, "you could use some shut-eye, too."

"I'll grab the extra blanket and lie on the couch," he said.

"You're at least six feet tall, Ian. There's no way you'll get any sleep on this tiny couch. Why don't you just sleep in the bed . . . with me?" My own suggestion made me blush.

"Victoria . . ."

"We're two grown people who can handle crashing in the same bed." I looked him square in the eyes, trying to convince both of us that what had almost happened would never happen again.

Ian sighed. "I don't want you to be uncomfortable. I didn't mean to make you uncomfortable earlier," he said apologetically.

"You didn't make me uncomfortable," I said. "Really."

"Well, in that case. I am six foot one, so yes, this couch would be tricky. I'm sure we'll both get a great rest and be ready to dive into the journal with clear eyes."

I showered and changed in the bathroom, and then tucked myself into bed while Ian showered and put on fresh clothes, too. It was eight o'clock. I don't think I had gone to bed at eight o'clock since I was ten years old.

Ian came out of the bathroom and stirred around for a minute before climbing into bed. He left the sheet down and covered his body with just the blanket, forming a barrier. Then he turned on his side, facing away from me.

I opened my eyes and stared at the back of his head, his neck, his shoulders. I didn't want to be distracted by Ian, but I was. My head swirled with thoughts of how it would feel to kiss him, his arms wrapped around my waist, his hands in my hair. My body trembled remembering the grip of his hand on my side. I wanted to know how that grip felt everywhere else, too. Would he be gentle or would he take command of my body, the way he did with everything else?

I closed my eyes, relishing the fantasy. I lifted my hand and inched it closer to him, daring myself to touch the smooth skin of his shoulder.

"Happy birthday, Victoria," Ian said without turning.

I pulled my hand back and turned over. My face burned with embarrassment. Had he read my mind? Was he thinking the same thing I was? It didn't matter. Like the knock at the door, his voice had come at the perfect time, reminding me where I needed to be. I moved closer to my side of the bed and closed my eyes.

"Thank you, Ian."

CHAPTER 10

I woke up to the aromas of a hot breakfast. It smelled like my last morning with Tiffany, and I smiled. Light was forcing its way through the gap in the curtains, casting a single beaming line down the bedroom.

I stretched and turned toward Ian's side and noticed that he and his pillow were missing. I peeked over the edge and saw a crumpled pile of pillows and blankets on the floor.

"What time is it?" I asked as I entered the living room.

"It's seven. I was just about to come get you," Ian answered. He was sitting on the couch in the sweatpants he wore to bed last night and an undershirt.

"You didn't sleep in the bed," I said.

"No."

"The whole point was for you to have a comfortable, good night's sleep."

"We met three days ago," he said gently. "I'm not in the

habit of sharing a bed with a woman I just met. I was fine. How did you sleep?"

I guess I shouldn't have been surprised. It was kind of nice, actually.

"I slept like a rock," I answered. "You got food!"

"I hope it's okay. Pretty basic American breakfast: eggs, bacon, pancakes, fruit, coffee."

"Wow. This is great, Ian. Thank you." I smiled sleepily and poured myself a cup of coffee from the carafe. "Speaking of—"

"Breakfast?" he interrupted, smiling then taking a sip of his coffee.

"Not quite. You're British, but you don't act like a Brit. What's up with that?" I folded over a piece of bacon and put the whole thing in my mouth.

"What, exactly, is your point of reference for how I'm *supposed* to act?" he asked.

"Movies and TV, what else?" I snickered and gave a crooked smile.

"Oh, well that's reliable," he laughed. "You want me to talk about tea and crumpets, and say things like 'cheerio' and 'Bob's your uncle'?" he laughed.

I laughed with him. "I guess I just got thinking that you speak much more like an American than you do an Englishman. I mean, you've got the accent and all, but—"

"I've spent a lot of time all around the world. I learned how to adapt. When I'm in London, I fall back into using English—true English—terms pretty easily. If it'll make me look more authentic, I'll throw a *bollocks* in here and there. How's that?"

"Yeah, that'd be great. Thanks!" We chuckled and finished eating. Ian put our dirty dishes back on the cart and wheeled it outside to the hall to be picked up later.

"So," Ian started. "*Oxblood*. Care to elaborate?"

"Yeah," I began. "It's a color. Our mom was an artist. She believed wholeheartedly in colors being the best way to describe feelings and emotions. When Gil and I were kids and fighting, she would intervene and make us say things like, 'When you took my toy, you made me feel gray.' We thought it was dumb and refused to do it after a while, like when we were teenagers. After they died and I went into foster care, we started it back up as a way to let me speak honestly to Gil. My foster parents weren't too keen on me dogging about my living conditions or talking about my feelings. So when Gil and I would talk on the phone, I could tell him exactly how I felt without getting in trouble."

"That's really beautiful," Ian commented softly. "And so *oxblood* must mean something serious."

"Yes. My mother always said the color felt dark and menacing to her. She only used it when she was painting someone who was troubled. It was the word we used to communicate that something was seriously wrong."

"Well, it's clear you and your brother have a special relationship." Ian gave a small, tight-lipped smile and a determined nod. "Have you read the journal yet?" He opened the journal and flipped through the pages.

"Not entirely. I got about three quarters of the way through on the plane when I gave up. Now I can only assume that Gil was mapping something out. His moves with the crime family, maybe?" I sat cross-legged on the floor in front of the coffee table.

"There has to be more to it than that," Ian mused. "He had been meeting with me and filling me in on his findings. He must have put something in the journal that he couldn't tell me in person."

"Explain to me the theory here. Gil made a connection to a larger mob family? Did he do this before or after he got here?" I asked.

"I don't know what he knew before he got here. We'd already identified some mob families that are becoming involved in more dangerous, violent activity."

"What does that mean?" I asked. "I thought the mob was synonymous with danger."

"Where your traditional mob families are about give and take—with a focus on the take—they usually don't go much farther than the customary beat the living daylights out of you and toss you in a trunk so you come to your senses and find a way to pay up. If you don't come up with a way to repay your debt, it's neat, clean. They might cut off a finger or two. But you're alive. The more aggressive families tie you to a chair and torture you for a few days, and then you get two in the back of your head before they dump you off a boat in the closest sea. These new families though . . . They're even worse." Ian shook his head.

"What's worse than being tortured and getting two in the back of your head?"

"Having it all done in front of your wife and child. And knowing that if they don't kill your family, they'll spend the rest of their lives being trafficked."

"Oh my God!" My stomach churned at the thought. The parents trying to tell their kids to look away, that everything would be okay, then boom.

"I'm sorry. I was too blunt there. I should have——"

"It's fine, Ian," I said, lifting my head. "So why do you think those families are becoming more violent?"

"That's our current problem. We're working on infiltrating one of those organizations, but it's taking longer than I'd like. There's no way for us to know what's changed in their business without having eyes on the inside."

"And that's what Gil was: your eyes," I said.

"Yes and no. We started out watching the Cappola family's import-export activity. But the last time I met with him, Gil said they had asked if he was able to work out some immigration papers for a friend. That was the same day he heard them mention Paolo," Ian said. He sat forward and took a long sip of what I was sure was lukewarm coffee at best.

"You think Gil's journal will connect the dots to Paolo, and then to this mystery person?" I asked. "Which will also lead us to Gil?"

"I don't know," Ian admitted. "In the journal, does Gil mention going anywhere out of Florida?"

I shook my head. "Not that I saw, but I didn't read the whole thing."

"Well, that means, if we have the code right, everything that happened, happened in Italy. But Paolo's activity spans the globe." Ian handed me the journal and I took it from him, moving from the floor to the couch.

"I guess we should just start at the beginning. None of it makes sense to me anyway. The only way we're going to decipher Gil's message here is by working together," I said.

Ian straightened on the couch, steeling himself. "Right. Let's get to work then."

First, we sized up the maps again so we could figure out *where* Gil was talking about. Gil had been all over the place: Genoa, Rome, Venice. Then we had to break down Gil's stories to decode all the people he had been in contact with.

"Shouldn't we flip to the back? I mean, it seems like Paolo would have been one of the last people Gil came in contact with, right?"

"A month ago he overheard the Cappola family mention Paolo, but we have no idea of the time frame in the journal. We need to figure out who each and every person is because any one of them could be Paolo—or the person Paolo is working for. Once we can confirm the identity of the first person, we can go through the rest of the figures and places, widening the circle."

I was already getting antsy. I had been in Italy for almost five days and it felt like I was still no closer to finding Gil. I realized now it had been naive of me to think that I'd have any answers so quickly.

"We'll find him, Victoria. It's going to take some time, but our chances greatly improved the moment you revealed his journal." Ian covered my hand with his. "Be glad. The journal keeps my team on task and gets us closer to finding Gil at the same time."

"Okay," I said, readying myself. "Along with physical descriptions, I need to think of other traits. Jobs, hobbies, quirks even. Right?"

"Excellent! And since it looks like Gil hasn't been outside of Italy, we can narrow it down to organizations based here," Ian added.

"That still sounds pretty overwhelming, Ian." I dropped my head and Ian lifted it with his palm.

"It's not as overwhelming as it sounds. Across the country, there are ten major crime families. He was most likely brought here by a lower-level family, but I don't believe that the mob families from the smaller villages have the manpower, money, or interest into the higher-level stuff we're looking into, so we can rule them out."

With that, Ian pulled up his file of pictures and nodded at me. With my mouth set in a thin line, I picked the journal back up and turned to the next page.

I stood and walked around the small living room and read the passage about our great-uncle Ricky, the dinner party, and the cut of meat he couldn't get from the butcher, who then ended up dead. I described Ricky in all his glory as a linebacker of a man with a weakness for my mother's profiteroles and a well-glazed honey-baked ham. I read about the fight over the shelter at the beach on the

Fourth of July and about my cousin Mickey jumping in. I described Mickey as a short and stocky guy with movie-star good looks but a glandular problem that made him sweat like a horse.

Ian typed away at his laptop, and I watched the right side of the screen flip through headshots with milliseconds between each one.

"Does your great-uncle Ricky look like this?" Ian asked. I bent down and put my face closer to the screen. The match was uncanny.

"It's kind of scary how much they look alike," I said.

Ian typed something else and another picture popped up. "What about him? Does he resemble your cousin Mickey?"

"No," I said immediately. "Mickey is a good-looking guy. This guy would make me cross the street."

"Doesn't matter. These are our two guys. Based on your physical description, we can safely say that Ricky is Antonio CancioBello. And thanks to your added comment about Mickey's sweating issue, we can rule out Antonio's other two sons and point the finger at Giorgio as our next match."

"Really?" I smiled a little at having accomplished one small step in this process. We were just a few pages in, but I was feeling hopeful.

"Really," Ian smiled back.

"So who are these guys? Are they lower level like you thought?" I asked.

"Not as low as I had initially thought. Gil clearly skipped

them and went straight for the meat. The CancioBellos are your typical mob family. They staked their claim on a small area of Genoa and shake down the business owners there for 'protection.' They use their businesses for money laundering and as fronts for whatever they're bringing in or sending out."

"So they're not dangerous?" I held my breath while I waited for Ian to answer.

"Not any more than your run-of-the-mill mobster," he smiled.

I moved on to the next entry. More strange family members and gruesome endings. As we continued, it got more complicated. Not everyone had a physical doppel-gänger, and I had to think harder about small traits like how people walked or talked. I finally remembered that my mom's friend Mary Jane had a weird twitch in her left eye every time she drank too much wine—a trait shared by her Italian counterpart, the wife of Rinaldo Fidorro.

Gil even used Sam from the diner. Fortunately, his counterpart is a nice old man who owns a bakery. Unfor-tunately, the bakery is constantly being shaken down by a mob from Rome. But it was brilliant of Gil to focus on him so that Ian could identify his location and, subsequently, the family who had staked claim in a part of Rome.

We had been at it for a while and weren't as far along as I had hoped. We hadn't identified anyone as the Cappolas yet but did find seven of the ten major crime families. The bad news was of those seven, three of their leaders were recently found dead.

3

"This is better than you think," Ian said reassuringly. I raised my eyebrows, asking him how. "Knowing who *isn't* in play is just as important as knowing who is. And based on the information that I already have, none of the families left have strong enough ties with Paolo that Gil would go back."

"If you say so."

I pressed on.

"Oh, this is about Leo, my dad's best friend." I was reading a passage about a guy who played poker in a bar with unsavory characters. "My dad had a regular poker night and Leo was there for every game. Gil and I used to refer to him as 'Uncle Creepy.' He didn't have any respect for anyone's personal space, if you know what I mean. And, eww!" I winced and made a face as I recalled a specific physical trait of Leo's. "He had this gross mole with hair growing out of it, right on the side of his face."

"Did he look a little something like this?" Ian entered something into the laptop and turned it to show me a picture of a tall, beefy man with greased-back hair and an unsightly hairy mole on the side of his neck. I wrinkled my nose and nodded.

"Lenny Scarpone." Ian's face twisted in worry.

"What's wrong with Lenny Scarpone? Is he a higher-level guy we should be concerned about?" I asked.

"His father, Leo, is not a high-level anything. The Scarpones have been running into some trouble getting certain products into the States. Someone like Gil, who knows about US customs laws, would be a good asset."

When I asked Ian what the products were, he laughed. "Honestly? It could be anything from prosciutto to olive oil to more cash than one is allowed to carry into the country."

"Cold cuts and olive oil? Really?"

"You'd be surprised about the regulations regarding importing cold cuts from a foreign country."

"So why would the Scarpones let Gil go? I mean, if he's such an asset . . ."

"They're not a family looking to branch out. They like their illegal import/export business just the way it is. So, once Gil got them set up, they could have easily referred him to a brother family in need of Gil's expertise, like the Cappolas," Ian explained.

"The Scarpones aren't so much the problem as is their youngest son, Lenny," he continued. "He's become known as a bit of a sleaze, willing to hire himself out for anything from shakedowns to kidnappings. If Gil went snooping around for a way into the mob, it's likely that Lenny was his contact and the one who invited your brother to come to Italy. The fact that Lenny showed up this far into the journal is a little worrisome. I'm going to have Damon look into it."

Ian stood and picked up his phone from the coffee table. Damon answered quickly, and Ian went directly into his instructions. Damon was to find Lenny Scarpone and ask what he knew about Gil.

"So he's been bouncing from one mob family to another, advising them on US customs laws," I said to Ian as he sat back down.

"Yes," Ian said after a beat. "At least that's how it started."

"But now he's following leads to try and find Paolo and his mysterious boss." I sat down next to Ian and tried to wrap my brain around my brother having decided to become some sort of contract worker for the mob. I couldn't make sense of what Gil had been doing, but mostly *why* he was doing it. "So he's been climbing his way up the mobster corporate ladder?"

"Essentially. Word gets out on the street about the business needs of a family and people get referred out. The problem is that the higher up the pyramid he goes, the more dangerous it gets. We stop talking about cold cuts and olive oil and start talking about drugs, guns, and other things."

"That means Gil is in danger," I said, my voice shaking. I was trying not to be, but I was scared. I didn't want to think about the things the mob did to those who crossed them. But the more Ian told me about these families, the more determined I became to find the crucial information Gil had hidden away in the journal.

"Why don't we take a break?" Ian offered. "We've been at this for hours, and I think I just saw actual steam seep out of your ears." He smiled the friendly smile that made me involuntarily reciprocate. "Why don't you go downstairs and get a soda or something? I'll follow up with Claudia and Damon."

I changed my clothes, pulled my hair into a ponytail, and strolled to the elevator. There didn't appear to be any alcove with soda machines, not that I knew what kind of money to insert anyway. I walked through the lobby and noticed it was strangely empty. Neither of the hotel clerks was at the front desk.

I entered the lounge, contemplating something stronger than a soda despite the fact that it wasn't even noon. That wasn't stopping the other patrons in the bar, either. I guess in Italy a glass of wine for breakfast is totally cool.

As I waited for the bartender to return, I scanned the lounge: An older couple sitting and chatting with each other. A few men drinking wine. A man reading an Italian magazine and another man playing with his phone.

All perfectly normal, and yet . . .

The guy in the corner wearing a T-shirt and jeans hadn't been turning the pages. The man sitting opposite him was focused on his phone, but instead of holding it in his lap, he was holding it up, in front of his face, the camera aimed in my direction.

I'd played a game with Tiffany at the mall: Pretend you're looking at something on your phone when really you're taking pictures of a hot guy. Was that guy taking pictures of me?

In Miami, maybe I'd be flattered, I thought. No, I'd still be creeped out. And after all my training, I couldn't help but get worried—especially when the magazine guy quickly glanced up at me.

I turned back to the bar, breathing fast. Was I imagining things, or were those guys surveilling me?

That's when I saw the old woman from the day I'd arrived. She was wearing the same dress and a scarf over her head, still knitting her heart out—or was she? That was three days ago, and it didn't look like she had made any progress.

My gut started doing flips. Were these people associated with the mob families that Ian and Gil had been trying to infiltrate? But Ian hadn't said anything about their cover being blown.

On the other hand, Gil *had* disappeared. If he'd talked . . .

The thought of Gil being tortured made my stomach, already aflutter, drop to my toes.

I couldn't think about that now. Whoever these people were and however they came to be here, they were watching me. Something was off. They might not be after me, but they would certainly be after Ian.

Breathe, Vic. Just breathe. Let Ian know what's going on ASAP.

I waited another minute or two before I shoved my hands in my pockets and walked to the front desk. There was still no one there.

As nonchalantly as I could, I picked up the phone and tried to figure out how to dial up to my room. I put my hand down on the desk, rummaging for instructions, and my hand slid as if it were in a puddle of water. I turned it over to look, and my palm was red and wet. A dark puddle of what could only be blood had pooled amid the pencils and receipts. It wasn't a paper cut amount of blood; it was like someone got her face smashed onto the stone countertop. I bit my lip to keep from screaming.

I wiped my palm on my pants and slowly walked toward the elevators, my eyes focused on my route. I saw movement in my periphery as I turned the corner into the elevator car. I punched my floor. As the doors slid closed, the magazine guy and cell phone guy came into view, walking quickly toward the elevator.

The car started up. I pressed the button for my floor over and over again, willing it to move faster. As soon as the doors opened, I squeezed myself through and ran to my room, all the way at the end of the hall.

Then I heard the *ding* of the elevator and did the most foolish thing: I looked back. It was the two men. We locked eyes, and I watched as they reached behind their backs. I turned and ran.

"Ian!" I screamed.

The door crashed open and Ian leaped out, a pistol in his hand. "Down!" he shouted.

I dropped to the floor and heard a *THUNK THUNK* as Ian fired twice. The gun's exploding sound was muffled by a silencer. Then Ian grabbed my arm and pulled me up. I glanced back as I stumbled into the room. Both men were sprawled out on the hallway floor, facedown.

"What happened?" he asked with no emotion as he closed the door.

"I was . . . I was . . ." I stuttered.

"Breathe, Victoria." Ian took me by the shoulders and looked me square in the eye. "What happened?" he asked again, punctuating each word.

"I was just standing there at the bar, waiting. I noticed those two men watching me. And there was a third. A woman, I tried to call the room from the front desk—"

I lifted my hand, the palm still stained red.

Ian drew a sharp breath and gripped my wrist. "You're bleeding!"

I shook my head. "It's not mine. The poor girl behind the counter." I began to cry.

"Was that it?" Ian asked. "Just those three?"

"Um . . ."

"Victoria!" he demanded.

"I think so!" I said. Ian narrowed his eyes at me, demanding a definitive answer. "I'm sure. Just those three."

Ian looked at me then nodded. "Okay."

I started to cry harder as the shock began to wear off. "Hey, hey," Ian said, wrapping his arms around me. "It's okay. You're okay."

"I thought I was prepared, but I'm not," I wailed into his shoulder.

He stroked my hair. "I didn't exactly prepare you for this scenario. We had no reason to believe there was a threat here. Victoria, are you sure I can't send you home?"

I pushed away from Ian, struggling to control my tears. "No. You can't send me home. I can't go home without Gil."

"Okay," Ian said. He brushed the hair from my tear-stained face and steadied me. His eyes were strong, and as they locked onto mine, I knew in that moment that Ian Hale was a man I could trust.

Ian sat me down on the couch and then pulled out his phone. It was a quick call to Damon before he was addressing me again.

"Outside of the journal, is there anything in this room you can't live without?" he asked.

"My laptop."

"Grab it, and let's go." Ian shoved his laptop in his backpack and slung it over his shoulder, while I stuffed mine along with the journal into my backpack. He had changed while I was gone and was wearing jeans and a T-shirt.

With his gun in one hand and my hand in his other, we left the room and walked to the stairs.

The two men were still sprawled on the floor just a few steps from the elevator. Except now pools of dark liquid stretched from wall to wall.

He opened the door to the stairwell slowly, looking above and below. When it appeared empty, we stepped through and closed the door quietly behind us, taking the stairs down quickly. We reached the bottom and hurried from one door through another until we reached the service area of the hotel. Ian weaved us in between crates of food and industrial-size laundry carts before we made it through the back door and to his car.

We screeched out of the parking lot in the direction of the factory headquarters. Once we were sure no one was following us, Ian pulled his phone out to make another call.

He looked worried. Now that we were in the clear, he was trying to get in touch with the team, but no one was answering. If whoever was in the hotel had come after us, Adam, Claudia, and Damon could be in danger as well. Despite our entire conversation about friendship being a luxury he could not afford, it was clear Ian was scared for them.

I took his hand and wrapped both of mine around it. "I'm sure they're fine," I said.

If I thought Ian could be comforted, that he'd accept it, I was wrong. The professional Ian who was able to shoot down my assailants was back, and he didn't need to be comforted. Without a word, Ian pulled his hand from mine and gripped the steering wheel.

We arrived at the old factory, and Ian jumped out of the car. Since no one from the team had answered his calls, he couldn't be certain that the building hadn't been compromised. He popped the trunk and pulled out a gun, loaded it, and handed it to me. He drew his from the holster behind his back. My nervous gaze caught his before we could move.

"You're going to be fine," he said. I nodded and followed him. He pulled the door open slowly. We both winced as the metal door squeaked against the frame. When we reached the top of the stairs, Ian turned to me. He put his palm out like a stop sign and then put a finger to his lips. I was to stay put at the end of the hall and keep quiet. I watched him inch down the hall and through the door into the main office.

After what seemed like plenty of time to check the back office and all the nooks and crannies, Ian still hadn't returned. My nerves began to tingle, and I knew something was wrong. I couldn't leave him in a potentially dangerous situation, so I walked up the rest of the steps softly until I reached the door. I listened closely for commotion, but it was as silent as it had been since we arrived. Perhaps Ian had found something and gotten so involved in examining it that he forgot about me. I pushed the door open slowly and stepped inside. My gun was drawn, and I was hopeful that I was holding it in the way Adam had trained me.

When I walked into the room, I couldn't help but gasp. Ian was unconscious, his body spread across the floor, with a man standing over him. The man looked up at me, then at something—or someone—behind me. Then everything went dark.

CHAPTER 11

The only sound I could hear when I regained consciousness was the pounding in my head.

I tried to remember what had just happened. Ian on the floor, unconscious. Someone standing over him, looking past me . . .

Someone must have been behind me. Someone who then hit me over the head.

I tried to reach up to check the damage, but my hands were bound together. Eyes burning from the light, I glanced down.

Duct tape. My wrists were bound with silver duct tape. My ankles were also bound, and I was slumped in a corner at the back of Ian's team's headquarters. Next to me, hanging by his wrists with his feet just grazing the floor, was a bruised, battered, and shirtless Ian. His shirt was torn and crumpled on the floor.

He looked at me, his eyes intense. "Victoria," he whispered.

The men who'd attacked us didn't appear to be in the room, but Ian was doing his best not to be heard.

"Victoria, are you okay?" he asked.

"I think so," I said. "My head really hurts though. How long were we out?"

"A few hours from what I can tell."

Ian's wrists were bound with rope, and the rope had been lassoed on a hook hanging from the ceiling. His wrists were rubbed raw. His sides were red and bruised, and there was a cut above his eye.

Whoever had ambushed us had worked Ian over.

The room was relatively empty. Were it not for the big-screen televisions hanging on the wall and the equipment on Claudia's desk, you would never know the place had been inhabited so recently.

There were no bags on desktops, no coffee cups, no coats tossed in the corner. Ian hadn't been able to get in touch with the team, but had they managed to get out before Thug One and Thug Two arrived?

Our backpacks lay against the wall behind Ian, unopened. I prayed that our laptops and Gil's journal were still tucked inside.

I rolled to my stomach then pushed myself onto my knees. Ian gave me a stern look.

"There's a hidden panel in the closet of the back room—"

"I'm not leaving you, Ian," I declared.

"I'll be fine," he argued.

"Oh yeah, because you're so comfortable hanging

there? We're in this shitty situation because of me, and I'll be damned if I'm going to let those assholes come back and use you for a punching bag and then do only God knows what with me."

"It's not your fault, Victoria," Ian said.

"I had a gun. I could have shot the guy standing over you, but I froze." I looked down, ashamed. I also couldn't stomach Ian's abused body. It broke my heart to see him like that, especially since I knew I was to blame.

"Look at me, Victoria," he said. He wouldn't speak again until my eyes met his. "Things happen. We both entered an unknown situation. You'll recall I was the one lying unconscious on the floor when you walked in." Even in his battered state, Ian had an uncanny ability to make me feel better. While I didn't think I'd ever relinquish responsibility, his words took the edge off.

"Okay," I agreed reluctantly.

"Now, they left about twenty minutes ago and could be back any minute," he said.

"Then I guess I'd better hurry."

Ian opened his mouth to speak again, but I cut him off before he could utter a single syllable.

"I already told you I'm not leaving you here. I'm our only hope of getting out of here, Ian, so let me do everything I can to make that happen." Here was my chance to make things right, and I hoped I could figure out and execute a plan before our attackers came back.

I pushed myself to my feet and hopped over to Adam's station. The secret panel to the weapons arsenal was voice-activated by Adam. I turned to Ian, who just shook his head and looked apologetically at me.

Frustrated, I shoved my body as hard as I could against the wall. It didn't budge. As if my 130-pound frame would somehow open Adam's military-grade secret panel. Every weapon we needed to defeat our attackers was just out of reach, made completely useless by the impossible wall. At least I wasn't the only one who couldn't get to Adam's weapons. I didn't want to imagine what our attackers would do with this arsenal at their disposal.

I sat in Adam's chair and searched his drawers. They were empty. Of course they were. In high-tech, digital, and heavily armed headquarters, who needs scissors?

I lifted my hands to my eyes and rubbed them as best I could. Suddenly, I remembered a YouTube self-defense video Tiffany and I had found one night.

I raised my hands as high as I could and said a quick prayer that these guys used cheap duct tape. With as much force as I could muster, I thrust my hands down and sharply twisted my wrists.

With a rewarding shearing sound, the tape snapped in half. My hands were free!

Ian raised an eyebrow. "Impressive," he said.

I shrugged. "I told you. I live in a gritty neighborhood. A girl's got to have survival skills."

Ian looked at my ankles, then back at me, tilting his head skeptically.

Good point. That move wasn't going to work down there.

I hopped over to Claudia's desk, praying that *someone* would have a pair of scissors. Her drawers looked similarly empty. But as I started to close her top drawer, something glinted in the light.

"Thank you, Claudia, for caring about your manicure!"

Office supplies? *Nada.* Beauty products? Better bet. A metal nail file was wedged at the back of the drawer.

It seemed to take forever, but I was able to use the nail file to start enough of a tear in the duct tape around my ankles to rip the rest away.

"All right!" I said, starting toward Ian. Then I froze, and Ian and I locked eyes. We both could hear it. The sound of someone coming up the steps.

"Victoria, go," Ian said. "The other exit—"

"No way," I said, surprising myself, because frankly, all I wanted to do was to run and never look back. I grabbed Ian's legs and tried to push him up so he could free his wrists from the hook. "I'm not going anywhere without you."

Ian struggled with the rope, but it was caught on the edge of the hook. The sound of footsteps reached the door.

"Victoria!" Ian hissed.

We were out of time. "Pretend you're unconscious!" I said.

"What?"

"Just do it!" I locked eyes with Ian. I had a desperate idea, but this was a desperate moment. It was time to put all that self-defense training to the test.

Ian glanced at the door, closed his eyes, and let his head hang.

OXBLOOD

I dropped my arms and kept my back to the door as it swung open. I heard Thug One or Thug Two come through the door and stop.

He said something short and harsh in Italian. He either swore or told me not to move. I decided to take it as the latter and stayed right where I was. My plan would only work if I didn't turn around.

"I don't speak Italian," I said, willing him to close the distance between us. Meanwhile, I was rehearsing in my mind what I was about to do. A cold sweat rolled slowly down my back.

The man said something else and crossed the room quickly. I felt a hard grip on my shoulder—right out of the assailant handbook. That was my cue.

I pivoted hard and jabbed an elbow into the man's ribs, then immediately swung that fist down and into his crotch.

It was Thug One, the guy who I'd seen standing over Ian. He crumpled to the ground, both hands cradling his groin.

"Quickly now!" Ian hissed.

I grabbed Ian's legs and lifted again. Ian struggled with the rope on the hook.

I stepped back, and he dropped to the ground.

"Get his gun," Ian said as he tried to free his wrists.

I glanced down at Thug One, who had gotten his knees under him but was still facedown, writhing in pain. There, tucked into his belt at the small of his back, was a pistol.

I reached down and pulled it free.

165

"Keep it on him," Ian said, pulling his wrists apart.

Then Thug Two burst through the door, gun up and blazing. Bullets whistled through the air around us as Ian grabbed the gun from me. He pushed me to the ground and fired in the same moment.

I saw Thug Two stagger and drop his gun. Had he been hit in the arm? He spun and kept coming. Ian got off one more shot before Thug Two tackled him, and they both went to the ground.

Before I could think about my next move, I felt a steely grip on my calf. It was Thug One, leering at me.

I did what was only natural. I lifted my free foot and stamped it as hard as I could into that ugly face. I wanted to break his teeth. I succeeded in breaking his nose. I think. Blood was everywhere as Thug One's body went limp.

That's when I realized I'd heard another gunshot. My stomach dropped. Ian?

He was up and walking toward me, the gun in his hand. Thug Two lay motionless behind him.

I stood up on rickety legs and grabbed our bags and Ian's shirt, then followed Ian to a back room that looked like it had once been a walk-in storage closet. He dropped an old-fashioned beam across the door, locking it, before pulling a panel from the wall. From inside the hidden space, he pulled a gun, a cell phone, and some cash.

"Is everything there?" Ian asked. I checked the bags. Our laptops and Gil's journal were still inside. I passed him his backpack, and he threw it over his shoulders.

I suddenly realized I was trembling and gasping. Ian looked as cool as a cucumber—he was a trained soldier. I, on the other hand, was a waitress from Miami who had barely survived by implementing YouTube self-defense training.

Ian cupped the back of my head and looked me in the eye. "Breathe with me, Victoria," he said. It took two long, deep breaths before I was able to synchronize our breathing.

Ian smiled ruefully and gave a slight shake of his head. "That was very well done."

"Did you kill him?"

"Yes."

"Did I kill the other guy?" I wasn't actually sure if I wanted to know the answer.

He paused before replying. "No. But what you need to remember is that unless you defend yourself and your team, whoever it is that is coming for us *will* kill us once they get what they want."

Ian was right, and I knew it. I couldn't focus on the condition of that man out there. My only objective was to find Gil, and I couldn't let anything get in my way.

I took a deep breath and pulled myself together. "And you said I was going to need more than self-defense moves to survive."

Ian smiled again. "I stand corrected."

"I'll be sure to alert the team to your confession." I smiled bravely back. "So, what now? Unless we're going to play Seven Minutes in Heaven, we have to get out of this closet."

"As tempting as that sounds, I'd like to get as far away from this place as possible." Ian cocked his head at me. "How good are you with a pole?"

I raised an eyebrow. "I'm going to need a little more information before answering that."

Ian grinned and reached behind the panels again. With a click, the wall at the back of the room indented, then slid aside to reveal a long silver pole that stretched to the ground floor.

I stared at it for a moment, then turned to Ian. "Just one? We don't each get a pole, Batman?"

"I'll go first," he said. "It's a long way through the dark, but there are motion-sensor lights once you near the bottom, and they'll click on for you once I've made it down."

"How far are we talking?"

"We'll be going down the equivalent of four stories," he answered.

"Well, we haven't got all day. Let's go."

Ian nodded. He wrapped himself around the pole and slid out of sight.

Trying to breathe steadily, I reached out over the dark abyss, grabbed the pole, and looked down. After a few moments, the lights Ian had promised clicked on. Forty feet down, Ian stepped away from the pole and looked up at me.

I repositioned my backpack and took a long breath, focusing on Gil.

OXBLOOD

It's now or never, I told myself. I jumped onto the pole and began to slide.

Ian had a big smile on his face when he caught me at the bottom. "Tell me that wasn't fun."

I twisted my mouth before I answered. "Okay, yeah. That was pretty badass."

Ian laughed and led me down a long tunnel. All the lights were on motion sensors, and sections clicked on and off as we progressed. I could tell Ian was hurt, but he never winced or said a word about it.

"Do we have any idea who those guys were?" I asked. "What about the ones at the hotel?"

"I didn't recognize any of them," Ian said. "It's hard to say who they work for, but we've made a lot of enemies over the years."

The floor was uneven in some areas, and there were random rocks and pebbles that I kept stumbling over.

"But those two were part of the same crew that were at the hotel," Ian continued. "I heard them say that their boss had to clean up the mess we left there."

We walked for another few minutes before Ian noticed my silence.

"Do you feel okay? Want to stop for a moment?" he asked gently. It was nice of him to be sensitive to my unconditioned body, and I had no doubt I was still in shock from my first fight, but it was the vision of Ian's body, unconscious, bleeding, and hanging from the ceiling, that was bothering me.

"I'm so sorry, Ian. You counted on me to back you up, and I let you down," I blurted.

"Stop it, Victoria. We've been over this." He moved to face me, bringing us to a halt. I couldn't lift my head to look at him in fear of opening the emotional floodgates.

"I just can't get the image of you hanging there out of my head," I told him.

"Hey," he said softly.

"I know, I know. I'm being weak."

Ian took my face in his hands and forced me to look at him. "You are not weak. You are human. And you're . . . you. I would be concerned if seeing me like that hadn't upset you." He studied my face for a moment before he spoke again. "You saved us in there. You followed your gut and were incredibly brave, and I will be forever grateful for that."

"So my stubbornness came in handy, huh?" I gave him a crooked smile.

"Yes. It most certainly did." Ian brushed my hair out of my face and sighed. "Now, are you okay to continue? It's not much farther."

"Yes, I'm good. Thank you, Ian." We mirrored tight-lipped smiles at each other and kept walking.

We climbed two flights of stairs at the end of the tunnel and emerged inside an old, abandoned house—completely empty and all kinds of creepy—before continuing outside to a barn. A keypad was hidden in the paneling, and Ian flipped the cover open and entered a six-digit code.

As we passed through the door, it became clear that the barn was just a shell hiding the true interior. We had entered a showroom with two cars parked with space for a third car between them.

Ian entered another code into a different keypad. Suddenly, the floor shifted, revealing that each car was parked on a massive plate. The car on the left lowered, and the middle plate moved into its place. The car on the right moved left. As each car replaced the previous one's place in line, a new one appeared from below on the right. A hydraulic, Ferris wheel–type system rotated several cars until a black SUV arrived.

Ian moved to the driver's side door.

"That. Was. Crazy," I said.

"Get in," Ian said, ignoring my amazement. More whiplash. Sweet to sour in the blink of an eye.

Once we were on the road, Ian pulled out the new cell phone and dialed. I saw relief flood his face when someone answered. "Claudia! What the hell is going on?"

I heard the muffled sounds of Claudia talking. Ian nodded a couple of times, told her to stay put in the new safe house, and then hung up.

I looked at Ian expectantly, but it appeared that he had no intention of filling me in. "What did she say?" I asked.

"Not now," he said tersely. He kept his eyes on the road, his knuckles white on the steering wheel.

"What did she say, Ian?" Did my friendship with the team suddenly not matter?

"I said, *not now*, Victoria!" He brought the car to a screeching halt in the middle of the road, jerking me forward into my seatbelt.

I looked at Ian in shock.

He calmed himself, but not before his nostrils flared with frustration. "Now that I know everyone is fine, I am trying to figure out the next move. I can't do that if you're asking questions incessantly."

"I'm sorry if I want to know what's going on! Two gunmen just chased me down a hallway, I was knocked out and tied up, you were hanging from the ceiling, I kicked a guy in the face and broke his nose, you just killed a man, and the team has gone MIA. Now we're driving toward I don't know what, and all you're doing is telling me to shut up!"

"Your job is to take orders and do as I say. I'll give you information when it's time for you to have information." His face was hard and steady. That was when I understood what it was really like to be a part of this team.

I realized that to be around Ian was to be around two different people. When it came to his team or the mission, he was one person. And, for whatever reason, when he was alone with me, he was someone else. A guy who *didn't* want to be that other guy all the time.

I turned my body to face the windshield and steeled myself. I wasn't going to become the two-faced machine Ian had become, but I could become the good little agent he needed me to be.

"You're right. I'm sorry. You'll give me information as I need it," I said coldly.

"Victoria," he began apologetically.

I had to let Ian work the way he worked. That was my only hope of finding Gil.

"It's fine, Ian."

Ian nodded once and turned to face the road. He took the car out of park and took us from zero to sixty in a matter of seconds.

CHAPTER 12

We drove for a long time. We passed farmhouse after farmhouse with nothing much in between. While he drove us to undisclosed location number two, I combed through the journal and came to a familiar story at the end of the book. The names had been changed, but I recognized the people and the events.

In the journal, the girlfriend of a man who Gil identified as a distant cousin had to leave Miami and go home to Indiana with her family. Weeks went by, and the cousin received no replies to his almost-daily emails. The cousin became consumed with worry, until one night, his worry turned into a nightmare.

Watching the evening news, he saw a story about the body of an unidentified young girl found inside a brothel in Miami. When a sketch of the girl's face appeared on the screen, the cousin fell apart. It was his lost girlfriend.

Gil's lost girlfriend.

We never got any clear answers about what happened to Maria or how she ended up in that brothel. All we knew was what Maria had told Gil: Her family was being deported back to Cuba. It was such a hard time for Gil. They had dated for two years and when he found out that she'd been murdered, it nearly killed him. He didn't eat and he barely slept for days. He snapped out of it, though, when he realized that I needed him. Dad and Mom had already been gone for more than two years by then. So it was just the two of us, and he couldn't check out on me. It was after her death that he became so laser-focused on school and research.

Poor Gil, I thought. *Maria's death still haunts him.* But what did her story have to do with Italy? Had Gil found himself in a mob family that ran a prostitution ring?

I logged the Maria story away and put the journal back in my bag.

We were entering a town that looked similar to Bologna. The farmhouses and pastures were slowly being replaced with rows of homes and businesses. It seemed like a nice place to explore someday—when I wasn't searching for my missing brother and running for my life.

After several turns, including a few extra that I'm pretty sure Ian took to be on the safe side, we pulled into an alley.

"Let's go," he said, his game face still on.

"May I ask where we are?" I shut my door and followed him into a building and up two flights of stairs. My still-fatigued legs were not thrilled by the lack of an elevator.

"We're almost an hour southwest of Venice in a city called Padova."

He pulled out his phone and began typing, but instead of putting it to his ear, he held it flat on his palm while we stood in front of a door. A moment later, the door unlatched and popped ajar.

"Fancy," I muttered under my breath.

"Damon!" Ian called as he strode across the room.

The setup here was different. This was a huge apartment with rooms and furniture. It felt almost welcoming until I spotted Adam's artillery on the coffee table. Although, it probably felt like home to Adam to have his "babies" right at his fingertips. Claudia's scaled-down tech was spread out on the dining-room table, a fraction of what she had at the other location. There were no flat-screen televisions. Only a lonely TV with bunny ears like the one my grandmother had in New York.

"Thank God, you're both okay," Damon said as he rushed in from a back bedroom. "We couldn't reach you when it all started."

Damon kissed both my cheeks and threw his arms around Ian in a manly hug.

Ian looked angry. "What happened? Why didn't the surveillance security on the building work, and why the *hell* didn't any of you answer your cell?"

Claudia was feverishly clacking away at her computer. "I don't know what happened, Ian. Our cells were fine when you called Damon after you got ambushed at the hotel. Then we got raided within minutes of Damon hanging up. After that, we hit the tunnels. They went dead down there and didn't come back up until we were already here. We tried calling you, but there was no answer," she explained. One of the thugs probably destroyed Ian's phone when they strung him up. "And I have no idea how they got in, but I'm going to find out. *No one* cracks my system!"

"I've pulled a few things you need to see," Damon began.

"Is there anything I can do?" I asked. I didn't know if Ian was going to bark at me or ignore me altogether.

"Just sit tight," he said before he walked away with Damon.

I sat down next to Claudia, and Adam joined us. "You okay, kid?"

"Yeah," I answered him. "What about you guys? What happened?"

"We were totally freaking ambushed, that's what happened!" Claudia said as she continued working.

Adam explained, "The trip wires at the other end of the building went off. Claudia pulled up the surveillance feed, and once we knew a rat wasn't the culprit, we grabbed everything and were in the tunnel in less than a minute."

"That tunnel is nuts!" I said.

"Right? That building used to be a factory. Rumor has it that the tunnel connected the factory to the designer's house. Shipments had to be brought through the tunnel to his home for his personal approval before they went out."

"Who was the designer?" I asked.

"The Prada family," Adam answered. "Ever heard of them?"

"Oh, I'm more than familiar! My friend Tiffany would

have a heart attack if she knew I stood on the same ground as a Prada," I laughed. "But, I hate to break it to you, the Prada business has pretty much always been in Milan."

Just then, the door flung open, and I thought for sure that we were being attacked again. A woman with a blazing red pixie-cut and a broad-shouldered wall of a guy with dark brown hair entered the apartment like they owned it. They were both dressed up and looked like they had come from a fancy party. His white dress shirt was undone, and his tie was draped around his shirt collar. Her strapless, skin-tight cobalt-blue dress didn't leave much to the imagination. They both looked a little rough, but not enough to keep them from being embarrassingly good-looking.

"What the hell, Ian?" the guy shouted as he closed the door behind them.

"Carter. Eva. What are you doing here?" Ian asked.

"Well, let's see. We were solidly embedded in Rubio's family, enjoying the engagement party of his daughter Caramia, when all hell broke loose! A team came in, guns blazing, and took Rubio and his boys out. You know the procedure before you send a Rogue team in!"

"That's bull and you know it!" Ian shouted.

Carter was pissed, and Eva seemed just as angry.

"What's a Rogue team?" I whispered to Claudia and Adam.

"We are. We're R-14, *Rogue*-14," Adam answered.

"How many Rogue teams are there?"

"No one knows for sure. I mean, someone knows, but we don't." Claudia looked at her screen again and shook her head. "And no one knows how long the Command division has been around. All we know is that in the last year, seven teams have either been eliminated or disbanded, with the remaining team members sent to join other teams.

"Enter Carter and Eva. They were on a mission in Colombia when the rest of their team was found dead, execution style. They contacted base, were extracted, and got reassigned to our team."

"Ian's right, Carter," Eva said, calmer now. "We need to regroup. If that wasn't a Rogue team, then we were ambushed along with the rest of them. What happened out there?"

"It's a long story that starts with Victoria and me being attacked at the hotel," Ian told them.

Carter and Eva turned to look at me. "Who's this?" Eva asked.

"This is Victoria. She's a part of the team now," Ian said matter-of-factly. It was the first time he referred to me as a member of the team without sounding like he was sorry I was there.

"Hmph," Carter responded.

"Stop being a jerk, Carter," Eva said. She walked over and shook my hand. "I'm Eva. That's Carter. He's not usually so . . . well, *that way*. It's been an interesting day. Welcome to the team."

"Thanks, and I don't think *interesting* begins to cover it," I said.

Carter took Eva's hand and disappeared into a second bedroom, closing the door behind them. I wondered if they were together, like, *together-together*. While I would think that romantic relationships would be a no-no, if you are playing a part with someone for so long, the lines must get blurred.

While everyone else returned to their tasks, I sat on the couch, tense and worried. Why was Ian's team being ambushed out of the blue? Of course any mob family that realized it was being monitored by a Rogue team would surely want to eliminate the agents. But the attacks didn't seem very moblike, based on how Ian said they operated. And Carter's description of their ambush didn't sound like one mob family coming after another.

I thought back over the events at the hotel. I felt like I had missed something. I closed my eyes and pictured the hotel bar. I saw the two guys who chased me, the old lady knitting, the various couples and people around the room. I couldn't think of anything I had missed. The two men who chased me were the only ones I saw *do* anything. Except . . .

The old lady. She had been there the day I checked in and met Ian. She moved to the lobby just around the same time Ian did. And she was in the hotel today. It sounded crazy, but I knew in my gut that she was involved.

Oh my God! I whispered to myself. "Ian!" I stood up and shouted.

"What?" he asked, looking slightly annoyed.

"They want Gil," I said as if it were explanation enough.

"What is she talking about?" Carter asked. He and Eva

joined us in the living room, his bow tie hanging loose around his neck and Eva's feet bare.

"The old lady who was knitting—well, she's probably not an old lady, she's probably young and just dressed as an old lady to seem less assuming. She was there the day I arrived. She was in the lounge where I first saw you."

"She's probably a guest there," Carter said.

"She was sitting in the lounge not far from you, knitting. When I checked in at the front desk, you were behind me in line and she moved to the big bench in the lobby."

Carter looked annoyed. "There are any number of reasons why that woman was there. C'mon, Ian. Really? Have any of you wondered about her showing up within days of the attack on this team?"

Carter folded his arms and glared at me. "What are you even bringing to this team?"

I stepped forward and looked up at him. "You favor your left leg." I said.

Carter dropped his arms. "What?"

"You try not to, but you favor your left leg when you walk," I said. "You also have a scar behind your right ear. And you might want to consider a smaller weapon strapped to your ankle because the one you had on when you got here screams, 'I'm armed!'"

Ian folded his arms. "That's what she brings to this team."

All eyes were on Carter, with Eva adding a knowing smirk.

"We'll see," Carter said before turning on his heel and walking back into the bedroom.

"Well done, Victoria." Eva said with a smile. "He may be pissed now, but he'll respect you later for not backing down."

Ian waved his hand dismissively. "Carter is a hard-ass. He doesn't like taking orders from someone with less field experience than him. I trust your instincts. If you say the old lady was casing the hotel, then let's start with that."

"Why do you think they were at the hotel?" Damon asked.

"Maybe for the same reason Ian was," I said. "Maybe they were waiting for Gil. Ian heard me ask about Gil, maybe she did, too?"

"Then why not just follow you to your room?" Eva asked.

"I don't know," I answered. "Gil sent me his journal from *that* hotel, and he sent it to me because something was wrong. What if they, the two guys and the old lady, were closing in on him, and he sent it just before he was able to get away?"

"Claudia, pull up the hotel surveillance footage," Damon said. He leaned in over her shoulder. I could see she was not as comfortable with his proximity as he was. His cologne must have been too much for her, too, because she kept wriggling her nose and looked like she was about to sneeze.

"They wouldn't be after the journal," I mused aloud. "There's no way anyone would look at it and think it's anything but a family history. Besides, I'm guessing no one else knows about it. They must just want *him*."

I tried not to let my nerves get the better of me, but my

voice betrayed me. "This whole time, I've been thinking that Gil was relatively safe because his skills are so valuable, but what if he was trying to get away from them? What if they asked him to do something he just couldn't do? Either he didn't know how or couldn't morally do it? Do you think he tried to make a run for it?"

"First of all, calm down," Ian said. "Even though it might not seem like it, we've got this under control. And, honestly, I have no idea if Gil is hiding or if someone has him. He was sure he was getting closer to Paolo and had new information for me, which is why I had been sitting on the hotel when you arrived. Maybe the old lady knew what he had. But why come after you?"

"If she heard me ask about Gil, it makes sense that they would come after me thinking either one of us could get to Gil. The question is: What does Gil know?"

"I don't know," Ian said. "Damon pulled some information about the locations we decoded and the people of interest. We haven't gone through all of it yet, but so far, there's nothing we didn't already know. All of it showed up on our radar, but none of it was out of the ordinary."

"I read through the rest of the journal. We could go through that and see what else we find. Paolo has to be in there somewhere," I suggested. Ian was right, though. So far, we had figured out where Gil had been and what he had been observing, but none of it was getting us that much closer to Paolo.

"I've got the surveillance footage pulled up," Claudia called from the dining-room table.

We joined her, eager to find out if we could identify our hotel stalkers.

"That was fast! How did you do that?" I asked, peering over her shoulder.

"I'm insulted, but I'm going to let it pass since you're still new." She smirked. "It's the twenty-first century. All that stuff is kept in the cloud. No more of that ancient hard-copy crap."

We all huddled around Claudia and watched the footage from different camera angles and locations in the hotel. It was devastating to see the moment when the poor girl behind the counter was killed. One of the men distracted her while the other one came from behind, took a knife, and slit her carotid artery. That explained the pool of blood on the counter. But they were smart. Both kept their heads down so there was no clear shot of them.

When I walked into the lounge onscreen, I confirmed that the two guys who killed the girl were also the two who followed me into the hallway. And then I pointed out the old lady pretending to knit. We watched the two thugs, and it was clear that they were keeping a close eye on me. My skin began to crawl, reliving what it felt like to be watched and followed by two cold-blooded killers.

As soon as I moved into the lobby, the two men got up and spoke to the old lady. She must have given them some kind of instruction because they just nodded.

"I just need them to look up, dammit!" Ian said, frustrated.

I watched myself walk behind the reception desk and

quivered as my hand slid across the desk in a puddle of blood. Even on the black-and-white screen, it was easy to see my face pale.

Damon rubbed my back comfortingly.

We watched as I got into one elevator and nervously pushed the button over and over again, while the two thugs and the old lady got into another elevator. They said little to one another but then, miraculously, the woman looked up at the numbers above the doors, giving us a clear view of her face. I was right: the old lady was anything but.

"Pause," Ian instructed. He stared at the screen. It didn't take enhanced observation skills to tell he was working hard to contain himself.

"Do you know who that is?" I asked.

"Yes." His answer came out quick and sharp. "That's Bianca Moran. She's a Rogue agent."

CHAPTER 13

The room was deadly silent. Confusion passed over the faces of each agent as they tried to understand why a Rogue agent would turn on her own.

Ian walked slowly toward the back bedroom where he and Damon had been working. "Victoria," he said by way of asking me to follow him.

He shut the door behind me. I studied Ian's face. He was scared.

"Why is a Rogue team coming after us?" I asked, worried.

Ian shook his head. "This is bigger, no, worse than I could have imagined. At this point, I *wish* the mob were after us." He wouldn't look at me. "You can't be here, Victoria."

"We've been over this," I said. "I'm the only one who can decipher the journal. You need me. And I need you. I'm not leaving without my brother. I can't."

Ian turned and started pacing. "I don't know that it's

a Rogue team. It could be just her, but I'd be surprised. I worked with her a couple of years ago on an arms case. She was always a by-the-book agent. Something is happening here, and I'm not sure I can protect you. If she has bad intel, she's going to follow her orders until she hears differently. If she's going off the grid and trying to take us down because she's joined a mob family, it's the same thing. She will not stop until she completes her mission."

"Can't we just contact your boss and find out? I mean, we could get some help, some backup from another team, couldn't we?" Ian looked at me and I knew my naïveté was showing.

"I can't just walk down the hall to the Command division's office and file a report."

"Well, there has to be something we can do. Carter and Eva are here now, so maybe they can—"

"You can't stay," Ian said. "Claudia will get you to a safe house in France tomorrow. Then you can take the train to England and fly home out of Heathrow. I'll have an agent watch you once you're home until we quash this."

"I'm safer with you, and you know it."

"You're not safe anywhere. Not as long as whoever has Gil is still out there. If they don't know you're his sister now, it's only a matter of time before they do. And then they'll come after you to get to him."

"Why do you keep looking for reasons to send me home?"

"I don't need to *look* for *reasons*," he said defensively. "All I see is proof."

"You and Adam ran me ragged in training so I'd be prepared for a situation like this. For the most part, I succeeded. So why are you going back on all that and trying to get me to leave?"

"Because you're different." He looked up at the ceiling, exasperated. "You're not like us, Victoria. That's what I tried to tell you from the beginning. You have a family. You have a real life. This work is merciless. It hollows you out. It steals your soul. It kills your heart. I can't let that happen to you."

"I'm no different than you, Ian," I said. "You have a heart and a soul. I know you do. I've seen it. And those people out there? *They* are your family. *They* are your home. I saw the look on your face when you thought they'd been harmed. You love them."

"Maybe so, but"—he ran his fingers through his blond hair—"I used to have this all figured out. Then you show up and remind me what it was like to have people you would travel halfway around the world to save. I haven't seen that, haven't *felt* that, in a really long time. And now all I can think about is keeping you safe because I couldn't stand it if something happened to you."

Ian rested his hands on his hips and looked at the floor. It was like he was embarrassed to have let his emotions take over.

"Hey," I said as I moved closer to him. "You don't have to be a machine to do your job, Ian."

"Yes, I do. I can't . . ."

"You can't what?" I asked softly.

He lifted his head and swallowed hard. "I can't look at you and feel what I feel. Emotions get in the way. In the face of an impossible situation, I can't be sure I'll make the right decision. And that's unacceptable."

"What is it, exactly, that you feel?"

Ian shook his head. "That first night, when I sat across from you at dinner, you stirred up parts of me that I thought were long gone. The problem is I haven't been able to shut that valve off since then. I've tried being harsh with you, wearing you down, but damn it if you don't just get back up again."

Ian cupped my face with one hand and ran his thumb across my cheek. An electric current shot through me, and the emotions I'd been pushing down fought their way back up.

"It's been so long since I've felt like this I'm not even sure *what* it is. It's not that I haven't encountered beautiful women before. It's that I've never come face to face with Victoria Asher. Why do I feel like you're going to be responsible for my undoing?"

I was supposed to say Gil's name to get us back on track and remind us of why I was there. I was supposed to remove his hand from my face. I was supposed to tell him not to say the things he was saying because they made feelings that scared me bubble up in me.

But the truth was, when I looked at him and he looked back at me, I felt stronger than I ever had before. I wanted him to keep speaking from the heart, keep talking about the way we made each other feel. I wanted him to hold my face with *both* of his hands. And I wanted him to kiss me because I knew that a kiss from Ian Hale would be unlike any kiss I had ever had or would ever have again.

But I didn't tell him those things. And he didn't do those things.

"I'm sorry," he said. He lowered his hand and turned to the window.

"Don't be." I bit my tongue to keep myself from saying any more.

When Ian turned back around, he looked at me, and I wordlessly reminded him that I was there to find Gil and would leave as soon as that was resolved. My time in Italy would be a story that no one could believe anyway. A dream so vivid that even I wouldn't be able to separate fact from fiction.

"I suppose I would rather keep my eyes on you to ensure your safety," Ian finally said. "It's only right. Gil is your brother, after all."

"So it's settled. I'm staying. Right here. By your side," I told him.

"Yes." His eyes were still soft. I couldn't deny how I felt when Ian looked at me that way. I knew he felt it, too. I wondered how long we could keep up the facade of being just teammates.

"So now what?" I asked.

"Now we have to figure out what the hell Bianca is doing." He walked past me toward the door and I followed him out into the living room.

"That bitch! I totally saved her ass in Moscow, and now

she's a traitor?" Carter was fuming. Apparently, Damon's update on Bianca was enough to distract him from the shock of my presence.

"We don't know enough yet," Ian said. "Damon, what did you find on Scarpone?"

"I made some calls and tracked him to Parma, but my friend with the local police said they pulled his body from a burning car a week ago," Damon replied.

Ian sighed and gave me an apologetic look. "Okay. Thanks."

My heart sank at having lost what had been the only solid lead on Gil's location.

Claudia still had Bianca's face frozen on the screen. The black-and-white surveillance video didn't reveal too much, but from what I could tell, she was a small woman. With delicate, feminine features, it was hard to see her as a ruthless agent. Especially one who was spearheading a hunt for Ian's team.

"So how do we find out why they're after us?" I asked.

"We'll ask around," Damon answered.

"You'll ask around?" I replied. "We need to smoke out a potential hazard to our team, not find a good place to eat on a Friday night."

"Hey! Newbie!" Carter called to me. "You do whatever it is you do, and we'll do our job."

"You're so grumpy after you've been shot at," Eva yelled to Carter before she turned to me. "There are always a few locals who have their ear to the ground. Damon, Ian, Carter, me, we each have our go-to guys. We toss a little money their way, and they're willing to find out whatever we need."

The group broke up, each pursuing individual tasks. Eva gestured at me, and I followed her to a set of chairs.

"Thanks," I said. "Seriously, though, what is his problem?"

Even seated, Eva was wonderfully tall, just like Tiffany. "I wasn't joking when I said being shot at made him grumpy," she explained. "But outside of that, Carter is a suspicious person. It's the training. It's what we do, living among the enemy. And then this skirmish happens and suddenly you're here? It's just his natural instinct to question you. Don't take it personally. It'll wear off. In the meantime, expect more attitude, but don't be afraid to give it back to him." She leaned in closer. "What you did earlier was impressive. It's a natural skill? You don't have any training?" she asked.

I shrugged. "I've just always been observant. My dad used to have his buddies over to play poker when I was a kid. He would sit me on his lap and point out everything the guys did to show they were bluffing or had a great hand. I got really good at picking up little details about people," I told her.

She nodded. "It's a great skill. Just make sure you're focusing on the right things. It may take a while before you can differentiate between good and evil, safe and dangerous, trustworthy and devious. In this industry, the lines can get blurred."

Eva got up and disappeared into the kitchen. My mind

was buzzing with everything we needed to figure out, and quickly. Was Bianca after us or Gil? Or both? Where was Gil? Was he in hiding or being held captive? And who was the mysterious Paolo?

I looked around the apartment. Ian and Damon were speaking quietly, Claudia was still engrossed in figuring out how Bianca's team had gotten past their security, and Eva, Adam, and Carter were huddled around the kitchen table salivating over weapons.

I needed a break. I stood up, crossed the room, grabbed a hoodie from the hook next to the front door, and slid into the hall.

I moved quickly down the stairs and outside with the hood pulled over my head. I didn't know what I was doing or where I was going, but I knew I needed a little space, even if just for a few minutes.

It was a charming town, like the Italy I had imagined— before joining a Rogue team and trying to stay alive—with basilicas and bell towers, ancient Roman ruins and museums, piazzas and streets filled with people. I watched a man adjust the display in his wineshop, and above him on the second-floor balcony, a woman was watering pots of geraniums hooked over the railings. I listened to the voices in the streets and decided that Italian was the most beautiful language I'd ever heard.

I wandered into a small park and sat on a bench. I only walked about three blocks. I had no intention of getting lost, especially considering the circumstances.

Mothers held babies on their laps, while older kids ran

around them, playing. Although the sun was beginning to set, there was still plenty of time left for the little ones to get out all their energy before dinner. I watched the children, and it reminded me of afternoons swinging at the park and walking on the beach with my own mother. Even though I missed her, the memories always calmed me, probably because it was impossible for me to think of her without being reminded of the lullaby she always hummed. I had long since forgotten the words, but the sweet melody was there.

I took a deep breath and considered the last week of my life. How had I gone from having dinner at The Cheesecake Factory to flying to Italy and joining a secret organization within INTERPOL?

At least I wasn't in it alone. If I trusted my gut, I couldn't say I was 100 percent sure about Carter. My mom always told me that suspicious people were, in fact, suspicious themselves. But I knew I was absolutely sure I could trust Ian. As long as I had him, I was going to be okay.

"Do you want to tell me what the hell you're doing out here?" It was Ian. When I turned around, I could see he was panting.

"Have you been running?" I flipped the hood of my sweatshirt off my head.

"Yes, I've been running! I turn around and you're nowhere to be seen." He sat down next to me. "You realize it's incredibly dangerous for you to walk around completely by yourself without telling anyone—especially since another Rogue agent is after us?"

I narrowed my eyes at him. After all we'd been through, I was not in the mood for another lecture.

He seemed to get the point, and his face softened. "Why did you leave? What's wrong?"

I sighed. "I made a decision less than a week ago to hop on a plane and come to Italy to find my brother. I don't know what I was expecting, but it wasn't this. Everything at the hotel and the factory. Your team. You. It's all so much. I just needed some air." I hugged my knees to my chest. "I'm doing my best to follow your orders, and I know we've made progress on the journal, but I left everything behind to find Gil and we aren't that much closer. It just makes me feel . . . helpless."

"I'm sorry. I never considered you would feel that way. Rogue agents . . . we typically feel empowered when we give all that up. With no ties to anyone or anything, we find freedom in this life. At least that's what we tell ourselves." Ian leaned back on the bench and looked at me.

"I'm sorry I just walked out."

"It's understandable."

We sat there for a moment in silence. It was comforting.

"Ian," I began. I turned to face him on the bench. "Before we go back, I just wanted to say thank you. I just showed up here and took over and you kind of went along."

"You didn't really give me a choice now, did you?" he smiled.

"No, I guess not. But you really made me feel like a part of the team when we were going through the journal.

Believing that I was actually doing something to make a difference has helped."

Ian half smiled and sighed. His eyes found the ground and he shifted in his seat.

"What is it? Did I get weird and make you uncomfortable? I made it weird, didn't I?"

"I have to tell you something," he said, pausing. "I knew about the journal."

"What do you mean?"

"I didn't know how he was chronicling it, but I knew he was keeping track of his findings in the journal."

"What?" I barked, standing up. Blood began to boil inside me. I immediately felt like we had wasted time. When we could have been looking for Gil, Ian and I were poring over information in the journal he already had.

"Why didn't you just tell me? Why did you make me go through all of that?" I began to pace. I tried to stay calm, but I knew I was making a scene.

"Gil sent you the journal for a reason. There had to be something in there, some ace up his sleeve that he'd been holding on to for whatever reason. You were the key to finding it, but—"

"But what?"

"But, so far, I already knew everything that we've found."

"You put me through all of that for nothing. When you realized there was no new information in there, you could have said something. You could have been honest with me, but you weren't. You asked me to trust you and I did, but now I see that was a huge mistake!"

Ian took me by my shoulders, locking his serious eyes on mine. "You're drawing attention to us. Now, either you need to slap me across the face like we're having a lover's quarrel, or we need to take this inside."

Going back to the apartment was not an option, and my fury was just ripe enough to accept his invitation.

Without hesitation, I lifted my right hand and let it fly.

CHAPTER 14

Ian's head popped to the side, his eyes shut tight. He paused before lifting his head, which I thought was just for effect since I had been present for a bloodier brawl than this. He rubbed his palm over the cherry-red mark on his cheek and stared at me. I was about to let off another round of fury when Ian grabbed my shoulders again and pressed his lips against mine.

His kiss was hard and rough, like he was proving a point. Then he dropped his arms from my shoulders and wrapped them around my waist, pulling me closer to him. His kiss became soft and tender. He moved one hand to my face and then behind my neck.

I kissed him back, hard, then soft, too. I ran my fingers through his hair and gripped his shoulders. My body was humming with energy, responding to every point where his body touched mine. It was electrifying. It was everything I knew it would be, and more.

When Ian pulled away, we stood there in each other's

arms the way lovers do after a make-up kiss: dazed, goofy, fired up. We smiled like we were different people. People who weren't being chased by a deadly Rogue agent. People who would not be forced to say good-bye soon.

It didn't last long. Reality set in, and we let each other go.

"So," I said, bringing us back to the issue that catapulted us into that life-changing kiss. "You've known about everything in the journal?"

"Yes. I told you Gil had been reporting to me. He told me he was keeping everything meticulously documented. The journal entries aren't what I imagined, but it contains everything he had already disclosed to me."

"I feel like such an idiot."

"Don't. Like I said, Gil sent you the journal for a reason. There's got to be something in there that he knew only you could decipher." Ian took my hand and brought me to sit down on his lap. "We need to look like a couple who just made up. Italians are known for how passionate they can be. This scene is quite normal to them."

I couldn't tell if he was being serious or not, but I had no problem playing along. Being near him was addictive. Just the thought of letting his hand go was like a punch in the stomach. "Okay." He wrapped his arms around my body, and I rested my head against his.

"By the way, thank you for not slapping me again," Ian said.

"Day's not over yet." I smirked.

"Honestly, Victoria, I've really been waiting for you to come up with some insight that Gil didn't give me."

"I understand that, Ian. So what do we do in the meantime?"

"Damon is going to put out some feelers with his contacts, and hopefully we'll hear from a local or two about any out-of-the-ordinary activity in town," Ian answered.

"Won't Bianca and her people be following us?" I asked nervously.

"There are fifty safe houses in Italy. It'll take them a while to locate this one. Claudia also increased the sensitivity on the security system and is constantly monitoring it for any irregularities." Ian threaded his fingers through mine as we continued to put on a "show."

I sighed and turned my thoughts back to the journal and reading about Gil and Maria's sad story at the end.

"What's wrong?" Ian asked.

"I was just thinking about how difficult it must have been for Gil to have seen something so similar to his own story go down." I wondered what the connection was between the Italian mob and Gil's story about Maria.

"I know we're pretending to be a couple, but I really can't read your mind," he laughed.

I echoed his laughter to keep up the facade. "The story about the girl at the end of the journal. It had to have been awful to watch someone else go through that tragedy."

Ian's face turned serious. "What are you talking about?"

"You said you knew about everything in the journal," I stammered, my face puzzled.

"I said I knew everything so far." Ian stood, taking me with him. "But we haven't covered that story yet."

"Oh my God!" I covered my mouth as Ian and I both realized that Gil wanted me to share Maria's story. Ian took my hand, and we hurried back to the apartment while I told him everything I knew about Gil and Maria. "And just when he was already heartbroken enough from not hearing from her, we turned the TV on one night to find out she had been murdered, found dead in a brothel."

"So she tells Gil that her family is being deported, he doesn't hear from her for months, and then she shows up dead?"

"Yeah."

"Where are her parents?"

"Don't know. Gil never heard back from any of them when he tried to get in touch with her," I told him. "What's the connection here?"

We stopped in the middle of the stairwell up to the apartment, and Ian lowered his voice. The space was dimly lit and musty. "Do you remember when I told you how parts of some mob families were venturing into more dangerous territory?"

"Yeah."

"Do you remember me saying that Paolo was photographed at an all-girls school just before three of them disappeared?"

I nodded.

"What I didn't tell you is that wherever he goes, there

ends up being an increase in missing persons reports. The authorities have written off those last three girls as runaways. But there has also been a spike of children under the age of ten who have gone missing." Ian sighed. "I think they're kidnapping and selling these kids. The teens are most definitely being trafficked in the sex trade. The younger ones could be as well, but may be shipped off to sweatshops. If they're lucky, they're being sold in illegal adoptions."

"Oh my God, Ian. And you think Paolo is behind it?" I asked, matching his hushed tone.

"Remember, Paolo's just an errand boy. I want his boss," Ian answered.

"Okay. I'll grab the journal, and you open your database of bad guys. This is it, Ian. Gil found Paolo's boss. All we have to do is connect the dots." I started back up the stairs, but Ian grabbed my arm to stop me.

"You can't tell anyone about this," he warned.

"Why not? This is big and we need the whole team involved," I argued, confused.

"I've been tracking this on my own."

"Okay," I said, unsure of what that meant.

"I've been tracking it on my own because I've been forbidden to deal with cases involving children."

"Why on earth would you be forbidden to do something like that?" It was a strange rule for someone who was charged with keeping the world safe.

"It's a long story, and I promise to tell you. I just need you to trust me." He took my hand in his and brought it to his chest. "Can you do that?"

I looked into Ian's eyes and saw pain. Pain that made him so willing to fight for those who couldn't fight for themselves. How could I not trust a man who's willing to risk his career for such a noble cause?

"Of course," I answered.

I looked at the door and saw shadows moving across the crack in the bottom. Someone was definitely standing on the other side, listening. I had an idea of who it might be.

I gestured with my head. "Feet," I whispered to Ian.

Ian nodded, then unlocked the door with his cell phone and let us in.

I charged through, ready to put on an act. "Geez, Ian! I just wanted some fresh air!" I said.

There he was. Carter. Standing just to the side. He gave me the evil eye, which I happily returned.

"You don't leave this place without my permission," Ian countered, walking in behind me. "Do you understand me? Someone is trying to kill us, so I'd prefer not to risk my neck running after your impetuous ass because you *need some air!*"

"Fine!" I returned. "Then let's just get through the rest of the journal. Hopefully we'll be closer to finding Gil and then I'll be out of your hair!"

I stormed into the back bedroom and waited behind the open door, listening for any comments from the others.

"Don't be so hard on her, Ian," said Adam. "She may be a badass and pick it up quick, but she's not a real agent."

"He's right," I heard Claudia say. "She's overwhelmed. Give her some room to breathe."

I smiled. I was right about being able to trust Adam and Claudia.

"Cut her loose," Carter said harshly. "She's unpredictable and she's going to get someone killed."

That guy, I didn't trust.

"Are you hiding?" Damon appeared from the bathroom.

I was so startled I jumped. "No! Not hiding. Just waiting for Ian," I told him.

"Ah, I see. You two, you should play nice. Ian, he's a nice guy," Damon said sweetly.

"Right." I said with a nod.

Ian came through the door. "I need the room," he said to Damon. He still had his pissed-off face on.

Damon winked at me and I gave him a small smile as he left. I liked Damon. He seemed to always know how to put me at ease.

"Well done with the theatrics. You get an A-plus on your acting skills."

"Who said I was acting?" I smirked.

In a flash, Ian had pulled the journal from his backpack and flipped to the last few pages. He read it over twice before handing it back to me. I scanned the words again, seeing a part of the story I hadn't noticed the first time I read it. According to the girl's parents, a family friend had offered to let her stay with him, but she declined, saying that she didn't trust him. I wonder who that could be?

"Okay. Now tell me what you know about their relationship before Maria was supposedly deported," Ian instructed.

"Okay." I didn't know where to start so I went back as far as I could remember. "Gil and Maria met in school, at University of Miami. Gil was a senior and Maria was a junior. They struck up a conversation in the library one day, and after that they were always together."

"How well did you know her?"

"I knew her okay, I guess. He brought her around some, but I wasn't very social back then. I was still pretty reclusive after my parents' deaths. Anyway, what I knew of her was good. She cooked for us sometimes."

"Did anything strange or unusual happen while they were dating, before she was supposedly deported?"

"If there was, Gil never told me. Everything always seemed pretty normal," I told him.

"How long after she supposedly left the country did you find out she was dead?" Ian asked, getting straight to the point.

"I guess it was about three or four months after she left when we saw the report about the brothel being busted in the worst part of Miami. The reporter said that an unidentified girl had been found dead in the building and then they flashed an artist's drawing of her on the screen asking if anyone recognized her. We knew immediately that it was Maria. Gil went down to the morgue hoping to see her family; he figured if she was still in Miami, her parents might be, too. But no one came. He had to identify the body. The worst part was that the medical examiner said she had been dead for almost two days before they found her. They just left her in some room while they went on with their business." I fought back tears as I remembered the night I held my brother while he mourned Maria. He was broken inside. Another person he loved had died, and all I could do was be there for him and let him cry.

"I'm sorry, Victoria. I know this is difficult for you to talk about," Ian said softly.

"Thanks." I took a breath and shoved down the lump that was forming in my throat. "After that, he threw himself into school. That's when he started his journals. He's just as intense about his research now as he was when he started. Maybe even more. He was convinced that Maria had been forced into working at that place. He believed her parents had been deported but that she was kept behind. Nothing could persuade him that she had been leading a double life."

"And what about this person who supposedly offered her a place to stay?" Ian asked.

"That's news to me—so it must be specific to whatever's going on here. There'd be no way for Gil to have known if that happened to Maria."

"Then it sounds like he's trying to tell us that someone we know is untrustworthy." Ian furrowed his brow as he thought. "Of course! It's Bianca!"

"It's a shame we didn't realize that *before* we were ambushed—twice," I said.

Ian closed his eyes as he processed everything. I could

tell he was debating with himself about whether he was going to let me in on his inner monologue or not. Finally, he turned back to face me.

"What is it?" I pried.

"How was Maria murdered?" he asked slowly.

I would never forget the night Gil came home from identifying her body. It was so late when he got back that the sun was close to rising. I stayed on the couch all night waiting for him to walk through the door. He came in like a zombie, feet shuffling, dark rings under his eyes. I made us a whole pot of coffee, the good stuff we saved for Sunday mornings. We sat silently sipping at the kitchen table until Gil was ready to speak. That's when he told me that Maria's family never showed up and exactly how she died.

"Oh my God, Ian," I began. My heart was pounding inside my chest and it became harder to breathe. "He said she had been shot. Two in the back of her head."

"It's okay, Victoria. It's going to be okay." Ian sat next to me on the bed and rubbed my back while I put my head between my knees and tried not to hyperventilate.

"I can't believe this is what Gil got himself into." I sat up and took a deep breath, tears streaming down my face.

"It's obvious he went looking for the trafficking ring that killed Maria. And I think he found it but didn't know what to do once he did. I think they wanted him to forge documents to get these kids out of the country."

"No," I said, not wanting to believe it. "As heartbroken as he was about Maria, I can't believe he'd leave me on a quest for vengeance."

Ian shrugged. "Vengeance is powerful. And danger-ous. Maybe Gil believed he could do just enough, forge the documents just well enough that no one here would know the difference. But once the kid got to the other country, immigration would spot the forgery and step in."

"Did you have any idea about this before now?" I wiped my tears and dried my palms on my pants.

"No. I thought he was an overzealous law student doing something really stupid in the name of education. Had I known he was specifically going after traffickers, I would have knocked him unconscious and sent him home." Ian stood with an angry force. "I should have never told him about Paolo."

"I thought you said Gil was the one who overheard the Cappolas mention him?"

Ian was pacing across the room. I could tell by the anguished look on his face that he was giving himself an internal beatdown.

"He did. But I had been trying to find something, any-thing that would serve as a solid lead to Paolo. The sooner I got to him, the sooner I would be able to take down his boss. When Gil told me what he had heard, I stressed how important it was to find everything he could about the Cappola connection to Paolo. All I told him to do was keep his ears open. Had I known his true intentions, I would have pulled him out." Ian turned and dropped to his knees in front of me. "I swear, Victoria, I would have pulled him out and sent him home."

"It's not your fault, Ian. He lied to both of us."

My heart broke. Gil had not only lied to me, but he left me. He left me and walked right into a situation where he could be killed at any moment and I would be alone forever. Maybe he was already dead.

I didn't want to think about it. I wanted to believe that if avenging Maria had been Gil's objective all along, then he had prepared himself. That he had learned the lay of the land and knew exactly how to stay alive with these kinds of people. But Ian was right. There was a good chance that Gil's true character and integrity would keep him from putting children at risk. Normally, that wouldn't be a bad thing, but in this case, it may have already gotten Gil two in the back of *his* head.

CHAPTER 15

"I have to go out," Ian said as he moved around the room gathering essentials: gun, cell phone, and an envelope he filled with money that he pulled out from under a loose floorboard.

I watched him, overwhelmingly aware that I was now officially in way too deep. Part of me wished I had taken Ian up on one of his offers—instructions—to go home. The other part of me felt like I was so close to finding Gil that I could almost taste it. There was still the smallest chance that Gil had learned how to navigate the deadly crowd in which he had embedded himself. He had risen through the ranks quickly thanks to his skills, his *useful* skills.

"Where are you going?" I asked Ian.

"I'm going to see what I can find out from some locals. I won't be long."

"I thought Damon had already put some feelers out?"

"Not for what I'm looking for." Ian took my hand in his. "Just sit tight, okay? Please don't go anywhere."

"I won't, but what am I supposed to do?" I motioned to my puffy, tired eyes. "I mean, if I can't tell the others what's really going on."

"We've just been through the journal again. You're upset and overwhelmed. You miss Gil and are afraid for what may have happened to him. The best excuses are the most obvious."

"At least I won't be lying," I sighed, and collected my thoughts. "Be safe, okay?"

He snickered at my implication. "I'll be fine." The idea of Ian not being able to protect himself may have sounded absurd to him, but the image of him hanging by his wrists in the old factory would haunt me forever. "Damon has contacted Command. We haven't heard anything back from them yet, but if there's bad intel out there and they sent Bianca after us, I doubt we'll hear anything soon."

"Is that what you think is happening?"

"No. I think Bianca is a tainted agent, and she and her associates are trying to stop us before we can stop them," Ian said. Ian put his hand on my neck and ran his thumb across my cheek. "I shouldn't be long."

He passed through the living room in a blur with a short declaration that he would be back soon. No one questioned him, not even Carter.

The door shut loudly behind him as I walked out of the bedroom. All eyes were on me. Claudia and Adam watched me with compassion while Eva raised a suspicious eyebrow. I knew what she was insinuating, but I wasn't going to gratify her presumptions with any kind of defense. Damon was engrossed in his papers and something on his computer. Carter? Well, at least he was consistent: It was the stink eye all the time.

I just shook my head and walked into the kitchen for something cold to drink. The small refrigerator had two shelves, one stocked with bottled water and the other with beer, white wine, and containers of food. I grabbed a water and guzzled almost half of it.

I leaned against the counter and thought about the dots Ian and I had just connected. I didn't know if I wanted to beat the crap out of Gil or give him a medal. I'd probably know when I saw him—*if* I saw him. I decided that the best thing to do was focus on Gil being alive and ready for my wrath. Maybe I could get Adam to help me sweeten my self-defense moves for a more thorough ass-kicking.

"What's the word, newbie?"

I ignored Carter as he opened the refrigerator, grabbed a bottle of water, and then immediately pulled out two beers. "Have a drink, newbie. You'll feel better."

"Stop calling me newbie," I said.

He chuckled. "Everyone needs a nickname."

"In that case, which do you prefer? Jackass or douche bag?" I twisted the cap back on my water and walked out of the kitchen.

"Leave her alone, Carter," Adam said. "Don't pay any attention to him, Vic."

"Yeah. He's always got a stick up his ass about something," Claudia added.

"I do not have a stick up my ass." Carter said with a laugh. "Okay, okay. I'm sorry, newbie, I mean, *Victoria*. Tell you what. Since we don't know how long boss man is going to be gone, let's play a game to pass the time."

"What kind of game?" I asked suspiciously. I didn't believe for one second that Carter was actually trying to smooth things over with me.

"It's not really a game," Claudia interjected. "It's something we do when new people join the team, so not very often."

"Have you ever played 'Never Have I Ever'?" Carter asked.

I rolled my eyes. "Seriously? A drinking game?"

"It's a twist on that," Adam began. "We all have a story, a reason why we've ended up on a Rogue team. We play 'Never Have I Ever' as a way of telling our story. Sometimes we find that we have more in common than we think."

"Here's how our version works," Eva said. "I might say, 'Never have I ever run away from home when I was sixteen.' In the original version, the person whose turn it is says something they've never done. Those who *have* done it take a drink. In our version, you tell something you *have* done, then you and everyone who has also done it takes a drink."

She crossed in front of Carter and took the second beer out of his hand.

"You do know that you're all grown-ups, right?" I said. "I mean, I didn't wander into a frat house, right?"

Adam laughed. "Unlike at a frat party, the point isn't to get wasted. The point is to share things about ourselves," he said.

He, among everyone here, seemed the most out of place. With his fair skin and hair that looked reddish in the right light, to look at him, you'd think he was a dad from the suburbs, mowing his lawn and taking his kids to Little League practice on weekends. Instead, he was deceptively strong and had an inhuman ability to hit any target you put in front of him, regardless of the distance. Were he not a Rogue agent, it would be difficult to convince me Adam had done anything nefarious.

"There is only one rule," Damon said. "Once we talk about it here, we do not tell another's story without permission."

In answer, I went into the kitchen and grabbed a beer. I popped the cap, took a fast swig, and gave the performance of a lifetime. No doubt about it, beer was nasty.

I cocked my head and locked eyes with Carter. "Game on."

"Now *this* is a Victoria I could get on board with," Carter said with a leer.

"You're not getting on board anything of mine," I retaliated.

Carter laughed and took a seat.

"You don't have to do this, Vic," Claudia whispered to me. I loved how she seemed to instinctively look out for me.

"I'm not going to let him push me around," I told her.

"All right then." She gave me a tight-lipped smile. "I'll go first," she said to the group. Claudia took a deep breath and continued. "Never have I ever moved to Hollywood and tried to be an actress."

She took a swig of her beer. I took a minute to translate in my mind that, in this group's version of the game, *never* actually meant that Claudia *had* moved to Hollywood and tried to be an actress.

No one else drank. Of course. *Thank you, Claudia.*

"Really?" I said. "You wanted to be an actress?"

Claudia nodded. "Yeah. I had a few small parts on the stage and I was an extra in a national commercial. Nothing anyone would remember, but big for me."

"I think that's awesome." I smiled at her like a friend would.

"Can I go now?" Carter whined. "Never have I ever been on the run from the law."

He took a huge swig of his beer, as did everyone else in the room. I looked at Adam curiously.

"Yep," he said. "It turns out you can't take guns across the border into Canada."

"Really?" I asked.

"Well, you probably could if they weren't stolen . . . and loaded," Adam chuckled.

"Okay, *piccolina.* Your turn." Damon raised his bottle to me and nodded.

I twisted the bottle around in my hand nervously. "Never have I ever flown halfway around the world to find the only family I have left."

I took a drink. As I suspected, no one else did.

I bet they had all flown around the world many times over. But no one here had any family left. They were loners, runaways. Forging lives for themselves void of any real connections besides one another. That was how it worked, right? In order to be part of a Rogue team, you had to have no connections, no loved ones left behind to face your possible, and imminent, death.

"Would you do it again if you knew your brother had lied to you?" Carter took a condescending swig from his bottle, keeping his eyes locked on mine.

"How would you know anything about it?" I asked. I thought the only person who knew what was going on with my brother was Ian. Had he told someone else in the group, who passed it along to Carter, or had he told Carter directly?

I felt my blood beginning to boil at the betrayal, but Carter just raised his eyebrows. I looked around the room, eyeing Adam and Claudia, and then finally landing on Damon.

"I'm done." I stood up and walked to the back bedroom. I pulled back the sheer curtain and walked outside to the small balcony, just big enough for two people. The view of the city was lovely. The sky had the same orange glow it did back home. For a single moment, I didn't feel so far from Miami. I didn't feel so lost. So alone.

I heard a boot scuff on the wooden floor behind me. "*Piccolina*," Damon began.

"I don't know what that means, but don't call me that."

"He was just curious about who you were and why you are here," he tried to explain. He leaned back against the railing. "I was just trying to alleviate his suspicions about you."

"It wasn't your story to tell. It wasn't Ian's story to tell *you*, either." I could feel heat rushing to my face as I became angrier with them both.

"I know your brother. Ian had me teach Gil about gathering information," Damon said. "He told me Gil was helping some of the mob families. He wanted to know if I thought there was a connection between the places Gil told you he was going and the places he could be now."

Damon propped himself on the railing with an elbow and crossed one foot over the other, his Italian swagger in full force.

"Yeah, well, Ian still didn't have to tell you my business."

Damon thought for a moment. "The way you talk to Claudia, you see her like a friend, like a sister. *Amica sorella.* I see this team like a family," he said. "If we do not watch out for one another, no one will. I am sorry I told Carter about Gil lying to you. Carter is like a younger brother to me. An annoying, arrogant, younger brother," he chuckled.

The temperature of my blood began to cool. It was nice to hear Damon share my sentiment about treating the people you trust with your life as friends or family.

I nodded. "Okay. But next time someone wants to know something about me, you tell them to come see me. It's my story, and I'll tell it how I want it to be told."

I gave him a small smile and raised my eyebrows. Just

enough to let him know that we were cool, but I was serious about him keeping his mouth shut.

"I can handle that," he said.

We stood there together on the balcony in silence, enjoying the view of the sky. A café owner down the street was wiping off tables and setting out tablecloths and flowers. Mothers were coming home from the park with sleepy toddlers in strollers. It all looked so normal, so Italian Norman Rockwell. Little did they know that not far from here, and maybe in this town, children were possibly being bought and sold like property.

I wondered how long a person could handle being on a Rogue team. It all seemed crazy, so outlandish to me. But it stood to reason that, after a while, one would become desensitized to the atrocity of it all.

I wondered how long a person could handle being cut off from the world. Agents may not have any family left, but there had to be friends left behind. You would have to accept that your future would consist of the same three or four people who made up your team forever. Or until you—or they—were killed.

"I was *polizia*," Damon said, breaking the silence. "A police detective."

I turned to look at him. He was volunteering his story to me.

"There were so many Mafiosi in my town. They came to us. They said they wanted to work with us. They said they could give us protection." He stared into the street below. "We told them, 'we are the *polizia*. We do not need your protection. We protect the people of our town from *you*!' They did not like that. They made an offer to the men of my unit. What is it that gangster movie said? Oh yes. They made an offer that couldn't be refused."

"So the men accepted their offer, and the mob took over?" I asked.

"Not everyone. Those who didn't accept paid the price. Some were never seen again. Others had brothers and sons beaten, mothers and sisters raped. They were left with no choice but to do what had to be done to keep their families safe."

Damon turned his head to hide the emotions welling up in him. "It was a very difficult time for me."

I realized that, as a member of Rogue, his biological family was gone.

"I'm so sorry, Damon," I said.

He took a deep breath and looked at me. "Now you know my story. Perhaps one day you will share all of yours with me, not just the parts that Ian told me." He smiled and patted me on the shoulder before he stepped inside.

I turned back to the railing and smiled. This was the kind of thing that connected the team. Knowing one another's stories made us real. Not divulging secrets through a lame pseudo-drinking game, but on our own terms, in our own way.

Suddenly, I was reassured. We were closer to finding Gil, and I knew that however it played out, Adam, Claudia, Damon, and I would have one another's backs.

CHAPTER 16

Cabin fever was setting in and everyone was starting to go a little crazy. It had been two days since Ian "had to go out." We hadn't heard from him or from Command. That's when I became the subject of my own personal Spanish Inquisition.

"Did he give any indication as to where he was going?" Adam asked me. "It's not like him to be gone this long without communicating."

"Who was he going to find? Are you sure he just said 'locals'?" Claudia asked.

"What about the journal?" Damon added.

My stomach churned at the mention of the journal. I could handle everything else they were throwing at me, but as soon as they brought up the one thing I wasn't supposed to talk about, I was afraid I was going to involuntarily vomit up information.

"You were exploring that further yesterday, were you

not?" Damon continued. "Perhaps something in there triggered his need to go out?"

The best, though, was when Carter all but pulled me into a dark room and turned on a bright hanging lamp so he could question me relentlessly.

"What are you hiding, newbie?" he barked. "Where's Ian? He doesn't leave like this, and you were the last one to talk to him. Where did he say he was going?"

"He just said he had to go out," I told him. "Like he would tell me where he was going! I'm the newbie, remember?"

"I don't trust you."

"The feeling is mutual."

"Back off, Carter!" Eva intervened. "Geez!"

"What if she sent him into another ambush?" he said. "My gut tells me something is off, and my gut is never wrong."

"How about that? We have something in common," I said. "I didn't send him into anything and you know it."

Carter examined me with as much skepticism as I did him. I couldn't decide if he was just an ass, or if something about him was off. All I knew was that Ian had been gone too long and that could only mean one thing: trouble.

Eva finally pulled Carter off me and sent him to his room. With a look of frustration on her face, she followed him, closing the door behind them.

As the hours went by, I struggled with the idea of telling them about the kidnappings and Ian's theory about Gil's quest to avenge Maria's death. I understood Ian's reasoning for keeping it from them. Having been forbidden from touching cases like this, it was best to have something solid to take to Command—without getting the whole team into trouble. On the other hand, Ian had been gone a long time, and it wasn't a good sign how worried everyone was. And if I told them, they would know where to start looking for him.

Damon worked nonstop. When he took a break to eat, he was surprisingly jovial. It seemed everyone else was constantly on edge, but Damon was able to flip the switch between working and relaxing. He told me that if I were going to be in Italy much longer, I would have to learn some conversational Italian. He taught me phrases like *"Dov'è il bagno?"* for "Where is the bathroom?" He said this might be the most important phrase I learn. He also taught me *"Sì, per favore,"* for "Yes, please" and *"No, grazie"* for "No, thank you." And then, just for fun, he taught me two of his favorite Italian curse words: *merda* and *stronzo*. I decided I wouldn't use either one of them. If I really needed to let the sailor in me out, I was sure English would do just fine.

Adam and Claudia tried to teach me the fine art of waiting.

"We wait a lot," Claudia told me.

"How do you pass the time? I'm guessing you can't exactly go to a movie," I said.

"Oh my God! Do you know what I would give to see a movie?" Adam said.

"I know, right? Unfortunately, waiting usually means monitoring our surveillance or doing research."

"Well, I'm tired of waiting," I said. "There must be

something we can do. What about the locals Ian is checking in with? Do you know who they are? What if we tried to retrace his steps?"

"She is right," Damon said.

"I'll go," Carter announced, materializing from the back room. "But I'm not talking to Ian's contacts. I've got my own. If Ian's around, they'll have heard something."

"I'm coming with you," I declared. Keeping my eye on Carter seemed like a much better idea than sitting around the apartment with nothing to do.

"Even better," he said.

"I'm not sure that's a good idea," Eva suggested.

"It's not a mission," Carter said. "It's a drive into Venice and a conversation with some guys at a bar. It'll be fine. Besides, I'll look less conspicuous with her by my side."

Carter cupped Eva's face sweetly. "Don't worry."

Carter put on a fresh shirt, and I pulled my hair into a low ponytail. Then he picked up a gun and gestured for me to do the same. When I demurred, he said, "I don't care if you've been a member of this team for five minutes or fifty years. If you're with me, you're carrying. You need to be able to protect yourself and protect me."

When everyone else agreed, I let Adam secure a back holster with a pistol at my waist.

"We'll be back by morning," Carter told the team as we left.

We weren't five minutes down the road before I had to call out the elephant in the room.

"I thought you didn't trust me," I said.

"To be honest, I'm still making up my mind about you," he answered.

"Well, if I were being honest, I don't completely hate you."

A moment passed before Carter replied. "You don't completely suck, either, newbie."

As we drove into Venice, Carter laid out his plan. Twenty minutes later, he parked the car and came around to open my door. "Are you clear on the plan?" he asked.

"We are a happy honeymooning couple. Except to your contacts. To them, we are the most dangerous people they know." We took a few steps then I stopped. "You don't like Ian. Why are you doing this?"

Carter considered me for a moment. "My allegiance is to Rogue. For better or worse, Ian is my team leader. Looking out for him is part of protecting my team. It's my job."

I could see the worry in Carter's eyes.

"That was pretty convincing."

Carter rolled his eyes and shook his head. "There are a lot of people out here, newbie. I need your eyes and ears more than anything. Tonight's the night to prove your worth."

"But no pressure, right?" I said.

"I'm not worried a bit."

It was a busy night, and the streets were full of tourists. We walked the busy sidewalk, stopping at two bars where Carter had informants. According to Carter, bartenders made the best kind: They saw and heard everything. Usually, the thugs like the ones who'd grabbed Ian and me were just strong-arms for hire. They weren't part of an organized crime family. Carter referred to them as Thug Temps. He said they were known for coming into a bar, getting drunk, and spilling everything to the bartender.

After the first two bars, Carter's contacts had come up empty-handed. While Carter did the questioning, I kept my eyes and ears open for anything that struck me as odd. When two guys I noticed at the first bar followed us to the second, I figured that qualified.

"We're being followed," I told Carter.

"You sure?" he asked. I nodded. "All right. Let's hit this last bar and see if my guy knows anything. If they're still tailing us, we'll take care of them," Carter said.

We were in character, walking hand-in-hand up the sidewalk. A chill from the air made me shiver, and Carter put his arm around me.

We found the last bar and took a seat. When the bartender saw us, he flinched. The other two bartenders hadn't been happy to see Carter, either.

I scanned the room as I had at the other locations and watched as the creepy guys who had been tailing us followed us inside. The first guy was bald and had a scar on his chin. He had been obsessively checking his phone. The other guy was wearing a black leather jacket and had enough earrings to make a pirate jealous. He watched the door like the Second Coming was about to arrive.

"I'm looking for a friend of mine," Carter asked the bartender.

"He speaks English?" I questioned.

"Yeah. He also speaks money." Carter slid a folded

bill across the bar to him. "Tall British guy. You seen him around?"

"No. No Englishmen around here in a while," he answered.

"Any noise about someone matching that description? Maybe something about someone poking around and getting himself into trouble?" Carter prodded.

"I haven't heard anything, but I will keep an open ear for you," the bartender replied.

He was acting a little jittery, shuffling back and forth and wiping a cloth around a glass long after it had become dry. And then he darted his eyes to the guy with the scar.

Carter let the bartender go and put his arm around me. "Did you catch that?"

"Yep," I answered. I leaned into Carter's ear like a newlywed would. "Those *two* ugly mugs are failing miserably at blending in."

"I see them," Carter said, cupping my face.

"What do you want to do?" I asked.

"Let's just watch them and see what kind of trouble we can get into with them."

Great.

We sat there for another hour watching the two men and pretending to be in love. When they still hadn't moved, Carter declared that we had to "smoke them out" by making a move of our own.

Stepping back out into the night air, I took a deep breath, a nice break from the smoky bar. We were halfway to the car when I shook out my ponytail to give me an excuse to look behind us. In the glow of the streetlights, the baldheaded thug with the scar on his chin was impossible to miss. Across the street was the earrings guy.

"It's them," I said.

Carter just nodded. When we were a block from the car, and the crowd had dispersed, Carter pulled me into an alley.

"We have about sixty seconds," he said sternly.

"I can't believe I'm being ambushed twice in a matter of days," I bemoaned.

Carter grinned like a shark. "Sweetheart, it's only an ambush if you don't see it coming. If anyone's being ambushed here, it's them."

Then, without warning, Carter kissed me. It was a big, passionate, write-home-about kiss. It took my breath away.

"What was that for?" I asked, trying to catch my breath.

"Luck. I always fair better in a fight after kissing a beautiful woman."

He gave me a crooked, sexy smile, and I knew he was full of shit. He leaned down to my ear and whispered, "Time to up your game on those acting skills."

Carter snaked his arms around me, gripping me tightly as the two men rounded the corner. Then he kissed my neck and said things like, "C'mon, baby!"

When the two men following us hesitated, I understood the game Carter was playing. I shoved Carter away from me. "Not here!"

When Baldy grabbed Carter's shoulder, I launched myself at Earrings Dude.

Their moment of confusion was our opening. As Carter punched Baldy in the stomach, I summoned my inner Adam and gave everything I had into the right hook he'd tried to teach me. What I wasn't prepared for was the pain that shot through my fist and arm as I connected with Earrings Dude's chin.

He staggered back. I followed by raising my knee and plowing my heel into his foot. He cried out and brought his head around, right where I needed it.

Behind me, I heard grunts and punches, but I couldn't waste time wondering how Carter was faring. I had to stay focused. As Earrings Dude lifted his head, I reached forward, grabbed his hair, and brought my knee up into his face.

He dropped to his knees and held his face, giving me the break I needed to reach behind me and unholster my pistol. I held the muzzle to his temple.

"Stop!" he yelled to his partner, blood streaming from his nose.

I was glad the word *stop* was known internationally.

I turned to see Carter get one more hit in before Baldy fell to the ground.

"*Cosa volete?*" Carter demanded as he drew his gun.

Before either of the men could answer, we heard a rumble from the darkest end of the alley that sounded like garbage cans being knocked over. Carter reiterated his question, but the two men refused to answer.

Carter moved to stand behind the men with me and then said something in Italian that I assumed was a directive to stay where they were because neither of them moved.

"What do we do with them?" I asked, still pointing my gun at my attacker.

"Well—" Carter began but was cut off by the sound of two shots being fired and our captives falling to the ground.

Carter pushed me against the wall and fired into the darkness of the alley. The way he looked at me, I knew he could feel my body shaking. I waited to hear the explosion of a gun, to feel the burn of the bullet tear through my skin before everything went black. But nothing came. Only silence.

"You okay, newbie?" Carter whispered.

I straightened my jacket. "Yeah, I'm totally fine. I'm alive. Was that meant for us?" My voice trembled, betraying my best attempts at putting on a brave face.

"No." Carter pushed the two men over and revealed a single gunshot to each of their hearts. "It was meant for them. They failed their mission, and this was the price they paid."

"So why not just shoot us, too?"

"They need us alive so we can tell the team to back off. C'mon."

Carter took my hand and led us back to the bar where we first saw the two men. The place had been shot up. Chairs were broken, and pieces of wood and glass were scattered everywhere. Bullet holes riddled the walls, and a dozen bodies were slumped over tables or laying on the floor.

"How did we not hear this?" My breath was short and labored.

"You can put a silencer on an AK-47 these days," Carter answered. "Let's go. The local police will handle this."

Back on the sidewalk, we ran to the car and were back

on the road in moments. Carter gave me an appraising glance and patted my knee. "You've caught on quick, newbie. You did good."

"How can you be so calm after what we just saw?" I asked, trying to catch my breath.

"I've seen way worse, sweetheart. All part of the job."

I guessed so.

"Well, thanks. And I realize you may be a method actor, but if there's a next time, you probably don't need to actually grab my ass."

"Where's the fun in that?"

CHAPTER 17

"Where the hell have you been?" Ian shouted as Carter and I walked through the door. He was standing in the middle of the living room with the rest of the team. The scowl on his face matched the harsh tone of his words.

"We went looking for you!" Carter answered. "You left us here for two days without any word. Badass here and I sought out some of my locals to see if anyone had a clue where you were. No one had seen hide nor hair of your ass, but we did meet some unsavory fellas on the way back."

"What are you talking about?" Ian questioned.

"Two guys started following us as soon as we hit the bars. Newbie here held her own. Even put a gun to the back of a guy's head." Carter beamed with pride as if holding someone at gunpoint were a rite of passage I had just conquered.

"What did they want?" Damon asked.

"I presume they were there to send us a message. They

wouldn't answer my questions, and just as we were deciding what to do with them, they each got popped in the chest from at least a hundred yards away."

I couldn't read Ian's expression at the news that I had fought to live another day. So before he could respond, I changed the direction of the inquisition.

"When did you get back? And why were you gone so long?" I asked.

"About an hour ago." Ian stood stiffly in front of us, his eyes alternating between boring holes in Carter and then me. He turned away and took small, painful steps into the living room. "It was a little more *difficult* to get the information I was looking for," he said, winded. He was unsteady, almost hobbling along.

"You're hurt," I said as I went to him.

"I'm fine," he lied.

"You're not fine." I helped him into a small wingback chair. His face was pinched, sweating from the exertion. It couldn't have helped that he'd already taken a beating a few nights earlier. Bruises on bruises.

"It's nothing he hasn't dealt with before, right, boss?" Carter's tone showed no signs of sincerity, making me want to punch him in the face.

"What *did* happen, Ian?" Damon inquired. "Where did you go?"

Ian tried to take a deep breath, but it was too painful. I hoped that cracked ribs hadn't turned into broken ones. Claudia brought him a glass of water. He only took a few sips before he gave the glass back to her.

"I apologize for making you worry." Ian looked directly at me and then back to the group. "I've been working on something without Command's knowledge."

I watched Carter shake his head, an aggravated expression painting its way across his face.

"I'm confident that Victoria's brother has been working for the people responsible for the rash of kidnappings around the country. I've been tracking a man known only as Paolo."

"What would Gil be doing for them?" Adam asked.

"Forging documents. He's made himself an immigration and customs expert so he knows how to forge adoption papers," Ian answered. His voice was dark and raspy. "It's unlikely that the adoptions are going into the United States due to the checks and balances in place there. I followed a few leads and ended up in Venice. When I got there and started asking questions about the availability of a child for adoption, I was given a swift beating to make sure I was aware of the *confidentiality agreement.*" More wincing as he tried to breathe. "I said I had an American client living in southern Italy who was looking to adopt. A childless couple with means." He looked at Carter and Eva.

"Hell, no." Carter immediately responded to Ian's look. "I'm not going into a situation where Command isn't prepared to send an extraction team in if things get hairy. If you and your girlfriend want to walk into a minefield, be my guest, but I'm not going to risk my life for something you don't even have authenticated evidence for!" Carter stormed back into his room like a five-year-old. He was already pissed at Ian. This only exacerbated it.

"We can't do this without you two," Ian said to Eva.

"I know. But he's right, Ian. Without Command being involved, we have no real protection. No one will know we're there. If things go south . . ." Eva trailed off, leaving me to fill in the blank of just how terrible it could get.

"I've been tracking this on my own for several months. I finally caught a break when Victoria and I realized Gil's connection. We may never get another opportunity if we don't act on this now," he said.

"Can't you just order Carter to do it? I mean, you're sorta his boss, right?" I asked.

"It's not an assignment from Command, so I can't make him do anything. Not that anyone can make Carter do anything he doesn't want to do." Ian rested his forehead in his hand, defeated.

"I'll talk to him," I said.

"Victoria . . ."

"Let me talk to him. It certainly isn't going to make it any worse. He can't say 'no' any more emphatically than he already has."

Ian hesitated as he considered my suggestion. When he finally nodded, I didn't waste any time and headed straight for the bedroom.

"Wait." Ian reached out and grabbed my wrist before I could walk any farther. His eyes caught mine and dug in deep. I knew he was telling me to be careful. Carter could be ruthless and would only be interested in coming out the other side of this as a hero.

"Carter?" I said as I knocked softly on the door. He didn't answer. "I'm coming in." I turned the knob and opened the door slowly. He was lying on the bed with his shirt off and one arm behind his head. Even with the redness and bruising from the alleyway fight, his body was stunningly beautiful.

"Are you reading?" I asked, acknowledging the book in his hand.

"Yes. Does that surprise you?"

"A little. What is it?"

"Aldous Huxley. *Brave New World*. Ever read it?" he answered without looking up at me.

"Yeah. Laboratory babies. Daily antidepressants. No violence. Utopia, right?"

"If that's what you consider utopian."

"Do you like it?" I asked.

"Anything to keep my mind off the bat-shit crazy world we live in." He still hadn't looked up at me.

"That statement surprises me more than you being a reader." I moved farther into the room and leaned against the wall.

"Oh really. Why? You think I'm some mercenary who just *loves* running into a deadly situation with guns blazing?" He rested the book, pages down, on his bare chest.

"That's pretty much how you come off," I replied. "And you sure didn't shy away from that fight tonight."

"I do what I do because this is my job. If I could go home, I would." His voice was calm and commanding at the same time. "There's nothing left for me there, so I make the most of what I've got here."

"Ian said the same thing about not being able to go home."

"That's about the only thing he and I have in common," he said harshly.

"What's your problem with him?" I asked. "He's been pretty great since I got here."

"Well I'm sure he's *swell* with the ladies. I just don't think he should be leading a team."

"Why? Because he doesn't have as much field experience as you?" I raised my eyebrows as I challenged him.

Carter eyed me suspiciously. "He *doesn't* have as much field experience as I do. But I also don't like the way Command coddles him." Carter's jaw tightened, showing me he was more than just slightly bothered by this.

I wondered why Command coddled Ian. He was an incredible agent. Did it have to do with why he had been forbidden from cases involving children?

"That's not his fault. Ian would love to do more," I argued.

"They treat him with kid gloves, and he should be put to the test like the rest of us."

"Then help us," I said after a moment.

"Why would I want to do that?" He stood up and put his shirt back on before sauntering over to where I stood.

"Because you know Ian's intel is good."

Carter thought for a moment before he spoke. "I'm all for taking down the bad guy—through a sanctioned mission."

"Deep down, you know it's the right thing to do, Carter."

He shook his head and smirked. "It doesn't matter if I think it's the right thing to do. You have no idea how dangerous human traffickers are. If Command doesn't know we're there, the chances of us all dying are pretty high."

"I *do* know how dangerous they are. That's the whole reason Gil is out there. His girlfriend was kidnapped and forced to work as a prostitute." I watched Carter process the information as he looked at me. I didn't know if he believed me, or if he saw the gravity of the situation the same way Ian or I did. "There are kids out there being taken from their families. Teenage girls being forced to do things no one should ever have to do. So forget Ian"—I stepped forward and stood close enough to Carter that I could feel the heat from his body—"You *know*, in your *gut*, that the right thing to do is take these guys down."

"You think they're the only ones running this business?" he challenged.

"Of course not. But we can at least take out the group we have in our sights and save as many victims as possible—and I can get my brother back." Appealing to Carter's hidden sense of right and wrong wasn't working. It was clear the only way he was going to even consider helping was by stroking his ego. "You know we can't do this without you. No one has the skills that you have, and no one is going to be able to execute Ian's plan like you. You pull this off, sanctioned or not, Command will probably give you your own team."

Carter stared at me, considering his options. He moved to the door but didn't open it. "I'm not making any promises, newbie," he said over his shoulder to me.

"I wouldn't trust you if you did," I retorted. I joined him at the door. He opened it for me like a gentleman, and we caught each other's eyes before passing through.

Carter sauntered to the living room and plopped himself on the couch, stretching his arms across the back. "All right, boss man. Not that I'm agreeing to this unsanctioned suicide mission, but what's your plan?"

Ian looked at me and gave the slightest nod I think I had ever seen anyone give.

"It's really pretty standard," he began. He tried to scoot forward in the chair but he immediately realized that was a terrible idea. "I've set up a meeting for tomorrow. Carter, Eva, you're a wealthy American couple living and working in Italy wanting to adopt. You're looking for a little boy no older than eight years old, and you'd prefer that his parents were deceased so you don't have to deal with him looking for his birth parents when he gets older.

"They've promised they already have a child who meets your requirements. I'll go in with you as your attorney. Once they bring the boy out, we'll pay them, you'll sign the documents, and then pass the boy off to Victoria who will play your nanny. She'll take the boy to the rendezvous point with Claudia. Adam and Damon will be on the rooftops across the street covering us. They're not going to be happy that they just lost a piece of their inventory. They'll put up a fight to get him back—and to keep their trafficking business going."

"*Inventory?*" Gross.

"To them, that's all he is," Ian said, a sad look on his face.

"Why aren't we going to Command with this?" Carter questioned.

"We put in a request for communication from Command, but we have yet to hear anything," Ian explained. He slowly shifted his body and pushed himself out of the chair. "Any word, Damon?"

"Nothing. I'll keep checking and I'll send another request," he answered.

"What about Gil?" I asked hesitantly.

"I can't promise he's with them, but if he is, I'll do everything I can to get him out."

Ian scanned the room and made eye contact with each team member.

"So?" he said, prompting the team to weigh in.

"I'm in," Adam said without hesitancy.

"Me too," said Claudia.

"Of course," Damon replied.

Ian turned to Eva. "Eva?"

She looked to Carter then to me. When she finally looked to Ian she said, "Yeah."

"Carter? We can't do this without you," Ian said humbly.

"Of course you can't," he said, standing. "I'm in, too, I guess. But I am not saving any of your asses if this goes in the crapper."

"Thank you, Carter," Ian said.

"Don't thank me. Thank your girlfriend."

CHAPTER 18

I didn't know if it was the uncomfortable couch, the possibility of seeing Gil, or that my first real mission was approaching, but I couldn't sleep. And as long as I was awake, I figured I'd make good use of my time, so I ran through the next day's plan over and over again. Ian, Carter, and Eva would meet with the sellers first. Once they had everything signed, Carter would call for me, their nanny, using our burner phones, and I would come in and take the child. Once I had the little boy, I was to walk around the corner with him and get back into the van I had been waiting in with Claudia.

I lost count of how many times Ian made me promise not to react if Gil was in the room when I walked in. I had to pretend I didn't know him. I was Carter and Eva's nanny. We were not friends. I was their employee and I served a purpose. The angle they were taking was that they were rich, pretentious entrepreneurs who wanted an adopted child because they thought he would appeal to their shareholders.

After an hour of tossing and turning, I decided to get a drink. I tiptoed through the living room so I wouldn't wake Adam or Damon, who were asleep on the floor. Since we didn't know where Bianca was, I had been concerned about everyone being asleep at the same time. Bianca had ambushed us in broad daylight at the hotel—what was to stop her from launching an all-out assault on us in the middle of the night? It took some convincing from Claudia, but she promised me that the system on this place was much newer and even more sophisticated than what was at the factory. Having Adam asleep nearby with his favorite gun at the ready was helpful, too.

I opened the refrigerator slowly and tried to peek inside so the light didn't bother Claudia, who was asleep on the Murphy bed just outside the kitchen. I considered my beverage options: water, beer, or wine. Beer was out after my overly ambitious swig the other night. I wasn't a big wine drinker but had heard it could make you sleepy. I grabbed a bottle of white from the fridge and a bottle of red from the counter and stood there in the chilly light trying to decide.

"Can't sleep?" Ian whispered from behind me. I turned around and he was standing there, shirtless. A few days ago, it wouldn't have meant anything. But since Ian's kiss and our conversation about feelings, I knew I'd never look at him the same way. My heart caught in my throat, and my eyes hovered over Ian's bare chest and defined abs. I was happy for a revised shirtless memory of Ian to replace the one I had of him hanging in the old factory.

Ian cleared his throat and my eyes darted up to his.

"In my opinion, red is the better cure for insomnia," he smiled.

He took the bottle from me. Turning on a small light under the cabinet, he opened the bottle and poured two glasses. Then he picked up both glasses and motioned for me to follow him. As we approached the back bedroom where Ian had been sleeping, or not sleeping, butterflies swarmed my stomach.

"Did Damon ever hear back from Command?" I asked as Ian set both glasses on the small table in his room. I sat in the chair with my back to the wall, crossing my legs as Ian pulled a T-shirt over his head.

"No," he said, taking a seat in the chair across from me.

"Can't you email or call or something?"

"I left a message for Director Thatcher when I was out. I told her about Bianca and the ambush and that we were getting close to Paolo," he said.

"Why didn't you just tell the team that instead of telling them it was an unsanctioned mission?"

"Whether I left a message for Thatcher or not, the mission is still unsanctioned. Thatcher isn't going to call me back and suddenly give me approval for a mission that she has no intel on."

I nodded, still confused. I would have asked for a better explanation of how things worked in Rogue, but I would be leaving soon and it seemed like wasted breath.

"How are you feeling about tomorrow?" Ian asked, redirecting the conversation.

"I feel okay, I guess. I wish I was doing more. I just want to be useful, Ian."

"You are useful. And if you were going to be here much longer, I'd really train you," he said. There was sadness in his voice. It was funny, really. All that time he'd spent trying to get me to leave, and now it seemed like he wanted me to stay. "I wanted to thank you for whatever you did to get Carter on board."

"He just needed to feel like a hero," I said.

"You did well. Carter is a hard nut to crack."

"That's an understatement. I think we came to an understanding last night, though. We were actually a pretty good team." I took another sip of my wine. "But kudos to you for working with someone who doesn't care for you all that much. I think he respects your position, but—"

"But what? He thinks Command babies me? They do," he said.

He looked past me and through the open doors to the balcony to a clear, still night. The stars were scattered across the sky, and I could just make out a cathedral's spire in the distance.

"What happened, Ian? Why has Command restricted the types of cases they give you?" Working at the diner taught me that secrets had a way of coming out at night. They say hairdressers are like therapists, but I can't tell you how many stories about successes, failures, and regrets I heard at the diner, especially during late shifts. I poured coffee and customers poured out their hearts.

Ian covered his mouth with his hand as he leaned his elbow on the table, unsure of where to start. "My mother didn't always make the best choices in life. She got pregnant with me during a one-night stand, and by the time I was six, I remember at least four different men living with us. A few of them were nice to me, a few of them knocked me around, but they mostly just tolerated me."

"Oh, Ian. I'm so sorry." I reached across the table and took his hand in mine.

"But it also meant Mum ignored me because they required her full attention. If they didn't get what they wanted, she paid for it.

"When I was around ten, Craig appeared out of nowhere. Like a knight in shining armor. He treated Mum with love and respect. He showered us with gifts. Pretty soon he moved in and I was getting a baby sister. When Jacqueline was born, it was like seeing an angel. She was perfect in every way. It didn't matter that I was ten years older. I loved her so much. We immediately had this incredibly strong bond."

I sat in silence while Ian spoke and took breaks to collect his thoughts. I watched his face twist in recollection and tears pool in his eyes.

"Craig was always nice to me, but we never really connected. As I got older, there were a few times I heard him accuse my mother of cheating on him, which was crazy because she worked two, sometimes three, jobs. As if she had time to cheat. It wasn't long before Craig's accusations escalated to shoving my mother against the wall or slapping her across the face. I tried to get in between them a few times, but Mum would send me to take care of Jacqueline. I was fourteen, but she was just so little . . . and so scared. I would take her upstairs and we'd hide in her closet with all her toys. We'd play with her dolls and I'd make up funny voices to go with them. Those were frightening times, but we bonded during them."

Ian swiped his thumb across his eyes and breathed deeply.

"It's okay, Ian. You don't have to go on," I told him.

"I want to."

I nodded and sat back, waiting for him to continue.

"When I graduated, I wanted to join the Royal Marines. Things were worse at home between Mum and Craig, and I didn't like the idea of leaving her and Jacqueline with him, but Mum said she wasn't going to let me give up my dream. So I joined and then a year later I volunteered for training and became a Green Beret. When I accomplished the rank, I wrote home and told Mum, and she wrote back and told me how proud she was. She also told me that things had gotten so bad between her and Craig that she had to move out. She and Jacqueline were staying at a client's home while they were away on holiday. Mum cleaned homes for some wealthy people and, because she was Mum, they adored her and treated her like family. So it didn't surprise me that one of them had offered their home as a place of refuge.

"I wrote back and told her that was probably for the best and that I would see her in a few weeks for the Christmas holiday." He stood and took a breath. "I never saw them again. I got word a week later that my mother and sister had been killed. That my stepfather had shot them both and then killed himself."

"Oh my God." I covered my mouth in shock.

"According to the report, forensics believed he held my sister and made her watch him shoot our mother. Then he shot her in the head before he did the same to himself. He killed his own daughter. And based on all the scarring and bruises covering her body, she had a history of being abused. She was just a little girl. . . . Coward." Ian gulped down his wine and walked out to the balcony.

I sat there, frozen in place. For years, people had been saying trite, patronizing things to me about my parents' death. It was a game I had to play over and over. Sounding concerned always seemed to make them feel better about themselves. Who cared if some old acquaintance of my father's told me that they didn't suffer? Nothing changed. My parents couldn't come back, and I wasn't going to magically not feel sad anymore. I didn't want to do that to Ian. I didn't want to be someone else reciting the inside of a Hallmark card and expecting him to get over it.

I joined him on the balcony. The quiet reminded me of the first nights I was living with Gil. It had been a year since my parents' death, but starting over, just me and him, seemed to rehash all the horrific emotions I'd buried deep while in foster care. We hardly spoke; we were too afraid to say something that might make the other sad. Gil coped by diving into his studies. I coped by crying in the fetal position with my head on Tiffany's lap. Good friends simply let you cry and don't say anything at all.

It was probably a good five minutes with just the sound of the crickets playing the only song they know before I spoke. "I'm so sorry," I said gently.

"No one here knows, so please don't say anything."

"I would never say anything. It's not my story to tell."

It was a few minutes before Ian spoke again.

"About a year after I joined Rogue, I was on an assignment in Thailand," Ian began. "We were taking down a sweatshop that was committing all kinds of human rights violations, even for Thailand. I didn't have it in my initial intel, but among the men and women, there were five long tables of kids working until their fingers bled.

"The men in charge would beat the children with reeds when they didn't work fast enough. The workingmen would cower, too, as the reeds went up. And I watched the kids cry as the reeds made contact with their tiny bodies, their clumsy little fingers moving as quickly as possible. I will never forget that sound. But that wasn't the worst part. Some of the children didn't react at all. It didn't matter how hard they were hit, they didn't make a sound or even flinch. The constant pain and fear had forced them to numb themselves to their world. That's what broke me."

Ian shook his head.

"So I pulled my gun and killed anyone with a reed in his hand." Ian looked out into the empty street while he spoke.

"You saved lives that day. Who knows how many women and children the families of that city had buried already." I put my hand on top of Ian's and wrapped my fingers under his palm. He closed his hand around mine and squeezed.

"Command doesn't necessarily see it that way. They think my past makes me too fragile to handle an assignment where children are involved." Suddenly, Ian's body stiffened and he dropped my hand.

"Don't do that," I said.

"Don't do what?"

"Don't do that thing where you shut down when you get scared. I can appreciate your need to be unemotional, but geez, Ian, you've faced some serious crap in your life. And you watch terrible things happen to people all over the world. You can't experience the things you have and not *feel* something. And it doesn't make you any less strong."

A sweet breeze swirled around us, giving me goose bumps.

"You're cold," Ian observed, apparently ignoring what I just said to him. He rubbed my arms.

"Ian," I began.

"Can you just . . . come here?" Ian pulled me to him and wrapped his arms around me, his mahogany and lavender scent arousing my senses. I melted into his body and wrapped my own arms around his waist. I could feel his body relax instantly, the tension dropping out of him like he just released the weight of a thousand mountains. "I wish you couldn't read me so well. Hiding is so much easier."

"Aren't you tired of hiding?"

Ian didn't answer. We stood there in each other's arms, letting the insanity of the world happen around us.

"It's been a long time since I've held someone like this," he said after a while, whispering in my hair.

"You can hold me all night," I said softly. I leaned my cheek against his chest and closed my eyes. I was scared and overwhelmed and anxious for tomorrow, but right here, with Ian's strong arms protecting me, I felt like everything was going to be all right. Like I was in the safest place in the world. Tomorrow could wait.

"That is a very tempting offer, Miss Asher." Ian's cheek was resting on the top of my head and I felt him smile. "I was already convinced that you were going to be my undoing. It seems I'm beginning to unravel. How is it that you see me so clearly?"

I lifted my face from his chest and gazed up at him.

"Maybe it's because I'm looking."

Ian stared at me, caught off-guard by my answer. After a moment, he leaned down and kissed me. This time, it wasn't for show. There was no one watching. It was just the two of us, alone on a balcony in a beautiful Italian city.

His lips were soft and moved gently with mine. He combed his fingers through my hair and gently cupped my head with his palm, pulling me to him. Somehow kissing Ian felt natural. I knew it was ridiculous, but how could I explain feeling so connected to a man I had only known for such a short time? This wasn't a silly summer romance, something Tiffany and I could giggle about during slow shifts at the diner. This was real. My entire body was lit up like a Christmas tree, like the sky on the Fourth of July. There was something real between us, something earth-shattering.

"I don't even know what to say to you right now." He smiled as he pulled away and gently brushed my cheek with his thumb. "These feelings, it's secondary school behind the library all over again."

"I don't know what to say, either."

"And tomorrow?" He tried to step away, but I wouldn't let him.

I took his face in my hands to make sure he was looking at me. "Tomorrow doesn't change right now."

Ian searched my eyes before he kissed me swiftly and then wrapped his arms around me again. I had never felt like this with anyone before, or so quickly. When I looked at him, it was easy to forget where I was or what I was doing. But it scared me. I was scared because the thought of leaving him broke my heart. I was scared because Miami didn't feel like home anymore. I was scared because I had never wanted anything more than I wanted Ian Hale.

"Do you want to go back to sleep? You can have my bed if you'd like. I'll take the couch," Ian offered.

"I don't think I'll be able to sleep at all," I told him. I tightened my grip around his waist and he reciprocated.

"Good. Because what I really wanted to ask was if you would stay out here with me a little bit longer."

"I would stay out here with you all night."

CHAPTER 19

Morning came and everything seemed normal in a strange sort of way. The team milled around the apartment like it was a normal day and they were all getting ready to go to work. The fact that work meant making sure guns were cleaned and loaded and surveillance and tracking equipment was online and ready made for an *interesting* "normal."

Adam and Claudia sat at the kitchen table calmly eating toast and drinking coffee; Carter and Eva were in their bedroom "getting in the zone," and Ian was in the back bedroom putting together fake driver's licenses and passports for identification purposes.

"You want something to eat?" Adam asked. "Some coffee maybe?" He held out the French press before pouring himself another cup.

"No, thanks," I answered. "Too nervous to eat." I sat down at the table across from Claudia.

"That's normal," she said.

"Yeah. I threw up three times before my first assignment," Adam said.

"I want you to know how much I appreciate what you're doing. Putting yourselves out on this shaky limb means a lot to me."

"Hey," Claudia said as she covered my hand with hers. "Despite what Ian says about family, we are one. You, Victoria Asher, are totally legit, which means I'd walk a hundred miles in stilettos for you." She gave me a sweet, crooked smile, and I felt some of my anxiety melt away.

"You guys really are the best." I myself was beginning to get choked up. I would miss Adam and Claudia. When I left Italy, I'd never see them again.

Of course, the preemptive good-bye sentiments were all contingent on finding Gil during the mission—a hope I couldn't help but hold on to, even though I knew there were no guarantees.

"Everything is set," Damon announced, coming through the front door.

"Good," Ian said, joining him in the living room. Damon had been gone since the early morning hours, even before Ian and I left the balcony. Ian said it was protocol for Damon to check the meeting point and make sure everything was clear.

"How is everyone this morning? Feeling good? Ready?" Ian asked.

"Uh, good?" Claudia said curiously.

"What's wrong?" I asked her.

"In all the time I've known Ian, he's never asked how

we were doing before an assignment," she explained with a smile.

"Victoria? May I speak with you for a moment, please?" Ian asked.

"Sure." I followed Ian into the kitchen. "What's up?"

"I've been thinking, and I'm not so sure about you being involved in this. These guys are much more dangerous than your average Mafia families. If Gil is there, I promise you, we will get him out, but I just don't think it's a good idea for you to be with us." Ian's eyes pleaded with mine.

"I'm going to be fine," I said. I appreciated him being concerned about me, but I had come too far to *not* go. "I know where I'm supposed to be until you call for me. I've been practicing my poker face if Gil is there when I walk in. I can do this, Ian. And I trust this team to do what they're supposed to do to keep us all alive." I took his hand in mine and squeezed. "We're R-14, led by *the* Ian Hale. What could go wrong?"

"I don't want anything to happen to you," he whispered.

"I know I'm safe as long as you're leading this team."

He sighed, knowing I wasn't going to change my mind.

"You have to promise me that you'll stay in the surveillance van with Claudia until Carter calls you," he said forcefully.

"I thought you said we didn't hide out in unmarked laundry vans." I smirked, but Ian was less impressed by my humor. His glare said as much. "I promise," I conceded.

When everything was packed and ready, we left for our

assigned locations in Venice. Adam and Damon left first and took their places on opposite rooftops of the meeting point, a pastry shop known for being controlled by the mob. Claudia and I took the surveillance van that Damon had acquired for us and parked a block down from the shop. Finally, Ian, Carter, and Eva got into position for their meeting with the child-selling scum.

"So, what is all this?" I asked Claudia as I took in all the switches and buttons of the fake laundry service van. It was tall enough for us to stand in, but only by an inch. "It doesn't look like we'll be able to see them. No monitors."

"We won't. We didn't have enough time to install cameras, or someone on the inside to ensure that they'd meet where we could watch," she said. The disappointment in her voice told me she didn't like not being able to see what was going on. "The best we could do was put microphones in the guys' buttons and one in the brooch Eva is wearing."

"What do we do now?" I asked.

"We wait," she answered simply. "And since we don't have any beer in here, we can't play Never Have I Ever." She laughed and tweaked a few buttons, then held a pair of headphones to her left ear.

"Is that really how you all tell your stories to one another?" I asked.

"Not really. It's just something dumb we do sometimes to take the edge off. Are you asking because you want to know my story?" she smirked.

"Oh my gosh! No! I'm sorry if it sounded that way. I wasn't prying, really," I said, flustered.

"It's okay, Vic. I don't mind telling you. Everyone else knows. You might as well join the club." Claudia flipped a few more switches and then turned a dial from headphone to speaker. "After things with acting took a dive, I went back to college. I thought I'd major in theater and then teach. I had to take a theater tech class as part of the major's requirements.

"The school had this ultrasophisticated system to control the lights, curtains, stage, and props. I ended up becoming really good friends with a tech TA who was majoring in computer science but minoring in theater tech." I gave her a curious look. That was the weirdest combination I had ever heard of. "I know, right? Well, he would talk about all the things that can be done on computers and I would listen. Pretty soon, we were hanging out and he was showing me all these different hacks and teaching me how to code new programs, and it just made sense to me. It was like a light went on inside my brain. I started seeing things differently, experimenting with different operating systems, and even building my own programs."

"So how did that land you here?"

"I had been dating this other guy for about six months when I found out he had been cheating on me the whole time. When I confronted him about it, he totally lied. And when the other two girls came with me, he acted like we were all crazy and delusional."

"*Two* other girls? Jerk!"

"Yep! Well, after almost a year of working on my mad

computer-hacking skills, I was well equipped to make his life a living hell." She smiled sinisterly.

"Oh my God, Claudia! What did you do?" I had a feeling this story was going to be way better than the time I helped Tiffany let all the air out of her cheating ex's tires.

She twisted her mouth to the side in feigned nervousness. "I hacked into the college's system, changed his grades, and erased two entire semesters of his work."

"HO-LY crap! That is some serious vengeance," I said, amazed.

"That was just the beginning. I added a note on his school demographics form indicating that Steven would prefer to be called Stephanie because he was going through gender reassignment. I also had a subscription to a girly magazine sent to him at his parents' address." She gave a little snicker. "Too much?"

"Oh no. That is just enough crazy to know not to screw with you."

"If only that were the end." She raised her eyebrows and I began to realize that the sweet girl-next-door Claudia was anything but. "I changed his address with the US Postal Service to a biker bar on the other side of town known for its *unsavory* characters. When he found out where it was, he had to go all the way down there to get any mail they didn't toss."

"And that's what got you in trouble with the law," I surmised.

"Yeah. They aren't kidding when they say messing with

people's mail is a federal offense. So I created a couple of new identities and split town," she said.

"What about your family?"

Claudia's lighthearted manner in which she told her Carrie Underwood song–inspired story disappeared. Her expression turned flat and hesitant.

"They had already disowned me a long time before any of that happened. They're hardcore conservatives from South Korea. I was fresh out of high school and dating a white guy I met at an audition. They told me to break it off with him because he wasn't Korean. They put up with it for a little while. I think they thought it would be a phase, but when I broke up with that guy and started seeing a black guy, it got even worse. I moved out when I was nineteen and lived my own life, which was not what they wanted. It took a while, but they eventually realized that I wasn't going to take over the family store, marry a guy they picked out for me, and only eat traditional Korean food. I would never live the life they wanted, so they disowned me.

"So even though I technically have family out there, I don't really. I'm dead to them, which is why Ian let me on his team." Claudia switched the knob and put one side of the headphones back up to her ear. When she heard nothing, she pulled it off and switched the knob back again.

"Oh, Claudia," I said sympathetically.

"It's all good. I wasn't made for that life. I mean, they came to America for a reason, you know? I considered reaching out to them when I decided to go to college. I thought they might be proud of me, but then I remembered that I was going to college for theater, not business or law or medicine. And college probably wasn't going to sway my preference in men." She sighed like it was the period to her sentence.

"Thanks for being so open." Sitting in the surveillance van and listening to Claudia share her story reminded me of empty nights at the diner when Tiffany and I would sit at the counter and talk over pie and coffee. "All that's left is for Adam, Carter, and Eva to tell me their stories and I'll know everyone's. Although I'm pretty sure Carter isn't going to spill the beans anytime soon. He strikes me as the kind of guy who likes to be mysterious."

"Oh my God! I swear he's going to introduce himself as James Bond one of these days," she laughed. "So you know Ian's and Damon's stories?"

"Yeah. Ian told me last night, and Damon found me on the balcony in the back bedroom the night we played Never Have I Ever. I think he felt bad," I told her.

"You're a lucky girl. I've been on Ian's team two years and he still hasn't told me," she said.

"I'll be leaving soon, so he probably figures it's not a big deal," I said with hesitation.

"No worries. He'll tell me when he thinks I need to know." She pulled two bottles of water out of a small cooler under the counter with all the knobs and dials and handed me one. "So I know I'm breaking the rule and talking about Damon's story without his permission, but, poor guy, huh? Watching your whole family murdered. What an awful thing for a kid to go through."

"I know! Wait—he was a kid when he saw his family murdered?" That wasn't what he told me at all, unless I wasn't remembering correctly.

"Yeah. A Mafia family came through town and wanted his father's pharmacy in their back pocket. When he refused, they killed his family while Damon hid under the back counter. I thought you said he told you his story?" Claudia's face was as puzzled as mine.

"He did. But he said that he was a police officer. That the Mafia came in and killed any cops who wouldn't go along with them, and slaughtered their families as collateral. I assumed because he was still alive that he had gotten out somehow. But that they had killed his family."

I thought about my conversation with Damon that night on the balcony. "Damon never actually *said* his family had been killed. He said that some officers chose to side with the Mafia while others who didn't were either killed or their families were killed. I assumed because he was *here* that his family had been killed." I stood up in the tall van and shuffled my feet. "Why would he tell us two different stories?"

"Maybe his real story isn't as exciting as he thinks everyone else's is. Or maybe it's actually more horrific than what he told either of us," she said.

"Maybe." The uneasy wheels were turning in my head. "Did he tell you in a group setting, like Never Have I Ever, or alone?"

"He told me one night when we were both a little

lonely, if you know what I mean," she said sheepishly. "I was missing my little sister a lot. We shared stories about our families and that's when he told me."

"*Hmmm.*"

"What's going on in there?" Claudia pointed to my head like she could see the wheels turning.

"I don't know. Something doesn't feel right."

I thought about the stories Damon told us. What was the difference between the two? Both were about him losing his family. He was a little boy in Claudia's and a cop in mine.

"It's like he told us stories he thought we wanted to hear. You needed to feel connected to someone who understood what it was like to miss family. I needed to know that I was safe and that finding Gil was a reality. Who better to do that than a former cop?"

I searched my memory for all the times I was with Damon. He had always been so charming. Too charming. The way he kissed my hand the day we met. How he rubbed my back to calm my nerves when we discovered Bianca on the hotel surveillance. Laughing and teaching me Italian curse words when we were all worried about Ian. It was all to disarm me.

It finally clicked when I remembered something he'd said when he trained me:

You have to know who the imposter is. We take months, sometimes years, and embed ourselves into the enemy's family just so we can find out even the smallest detail about their organization. We become one with them . . . so much a part of who they are that they don't pay attention to the tiny details. You have to pay attention to the details, Victoria.

"Claudia, can you get into the account used to communicate with Command? Check if there's any recent emails," I asked. My gut was doing flips, and I could almost feel the pieces of the puzzle floating around my head snapping into place.

"Of course," she answered as she tapped away at the keyboard. "That's weird. There are no recent emails from Damon to Command."

"Are you sure?"

"Yes. There's nothing."

"Is there any other way he would have reached out to Command?"

"No, but Ian could have."

"He left a message for Director Thatcher, but as of last night he still hadn't heard back from her."

I thought for a minute before I spoke again. I let out an exasperated sigh. "I can't believe I ignored such blaring red flags! Damon was the only one who ever asked about what Ian and I had found in the journal. Command was mysteriously taking forever to respond to him. The only lead Ian and I had for Gil's whereabouts was conveniently murdered. And Damon lied to us about his story in order to lull us into a false trust. Claudia, Damon is the mole."

"What mole? What are you talking about?" she asked.

"Ian and I found something in the journal. Gil was telling us that there's a mole in Rogue. We thought it was

Bianca. But it's not. It's Damon! We have to warn Ian and the others before it's too late." Fear made my voice tremble and my heart pounded inside my chest.

"Okay." Claudia's voice had an edge to it. "Everyone is already in place so we're about to become an army of two." She pulled two guns from where they had been strapped underneath the counter and handed one to me. "This is a .22 caliber pistol. Do you remember Adam's training?"

"Yes," I said confidently. I already had two unplanned experiences with a gun and handled myself pretty well. However misplaced the feelings may have been, I felt in control.

"If you're not sure you can stay here if you want, Vic. I'll go in and—"

"No. I'm going with you. Gil may be in there, and now is not the time to sit back and see what happens. We are Rogue-14 and we stick together," I said resolutely.

"Okay. Take a deep breath and follow me."

She opened the back of the van quietly, slid out, and I shut the door behind us. The click of the latch seemed so loud, like an announcement for our enemy that we were on the move. We stepped onto the sidewalk. Five paces into our rescue mission and we were stopped cold in our tracks.

"Going somewhere, ladies?" the voice said, inches behind me.

CHAPTER 20

Bianca stepped around in front of us, the cold steel of her gun pressed to my temple.

Where the hell was Adam and his expert aim?

Rage boiled up inside me at the sight of the woman who had led the ambush at the hotel. The woman who was surely responsible for the thugs who had used Ian as a punching bag. The woman who had turned on her own.

"You're early, Victoria," she said in an Eastern European accent. The sun glinted off the gun's barrel. In one quick move, she grabbed me with her left hand and held the gun to my back with the right. "But since you are here now, we might as well go in—after you empty your weapons, that is."

"What the hell, Bianca? I thought you were one of us?" Claudia said through gritted teeth.

"I was, once. But I received a proposal that was much more lucrative than anything INTERPOL could ever offer," she hissed. "Now, the guns, ladies? Please don't make this any more difficult for me than it already is." She smiled at us, showing two rows of perfect teeth.

Claudia hesitantly released the clip from her gun. I did the same and Bianca snatched them, stowing them in the bag slung over her shoulder.

"Thank you, darlings. Now, Claudia, be a dear and walk ahead a few paces so I can get to know Victoria a little better." She grabbed my elbow, her fingers cutting into the flesh on my arm.

"Let Vic go, Bianca. She's not even a real Rogue agent," Claudia pleaded as we walked.

"Are you kidding me? Victoria is our ticket. No one on your pathetic little team is going to let anything happen to her. She stays," she replied harshly.

She directed us to an alley behind the pastry shop, then through the back door. We maneuvered around giant electric mixers and massive bags of flour until we entered the front of the empty store. It smelled sweet and sugary, just the way a pastry shop should. The glass case was filled with colorful treats, and the wooden shelves behind the counter displayed confections of every shape and size.

Bianca pointed to a small table with chairs against the front window of the shop. "Sit," she commanded, like we were dogs.

"Where are the others?" Claudia asked bitingly.

"They'll be here soon enough," Bianca replied, turning on her heels and leaving. Two armed men entered through the kitchen and stood guard when Bianca left. One of them had a bandage over his nose, and I recognized him as Thug One, the guy who I'd fought in the factory home base. He winked at me and I knew he was itching to settle the score.

I looked around the shop, taking note of any other escape routes, but couldn't find anything besides the front and back doors. Besides, making a run for it would be impossible with the goons standing over us. We had no weapons, no backup plan, and no support from Command. When Ian, Carter, and Eva arrived, they'd be stripped of their weapons, too.

I put my face in my hands and tried not to cry out of frustration. Ian kept me on the team because I was supposed to be observant and intuitive. Instead, I let my guard—and Ian and the team—down.

"What happened to Adam?" I whispered to Claudia.

"Adam is an expert marksman. He would have taken Bianca out if he saw her holding a gun on you. Damon must have gotten to him already." Claudia dropped her eyes sadly. "Adam is gone."

"Shut it. Don't make me use this before it's time." Thug One shifted his gun menacingly.

I was defeated. I had flown halfway around the world to find my brother only to be trapped in a pastry shop that was surely going to be my deathbed. I wouldn't let myself cry, though. If Paolo were going to kill me, so be it. And if Damon were the one who pulled the trigger, I'd never give him the satisfaction of seeing just how scared I was.

Voices echoed from the back room. The tone was

casual. I heard Carter's voice ring out a too-loud guffaw as he pretended to find someone's joke funny. Despite knowing they were about to walk into the same trap Claudia and I had, my body flooded with relief.

Eva emerged first. Her eyes widened when she saw that Claudia and I were not only there, but that we were being guarded by two men with guns. We got the same response from Ian and Carter as they followed her in. But the biggest eyes came from Gil as he walked through the door and saw his little sister being guarded by a trained gunman. It took everything in me not to respond.

Poker face, Vic. Poker face.

I took Gil in from head to toe. He was thinner than he was when he left home, and he had dark rings around his eyes like he hadn't slept in weeks. He was in desperate need of a haircut, but he was still my handsome brother. And most importantly, he was alive.

"Who is this?" Ian asked. "I thought this was a closed-door deal, Paolo?" Ian faced the last man to enter the room. "What's with the girls and gunmen?"

So that was the infamous Paolo. He was tall like Ian and Carter, but his short, graying black hair made it difficult to guess his age. He wore a khaki suit with a white shirt halfway unbuttoned. He didn't even try to hide the smug look on his face as he drew his gun.

"It is a closed-door deal," he answered. "The deal is that you're all going to die so we can continue our business without your interference."

"I don't know what you're talking about," Carter interjected as he held Eva close to his side. "My wife and I just want a child. You said you could give us a child!" He was good. If I didn't already know what a smart-ass he was, I would have been tempted to believe he was just another pretentious businessman used to getting whatever he wanted.

"Please. You said you could help us," Eva added, looking distraught.

"My goodness, Carter. That is one of your best performances yet!" Damon said as he sauntered through the doorway, gun in hand, three more henchmen fanned out beside him. As Ian, Carter, and Eva pulled their weapons, the armed men pointed their guns at Claudia and me. Damon trained his barrel on Gil. "You can put those on the floor and slide them over now, thank you."

"You're out of your goddamn mind if you think I'm going to hand over my weapon," Ian said harshly. His right arm flexed as he tightened his grip on the handle of his gun.

Damon motioned to the henchman guarding me, and I felt the firm grip of his hand on my bicep. In response, Ian took a step toward me while keeping his gun pointed at Damon. Carter and Eva alternated their aim between Paolo and the henchmen.

"I don't want to, but I'll kill her if I have to," Damon said flatly.

Ian looked at me as he, Carter, and Eva laid their guns down and kicked them away, but not without Carter using every Italian curse word he knew.

"You're working with Paolo, Damon? How could you?" Eva demanded.

"I'm not working with him," Damon replied. "He works for me."

Ian's nostrils flared and his face flushed with anger. Damon was the mysterious figure Ian had been chasing. All this time, he had been right under his nose.

"You should go say hello to your sister, Gil. She's traveled a very long way to find you," Damon said, his voice dripping with false sincerity.

"What the hell is she doing here, Ian?" Gil barked as he rushed across the room to me.

"Trust me, I tried to send her home," Ian told him. There was a bite to his tone, angry that he hadn't been more forceful or I hadn't been more agreeable.

Gil threw his arms around me. He stroked my hair and held me tightly to him. "Why didn't you listen to him? This wasn't how this was supposed to play out. You were supposed to tell him about Maria and he was supposed to send you home!"

"I wasn't going to just leave you—" The thug who had my arm let it go when I yanked it from him to hug my brother. I had missed Gil so much. I studied his face and brushed his messy hair to the side. He looked the same, but there was a hardness in his eyes that I didn't remember.

"When did you know Damon was part of this?" I asked.

"The Cappolas had me forging immigration documents for Paolo," Gil began. "When Damon showed up, I thought Ian had sent him to get me. He made it clear that was not his intent when he took his gun and cracked me on the head. I escaped a few days later and sent you the journal."

"I hated to be so aggressive with you, but I thought it best to establish what our relationship was going to be like going forward," Damon said plainly, his lips curling up slightly at the corners.

"*Going forward?*" I questioned.

"Yes," Damon answered. "I trusted Paolo to keep a hold on Gil, but apparently that was a difficult task. Now that both Paolo and Gil have learned their lessons, I do not anticipate any more trouble." I looked at Paolo and noticed that a bandage on his left hand covered the place where his pinky finger should have been. "It took us some time to find him. Fortunately for us, he never made it to the US Embassy in Rome."

"But you were part of this team—this family," Ian said with a glance at me. He finally got it. "I trusted you."

"And that was your mistake." Damon's stone-cold face matched his icy tone. "I did what was necessary to find out how close INTERPOL was to finding me. Being on your incredibly boring team gave me the access to everything I needed. Although I will say that things got much more exciting when Victoria showed up." The snakelike grin crossing Damon's face made me want to throw up.

"So what now? You're going to take Gil and just kill the rest of us?" Claudia challenged. "That's not very creative of you, Damon."

He let out an annoyed sigh. "You're right. It's not." He

grazed his eyes creepily along the length of my body. "I'm taking Victoria with me, too. I showed her picture to a few clients, and I've got a buyer lined up already."

"Like hell you're taking my sister anywhere!" Gil shouted as he stepped protectively in front of me.

"Take them," Damon said flatly to his henchmen. Within seconds, the thugs had Gil and me by the arms and were dragging us toward the front windows. The others made moves to save us, but their efforts were futile. Without guns, there was nothing they could do.

"It's going to be okay, Victoria," Ian said as reassuringly as he could, his eyes catching mine from across the room.

"I know," I lied.

"What do you want, Damon? You want to run? Run. Just leave Gil and Victoria. They're not part of this team," Ian argued.

"Don't worry. I'm not going to hurt them. Gil is far too valuable to my business. As for Victoria, if you come after her, I'll kill her. You've all come to love her too much to risk her life. Isn't that right, Ian?

Ian looked at me with soft eyes. Did he regret meeting me? Everything he told me—that you couldn't have friends in this business, that feelings just got in the way—was proving to be true. But we had found something in each other we didn't know we had been looking for. That was worth it, right?

And Gil. I had finally gotten him back, only to lose him again.

I wondered if Damon was right. Would they all stand

down just because they didn't want to risk me getting hurt? Or was I simply collateral damage, something not worth risking their entire operation for? Suddenly, I felt terrible, like I had compromised the integrity of the team. I worked to break down Ian's emotional wall, but I should have left him alone. I was the key, as Bianca told me. I was the weakest link.

"He wasn't there," Bianca said, storming in from the back room.

"What do you mean he wasn't there? Adam never breaks protocol. You must have been on the wrong roof," Damon chastised.

"I wasn't on the wrong roof. He wasn't there," she reiterated aggressively.

Claudia and I assumed they had already taken Adam out when he didn't save us from Bianca. If he was safe, we actually had a chance of escaping.

Damon thought for a moment. "Okay. Let's move." He motioned to the men holding Gil and me, and they pushed us forward. There was no way in hell I was going with Damon. I'd rather die than be treated and sold like property. More than that, I wasn't going to make the team compromise the mission. They had a job to do, which was to take Damon down and end his human-trafficking ring. I was just one person. The lives of countless children and their families were worth saving.

I looked down at the gun pointed at my side. *Someone forgot the second rule of gun safety.* I gave Ian a determined look and took a deep breath. He must have seen me evaluate the gun because the last thing I heard was Ian yelling for me to stop.

I grabbed the gunman's hand and jammed my finger on top of his in the trigger guard and pulled. I fell to the ground, the pain exploding in my body like a bomb going off. I gripped my side and saw warm blood seeping through my fingers. My vision blurred. I didn't know what damage I had done, but it didn't matter. With me down, Damon's card was out of play for the moment, and Ian and the others could act without hesitation.

I lay in a heap on top of the gunman for only a moment before Eva kicked him in the face. His blood spattered across my neck. He got up as fast as he could, rolling my body off of him. He was barely on his knees when the sole of someone's shoe connected with his chest and he went flying through one of the windows. He tried to come back through, but suddenly he fell, his lifeless body folded over the window frame, blood dripping down the shards of broken glass.

The door shattered around me like it had been broken from the outside. Wood from tables and chairs ricocheted around the room as they were hit by bullets meant for human targets. Bodies slammed against the display cases, splattering glass and pastry remnants everywhere. Then the gunfire stopped. All I could hear were the sounds of punches and kicks making contact.

Blood flowed from Paolo's face as Ian held him by the collar and punched him repeatedly. Paolo grabbed Ian's shirt and head-butted him, knocking Ian off balance for only a split second before Ian's retaliatory blow sent Paolo crashing into the already destroyed dessert case. Pastry bits exploded into the air, sweetening the iron smell of blood and gunpowder. When I licked my lips, I was taken back to my birthday dinner with Tiffany when we indulged on huge slices of cheesecake.

Hands were suddenly on my shoulders, dragging me, leaving a trail of blood in my wake. My side was on fire, and I was immobile, defenseless. Panic filled my chest until Claudia moved into my vision and gave me a firm nod as if to say, "We've got this."

Then she turned around and punched Bianca in the face, dodging the retaliatory fist Bianca threw back. A knock to Bianca's stomach and then another to her chin sent the former Rogue agent flying. She hit her head on the counter and her body went limp.

On the other side of the shop, Eva gave a roundhouse kick to one of Damon's thugs and then turned to right-hook another one. He punched her in the stomach, knocking her to the floor. Carter finished him off by twisting and snapping his neck.

I heard a gun fire again and knew it had to be Adam shooting from the rooftop across the street. The only intact front window shattered, and the thug whose nose I had broken took a bullet to his temple.

I couldn't see Damon anywhere. Had he been taken down or did he get away?

Claudia swept the floor with her leg and knocked Paolo down, stomping on his injured hand. Then one of

Damon's thugs came behind her and got her in a choke-hold. She fought hard, and I recognized some of the basic self-defense moves she used, but the guy had arms like tree limbs. Carter gave him a swift kidney punch, loosening his grip. When she was free, Claudia kneed him in the crotch and then palmed his nose.

Gil finally came into view. He was crouched down in the opposite corner of the room, and Ian was fighting off any-one who tried to get near him. Ian must have left his fight with Paolo to protect my brother. The last of Damon's men were coming at Ian relentlessly. Blood trickled down his face, and there was a gash in his cheek. Carter pulled one of the men off and slammed his head into the exposed brick wall. Ian took the last man down with a final punch to the face that sent two teeth flying from his mouth.

Finally, with his chest breathing heavily, Ian stared down Damon, who had been hiding like a coward and waiting for the dust to clear so he could grab Gil and run.

"Give it up, Damon," I heard Ian say. "You've got noth-ing left." Carter, Eva, and Claudia had each picked up a gun and had it pointed at Damon. Their faces and clothes were covered in blood. The shoulder of Eva's jacket was torn, and half the buttons on Carter's shirt had been ripped off.

Ian held his arms out to draw attention to the defeat of Damon's minions. Paolo was a disheveled mess on the floor, and most of his thugs were dead. Bianca, however, was nowhere to be seen.

"Not a chance." Quicker than anyone could respond, Damon aimed his gun at Ian. At that point, my head became too heavy to hold. And as everything began to go black, I watched my brother's body fly out across the room.

I tried to keep my eyes open as long as possible. I needed to know that Gil was okay. That Ian was still alive. I needed to tell them both how much I loved them before I died. It didn't hurt as much anymore. I was cold and could still feel the warm blood oozing from my side pooling next to me and soaking into my pants.

As if from a long shaky tunnel, Ian was calling to me. "Stay with me, Victoria. Please stay with me." I could feel myself being picked up. We must have walked outside because suddenly the light got brighter, too bright. I closed my eyes, my ears ringing with the echoes of gunshots or sirens, the bodies left to die in the obliterated pastry shop, my own life winding down.

"You didn't leave me," I managed in a breathy voice and laid my head on Ian's warm shoulder.

"I'll never leave you, Victoria," he said softly. Then everything went black.

CHAPTER 21

The first thing I heard when I came to was a steady, rhythmic beeping. I breathed deeply through my nose, but something scratched against it annoyingly. My eyes fluttered open, disorientated in the bright white light. I lifted my arm to rub my nose, but I couldn't bring it very far—it was covered in tubes and wires. It also made my side hurt. I had actually shot myself. But I was still alive.

I surveyed my surroundings. I was in a small room with tiled floors. A wooden door with a narrow window was to my left, and I could see people in lab coats and scrubs walking past. A hospital.

It wasn't until I tried to move my other arm that I realized Ian was attached to it. He was resting in the chair next to me, his body hunched over, his head on the bed, his hand clutching mine.

"You're not drooling on my bed, are you?" I asked in a raspy voice. My throat and mouth were dry.

"Oh my God! Victoria!" Ian darted up. "You're awake!" He stood up and looked like he was trying to figure out how to give me a hug. When it was clear that was going to be difficult, he leaned down and kissed my forehead. "Let me get a nurse."

Ian opened the door to my room and called out to someone. "*Infermiera! È sveglia!*"

A middle-aged nurse with a tight bun in her hair came in and took my vitals. She said something to Ian, who then quickly turned his back to me, then checked my wound.

"*La ferita si stia rimarginando. Sta guarendo bene,*" she said to Ian. He must have told her I didn't speak any Italian and not to bother talking to me. "*Ha bisogno di riposo. Il medico la controllerà domani e le fa sapere quando lei potrà tornare a casa.*" She smiled kindly at me and nodded to Ian before she left the room.

"What did she say?" I asked.

"She said your wound is healing nicely, and that the doctor will check you again tomorrow and let you know when you can leave," he answered as he brushed the hair back from my forehead sweetly.

"Where are we?" I asked.

"Salvator Mundi International Hospital in Rome," he answered.

"Rome? That's hours away from where we were in Venice. How did we get here?" Feeling stiff, I shifted in the bed, but my body screamed out in pain. I grimaced.

"We had you airlifted."

"Airlifted? How?"

"I know people, Victoria." Ian smirked playfully, which made me smile. "I'm glad you're okay. You had me worried." Ian took my hand in his again. He lifted it to his lips and kissed my knuckles.

"How long was I out?"

"Three days," Ian said quietly. He sat carefully on the side of the bed. "And you are officially the luckiest person on the planet. You managed to miss every major organ and your spine. You lost a lot of blood, but they were able to stabilize you in the helicopter and then replace what you lost when we got you here. I want to be furious with you—but you're still alive. And since that's all I've prayed for over the last three days, I guess I can't be too mad."

"Have you been here the whole time?"

"Yes." He nodded bashfully, making me smile just a little.

"I'm so sorry, Ian. I couldn't be the reason the team didn't do their job. And there was no way I was walking out of there with Damon." I took Ian's hand and squeezed it.

"You made a call, Victoria. That's what we do. Sometimes it works out perfectly. Other times, not so much." He ran his thumb across the back of my hand and gave a small, reassuring smile.

"How is everyone?" I asked of the team. "They looked pretty roughed up."

"They're good, and tough. They've encountered worse, so they'll bounce back just fine."

"Ian?" I began. "What happened with Gil?"

He looked at me for several long moments, unsure how to answer. I could practically feel his heart pounding through our gripped hands. He looked down, forming his words carefully.

"When Damon took his shot, Gil stepped in front of me. I tried to stop him, but it was too late. There was nothing I could do."

"So is he okay? Is he here in this hospital?" My heart was beating wildly in my chest, and it was all I could do to not rip the wires and tubes from my body and leap out of bed and find him.

"Victoria," he said softly, looking me straight in the eyes. "Victoria, I'm so sorry. Gil didn't make it. I promise you we did everything we could."

"No! He can't be dead. I just saw him, he was right there. . . ."

"You knew how much he loved you, Victoria, but he told me to tell you."

"What . . . What else did he say?"

Did it matter? No, nothing mattered. Not anymore. My world was over. I had one job to do and I had failed. I failed everyone, especially Gil.

"He told me to take care of you."

"And what did you tell him?" I asked.

"I promised him I would."

Gil throwing himself in front of Ian to save his life replayed in my head like a nightmare. It was brave and selfless and stupid and reckless all at the same time. How could he do this to me? Why didn't he let Ian do his job? Why didn't Ian protect him?

"How could you let this happen?" The beeping of the heart monitor was rapidly increasing.

"Victoria, you need to stay calm."

"Calm? You want me to stay calm? My brother is dead, Ian. After everything I went through, I still lost him. I failed." Tears were beginning to sting my eyes. I pulled my hand away from Ian's hold. "You were right there and you didn't save him!"

"I would have gladly taken that bullet to spare you this heartache." Ian's eyes were glassy with tears. "As soon as Gil's body hit the ground, I was focused on him. I tried to keep him alive, Victoria. I swear I did."

"What happened to Damon? Please tell me you at least got him." Panic began to rise in me that the entire mission was a complete loss.

"I wish I could." Ian's voice conveyed every bit of his disappointment. He looked at me with sad eyes like he was more concerned about letting me down than anything.

Instantly, tracking Damon became my one and only focus in life. Damon would pay for what he did. "So what happens now? How do we find him?"

"He'll go underground for a while. Then he'll move to another part of the world. That's the thing about human trafficking. Its global reach makes it easy to run from anywhere," Ian explained.

"So he's just going to relocate and terrorize people somewhere else." I closed my eyes for a moment to regroup. How could someone so evil kill my brother, get away with it, *and* go back to destroying people's lives?

"We'll get him, Victoria. It may take some time, but we will get him." Ian took my hand in his. "I will make Damon pay for what he did to you, to Gil, if it's the last thing I do."

"I need to be alone." I turned my head to the other side of the room, away from Ian.

"Of course. I'll be back in the morning. I'll bring Claudia and Adam. They've been begging to see you," he said. He walked toward the door and stopped. "Victoria," he said softly as he turned. "Gil said one more thing."

I didn't want to look at him, but Ian was the only person who knew my brother's final words. I had to know what they were. I moved my head and caught Ian's eyes.

"Sky."

Ian turned and left the room without another word.

Sky. It was our mother's word for peace. "There's nothing more peaceful than the color of the sky on a beautiful day." She used to tell us that just looking up at a blue sky would make all the worries of life disappear. I wished there was a window in my hospital room. I needed some sky right then.

Tears came and they came hard. I closed my eyes and let my life with Gil play through my mind like an epic documentary of every meaningful moment we ever shared. Riding bikes in our neighborhood as kids. Family day at the beach when Gil would hold my hand in the water because he didn't want me to get swept away. The day he rescued me from that awful foster home. Watching television from the floor in our crappy apartment. Saying good-bye at the airport.

Tears began to flow, streaming down my face in every direction. I didn't care. I was just glad I was already in the hospital. I wasn't sure how strong my heart would be by morning.

CHAPTER 22

"Hey, kamikaze!" Carter shouted cheerfully as he walked through the door of my hospital room.

It had been three days since I'd woken up and I was finally being released. Ian had been back every day, but I refused to talk about Gil. I didn't know what to say, so I said nothing.

"Hello, Carter," I smiled. "What are you doing here?" I threw the toothbrush and the last of the clothes Claudia had brought me into my bag and zipped the top.

"A guy can't come see his favorite girl?" he said as he flopped himself onto the hospital bed and crossed his ankles.

"Sure he can. Would you like me to call her for you?" I smirked.

Carter got up from the bed and came around to the side where I was. "No, really. I wanted to come see how you were. You were pretty badass the other day. I mean,

I'm *totally* badass, but I've never shot myself to create a distraction before."

"I saw some of your moves in there. You could have fared better," I teased.

"I probably should have kissed you then, huh?" We both laughed, but Carter turned serious.

"I thought what you did in the alley was something, but what you did in the pastry shop was nothing short of brave and heroic. You need to know that, Vic," Carter said.

"Yeah, well, it got my brother killed, so . . ."

"Your brother was killed because he took a bullet meant for another man. You two were clearly cut from the same cloth. He made the choice he did because he knew in a second that if he didn't, we'd lose one of the greatest leaders INTERPOL has ever pretended not to know. He knew that if we lost Ian Hale, this world would not be as safe."

"Wow. That's the first nice thing I've ever heard you say about Ian," I replied.

"Look, we've all got our own crap. Sometimes we put that crap on other people. Ian is a good man, and he's an excellent leader. I would be honored to stay on his team. But if you tell anyone I said that, I'll call you a liar." Carter smiled and threw his arms around me. I winced, and he quickly let go.

"My lips are sealed," I chuckled.

"What are we keeping under lock and key now?" Adam asked as he opened the door to my room. Claudia, Eva, and Ian followed him in. Adam was carrying the biggest bouquet of flowers I had ever seen. He handed them to me and then gave me a gentle hug and a kiss on the cheek.

"We were just discussing your awesomeness, Mr. Sharpshooter," I said, returning the hug and kiss.

"Oh, well, no need to keep that to yourselves!" Adam held his arms out to the side.

"No, really. Thank you for what you did. Actually, I need to thank all of you. I already apologized to Ian, but I wanted to make sure you all knew—"

"Stop," Eva said. "Part of being a Rogue agent means making judgment calls. I don't know many agents who would have taken as big a risk as you did."

I sighed, not sure how to respond to another congratulations when it just felt like I was the one who had screwed everything up—and lost my brother. "Tell you what—let's just move on. How does that sound? I won't apologize or even say thank you again, and you don't tell me how brave I was for shooting myself. Deal?"

"Deal," they all said together.

I grabbed the small duffel off the bed and started for the door.

"I've got this," Ian said, grabbing my bag. "You: Get in the wheelchair."

Before I could protest, the whole team was giving me the stink eye. Deciding to skip this battle, I sat.

"Thank you," Ian said. We nodded to one other and Carter pushed me as we all made our way out into the hall, down the elevator, and out onto the sidewalk.

"Good news, everyone. You're all on vacation," Ian declared.

"Vacation? What is this 'vacation' you speak of?" Adam joked.

"Go. Get away from me. Take a month and do whatever you want. Wait. . . . Do whatever you want that is *legal*. Please don't make me pull strings to get you out of jail . . . Carter." Ian looked at Carter over his nose and raised an eyebrow.

"I resent that you would think I'd actually get caught," Carter replied with a straight face.

"Let's go, troublemaker," Eva said as she pulled Carter down the street. "Thanks, boss! See you in a month!" We watched as the two of them made their way down the street and off to whatever adventure awaited them.

"What are you two going to do?" I asked Adam and Claudia.

"You ever been to Monte Carlo?" Claudia asked Adam.

"Nope."

"Wanna go?"

"Sure."

"We're going to Monte Carlo," Claudia answered back to me.

I smiled. "Well, have fun! Win big and bring me back a present."

Adam and Claudia walked down the street in the other direction and got into a parked car.

"God, I hope that belongs to one of them," Ian said

with a laugh. "What about you, Miss Asher? What are you going to do?"

"That's a good question. I don't have any family. No home to go home to. Maybe I'll just hang out in Italy for a while," I mused. "Or maybe I'll travel the world since the psycho leader of a human-trafficking ring is probably after me."

"Well, as long as you're here," Ian said as a black limousine pulled up next to us. Ian opened the door and invited me inside.

"This is a bit much, don't you think?"

"It's a company car. Get in."

I climbed in and Ian followed.

"Where are we going?" I asked.

"Here. You need to stay hydrated." Ian handed me a bottle of water while conspicuously not answering my question. I took the bottle from him and held it in my hands, the condensation soaking my palms. "Victoria, I really am so, so sorry about Gil. If I could have changed places with him, I would have."

"It's not your fault, Ian. And, *I'm* sorry. I shouldn't have blamed you. It was Gil's decision to seek justice for Maria. He could have studied his ass off in Miami and pursued his mission there. But clearly, we Asher kids don't take the easy way. When we're in, we're all in." I laughed to keep myself from crying. I would be sad for a long time, but I had already spent enough in a hospital bed soaking my pillow.

We drove for a while and I watched the city pass by

through the tinted window. Rome was beautiful; everything looked like a postcard. The buildings were detailed
with ancient stone, stained-glass windows adding dashes
of color.

I wondered how long I could stay before the guilt of
using the settlement money would begin to weigh on me.
But maybe it was time to let that go. I was alone now. After
meeting Ian and being a part of his team—even for a short
time—how could I return to a life of TV movies and the
diner's daily specials? And what could college possibly
teach me about life that a mob shootout hadn't already? I
could see now that the world would become my classroom.

I could start a new life, tour Italy, or France, or both.
Hell! I could tour all of Europe if I wanted to! I know
Mom and Dad would have wanted me to see the world,
and I'm sure they would be happy for me to use the money
to begin my adventure.

The car stopped in a busy section of the city. Ian got
out and helped me exit carefully. He took my hand as we
walked. I didn't protest.

"Where are we?" I asked. We were approaching a huge
fountain and an insane amount of steps that led to a church
high in the distance.

"These are the Spanish Steps. The one hundred and
thirty-eight steps lead to the Trinità dei Monti, a church
that was built in the 1500s. And this," he said, pointing to
the fountain where we had stopped, "is the Fontana della
Barcaccia. It means 'Fountain of the Ugly Boat.'"

"Wow. Italian really *can* make anything sound romantic," I chuckled. "What else is around here, oh personal tour guide of Italy?"

"Some famous people lived and died around here. Oh, and the Spanish Steps were made famous to non-Europeans in—"

"*Roman Holiday* with Audrey Hepburn!" I said excitedly.

"Very good," Ian said, applauding my limited knowledge.

"Tiffany and I have watched that movie about a dozen times," I explained.

"There are some shops down there. Feel like walking a bit?"

"Sure. I'm just happy to be outside again," I said.

As we walked, I tried not to think about our time together ending soon. Ian would go back to his Rogue team and I would go . . . somewhere. Preparing myself to say good-bye forever was becoming even more painful than the shot in my side. But at least that was already healing—I wasn't sure if the hole in my heart would ever heal. I took a big breath and tried to be grateful. I was walking through Rome holding the hand of a gorgeous Rogue agent. At least it would be a good story to bring home to Tiffany. I forced myself to smile at the thought, even if it made me sick to my stomach.

We passed in front of another clothing store. I gave it a cursory glance as I had a few of the others, but I certainly wasn't in a headspace for shopping. Plus, this was Italian fashion at its worst. But behind the loud blouses and tight leather pants, something caught my eye. I stopped and stared at them like they were the answer to an unspoken prayer and walked into the store.

"You like them?" Ian asked.

"Not as much as my friend Tiffany." Sitting on the display table were the grommet, suede, peep-toe Prada booties Tiffany had been coveting since they came out earlier that year.

"You should buy them," Ian said as if money were no object. He had also clearly forgotten that being wiped off the face of the planet meant not having access to my bank account.

"You haven't given me my bank card back," I said.

"Then Command will buy them for you."

"Why would Command buy me an insanely expensive pair of Prada shoes?" I asked curiously.

"Because they take care of their agents," Ian answered simply.

"I'm not a Rogue agent, Ian. I'm just a girl who impetuously charged into your team like I had any business being there. Now that Gil is gone, I don't have any reason to stay."

"Now that Gil is gone you have *every* reason to stay."

"I don't know what I'm doing!"

"We'll train you. Help you hone your skills," Ian countered.

"I'm not a mutant with superpowers, Ian. I'm just observant. It's not that big of a deal."

"It's a bigger deal than you realize." Ian paused and looked around the room. "Tell me what you see."

I sighed and looked around the small shop. There were a few women shopping. Some were trying on clothes while others were just browsing. "I don't know."

"*What do you see?*"

I scanned the store again, looking for anything that seemed out of place. "Her," I whispered. "She's not here to shop. She's dressed the part, but she doesn't have a bag." The woman I was assessing was wearing a light-blue pencil skirt with a white cap-sleeve top that flared at the waist and yellow floral stilettos. Her hair was pulled back in a pony-tail, and for a woman who appeared to be in her early fif-ties, she pulled off the young-and-modern look flawlessly.

"Maybe she's just looking. Or maybe her husband is meeting her here with his wallet," Ian suggested.

"No. If she were just browsing, she wouldn't have gone to this much effort with her wardrobe. Women who shop in stores like this come dressed the part from head to toe, earrings to shoes. She would want a bag to complete her outfit," I explained to him.

"She's as good as you said she was, Mr. Hale," said the woman I had just detailed, her British accent adding to her elegance.

"Victoria, this is Penny Thatcher. She's the director of the Command division for INTERPOL, also known as Rogue," Ian said by way of introductions.

I extended my hand and noticed how beautiful she was. She had fair skin and green eyes, and the most perfect bow to her lips. She smiled back at me warmly as she shook my hand. "It's an honor to meet you, Ms. Thatcher."

"I've heard a lot about you, Miss Asher. I'm very sorry to hear about your brother. He would have made an excellent intelligence agent. We would have been proud to have added him to our team, as we would be to add you," she said.

I volleyed my eyes between Ian and Ms. Thatcher. "You want me to join the team? My skill set includes cutting pie and pouring coffee. I'm not strong or brave, and I'm so afraid of flying that I'm fairly sure the air marshals are going to have to sedate me the next time I board a plane. Of the more qualified people around the world, why on earth would you want *me* to be a Rogue agent?"

"I can train anyone to use a gun, hack into a computer, or gather intelligence. I cannot train someone to do what comes naturally to you. But I *can* help you fine-tune those skills and turn them into more than a party trick," she said confidently.

"But I missed the mark with Damon. Had I been as observant as you think I am, I would have seen it all coming," I said uncertainly.

"No one saw it coming. I spent a year with Damon, and he had me fooled. He played the part because that's what he was trained to do." Ian shoved his hands in his pockets. "He played all of us, Victoria. Now, I don't know when he's going to rear his ugly head again, but if you stay with me, train with me, then one day, we'll get him."

I watched Ian as he spoke. He was serious and passionate and soft all at once. And I *definitely* heard him ask me to stay with him. Not with Rogue. Him.

"Well, I can see you two have some things to discuss. I have a meeting. After the incident with Mr. Pazzia, we're going to be revising some policies within the division. I do hope you'll stay with us, Miss Asher. From everything Mr. Hale has told me, and just the little bit I saw today, I believe you'll be a great asset to our organization." She smiled and extended her hand. "It was lovely to meet you."

"When do you need my decision?" I asked as she headed for the door.

"It seems Mr. Hale has given his team a much-needed break. I'd say you have at least that much time to decide if you're going to go home to your job at the diner, or if you are made for more than that." Ms. Thatcher nodded and left Ian and me standing next to Tiffany's favorite Prada booties.

"Well?" Ian prompted.

I hadn't considered that staying with Ian's team was an option. I came to Italy to find Gil and bring him home. I found him, but Gil was gone now.

"I don't know, Ian," I began.

He took a step closer and my heart fluttered. That was something else I would have to consider: If I stayed, what would happen with Ian and me? Would we have to close that door?

"What did you say to me the first day in the hotel when I wanted to send you home?" I averted my eyes because I knew where he was going with this. "You said you would rather feel like you were accomplishing something than merely existing. You told me to put you to the test. And you told me, in no uncertain terms, that you knew you could do this."

"You also told me that day that this was a lonely life you wouldn't wish on anyone," I reminded him.

"I did say that," he replied. "But somehow it hasn't seemed as lonely since you arrived."

I closed my eyes and argued with myself. If I went home, my life would be everything I didn't want it to be. I might go to college like Gil and I had talked about, but it was more likely that I'd stay in our crappy apartment and live out my days at The Clock.

Or I could stay here with Ian and be a part of a Rogue team. I could put my life in danger every day for the betterment of the world and to keep people safe—starting with hunting down Damon.

But what would I do about Tiffany? She'd be totally alone in Miami without me.

A light bulb went on in my head. If I wasn't there, she'd be forced to get out and move on, too. If Command was going to take care of me, then I could take care of her—just like she had for me when I was at my lowest. I'd make her promise to finally go to New York, visit all the agencies, and pursue her dream of modeling.

That was it. The final piece to the puzzle of what was keeping me in Miami, instead of joining the Rogue team and starting my life. My heart was happy and my mind was determined.

"Okay," I said. "I'll stay. But you have to do a few things for me."

"Anything!"

"I want half of the money from my account sent to my friend Tiffany. But there has to be a way to stipulate what she does with it. Leave the remaining half and have Claudia do that cloaking thing. Can we do that?" I asked.

"Yes! Absolutely!" Ian said. He hugged me and I winced. He immediately pulled away. "Oh my God! I'm so sorry, are you okay?" He smiled sheepishly.

"I'm fine," I laughed. "But you might need to take your excitement down a notch."

"Is there anything else you need?"

"Yes. I need these shoes, and I need them sent to Tiffany at my apartment," I told him.

"Done. Is that it?"

I thought for a moment, wracking my brain for one last thing that could possibly stop me from doing what I'd begun to love. "That's it." I took a deep breath and looked into Ian's eyes. They had become so familiar and calming to me, like I was finally coming home. I knew that wherever I was going and whatever I was going to face, if I had these eyes and the man they belonged to by my side, I could do anything.

Ian took both of my hands in his and grinned cautiously back at me, like he just realized what he had asked me to do.

"Do you feel strange now that it's all ending?"

"This is far from the end, Ian. This is only the beginning."

ACKNOWLEDGMENTS

To say I am thankful or appreciative is such an understatement. The entire process to bring *Oxblood* to publication is one that has changed me and made me a better writer. For that, I have to thank my amazing editor, Emma Pulitzer. Thank you for asking all the right questions and for making sure this story became the beautiful and exciting piece it is.

Thank you to my amazing agent, Italia Gandolfo. No one in this business works harder than you. Thanks for keeping vampire hours and making things happen. Now go take a nap!

I hesitate to boost his ego any more, but . . . Thank you to my incredible publicist at Red Coat PR, Rick Miles. You believed in me from our very first conversation. Thank you for being not only a great publicist, but also a wonderful friend. Best one hundred dollars I've ever spent!

Thanks to my PA Extraordinaire, Jewels Bromley. Even

an ocean apart, you still manage to keep me on track! Thank you so very much for all you do!

I couldn't exist in this industry without the solid group of fellow writers around me. Community is everything! Michele G. Miller, Amy Miles, Kristie Cook, Samantha Davis, Wendy L. Owens, and Stacey Rourke, you ladies are the peanut butter to my jelly and the Peter Pan to my Tinker Bell! Thank you for being the best traveling buddies on this amazing journey!

A huge thank-you to Adam Brown. Everything Vic knows about shooting, she learned from you! Thanks for taking the time to help me make sure Vic knew what she was doing. You are an excellent and patient teacher! And you're a pretty swell guy, too!

Thank you to my parents, my brothers and sisters-in-love, and my nieces and nephews. None of you gave me the side-eye six years ago when I told you I was writing my first book. Thanks for always being so encouraging and supportive.

Last, but never in a million years least, thank you to my husband, Donavan, and my two awesome kids, Truman and Claire. No one loves and supports me the way you do. There is no way I could do what I do without you by my side. I am so grateful that God created our amazing family and I can't wait to see what else he has in store for us. The best is yet to come!

ABOUT THE AUTHOR

AnnaLisa Grant is the author of the Lake Series (*The Lake*, *Troubled Waters*, *Safe Harbor*, and *Anchored: A Lake Series Novella*). She received her master's degree in counseling from Gordon-Conwell Theology Seminary in 2008 and spent two years in private practice as a therapist. Grant married her husband, Donavan, in 2001 and lives in Matthews, North Carolina, with their two children. *Oxblood* (2016) is the first novel in the Victoria Asher series.

INTEGRATED MEDIA

Find a full list of our authors and
titles at www.openroadmedia.com

FOLLOW US
@OpenRoadMedia

CPSIA information can be obtained at www.ICGtesting.com
Printed in the USA
LVOW07s1602120916

504264LV00001B/161/P